Nothing Breaks Like A Heart

BARBARA FREETHY

BARBARA FREETHY
BOOKS

Fog City Publishing

PRAISE FOR BARBARA FREETHY

"Barbara Freethy's suspense novels are explosively good!" — *New York Times bestselling author Toni Anderson.*

"A fabulous, page-turning combination of romance and intrigue. Fans of Nora Roberts and Elizabeth Lowell will love this book." — *NYT Bestselling Author Kristin Hannah on Golden Lies*

"Powerful and absorbing...sheer hold-your-breath suspense." — *NYT Bestselling Author Karen Robards on Don't Say A Word*

"Barbara Freethy delivers riveting, plot-twisting suspense and a deeply emotional story. Every book is a thrilling ride." *USA Today Bestselling Author Rachel Grant*

"Freethy is at the top of her form. Fans of Nora Roberts will find a similar tone here, framed in Freethy's own spare, elegant style." — *Contra Costa Times on Summer Secrets*

"Freethy hits the ground running as she kicks off another winning romantic suspense series...Freethy is at her prime with a superb combo of engaging characters and gripping plot." — *Publishers' Weekly on Silent Run*

"PERILOUS TRUST is a non-stop thriller that seamlessly melds jaw-dropping suspense with sizzling romance, and I was riveted from the first page to the last...Readers will be breathless in anticipation as this fast-paced and enthralling love story evolves and goes in unforeseeable directions." — *USA Today HEA Blog*

PRAISE FOR BARBARA FREETHY

"Barbara Freethy is a master storyteller with a gift for spinning tales about ordinary people in extraordinary situations and drawing readers into their lives." — *Romance Reviews Today*

"Freethy (Silent Fall) has a gift for creating complex, appealing characters and emotionally involving, often suspenseful, sometimes magical stories."— *Library Journal on Suddenly One Summer*

"If you love nail-biting suspense and heartbreaking emotion, Silent Run belongs on the top of your to-be-bought list. I could not turn the pages fast enough."— *NYT Bestselling Author Mariah Stewart*

"Hooked me from the start and kept me turning pages throughout all the twists and turns. Silent Run is powerful romantic intrigue at its best."— *NYT Bestselling Author JoAnn Ross*

"An absorbing story of two people determined to unravel the secrets, betrayals, and questions about their past. The story builds to an explosive conclusion that will leave readers eagerly awaiting Barbara Freethy's next book."—*NYT Bestselling Author Carla Neggars on Don't Say A Word*

"A page-turner that engages your mind while it tugs at your heartstrings ... Don't Say A Word has made me a Barbara Freethy fan for life!" —*NYT Bestselling Author Diane Chamberlain*

"*On Shadow Beach* teems with action, drama and compelling situations... a fast-paced page-turner." —*BookPage*

ALSO BY BARBARA FREETHY

Mystery Thriller Standalones

ALL THE PRETTY PEOPLE

LAST ONE TO KNOW

THE OTHER EMILY

Off the Grid: FBI Series

PERILOUS TRUST

RECKLESS WHISPER

DESPERATE PLAY

ELUSIVE PROMISE

DANGEROUS CHOICE

RUTHLESS CROSS

CRITICAL DOUBT

FEARLESS PURSUIT

DARING DECEPTION

RISKY BARGAIN

PERFECT TARGET

Lightning Strikes Trilogy

BEAUTIFUL STORM

LIGHTNING LINGERS

SUMMER RAIN

For a complete list of books, visit www.barbarafreethy.com

NOTHING BREAKS LIKE A HEART

For more information on Barbara Freethy's books, visit her website:
www.barbarafreethy.com

PROLOGUE

Rain and wind rattled the office windows next to my cubicle, drawing my attention from the computer screen before me. Southern California usually had mild Decembers, but the storm had blown in off the Pacific Ocean about an hour ago and made me think I probably should have gone home at five with the rest of my coworkers, but I'd decided to keep working on our new marketing campaign.

Turning back to my screen, I smiled at the completely opposite experience I was trying to sell—a beautiful summer wedding with a couple holding hands under a sunlit archway, all golden light and smiles. The woman was a pretty brunette with a blinding smile any dentist would be proud of. The man was tall and fit, with blond hair and loving brown eyes that were gazing with adoration at the woman he'd just married, the woman who would share the honeymoon suite with him at the Carrington Coastal Retreat, our new resort hotel on the island of Catalina, that would launch this coming May, in time for the spring wedding season.

I leaned back in my desk chair, staring at the glossy, impossible image of wondrous, joyful love and the headline *Your Dream Honeymoon Awaits.* The ad screamed effortless happiness: pristine beaches, champagne toasts, bikini beach days, and sensuous nights in fluffy beds with the ocean waves singing you to sleep.

The couple looked perfect, exactly how I'd wanted them to look when I'd conceived the marketing campaign, but I still hated them a little. Not because the ad was bad. If anything, it was too good, because I knew that couple didn't exist. They were a fairy tale, the kind of happily ever after I'd wanted to believe in but had never experienced. My relationships had all turned out to be a bust. And the last three years, I hadn't even had time to look for love while I'd been caregiving for my mother, who had passed away last Christmas, which was one reason why I was working at ten o'clock on a Friday night instead of doing anything else. I couldn't seem to shake the sadness inside of me, especially at the holidays. I felt numb and broken.

I wished I could be that woman in the ad: carefree, in love, looking toward the future... Maybe one day...

Sighing, I saved the file and clicked off the image. The cursor blinked at me, waiting for my next command or for me to finally admit I couldn't stall a second longer. The windows rattled again, and for a second, the lights flickered, sending a shiver down my spine. Thankfully, they came back on, but I probably shouldn't push my luck.

As I gathered my things, I heard more odd noises, and I wondered why I hadn't seen the security guard come through tonight. Usually, he made his rounds around nine, but I hadn't seen a soul in hours. Maybe security was busy downstairs. I was working on the top floor of the Carrington Newport Beach Hotel, which was also the headquarters for the Carrington Hospitality Group. The top two floors were office space while the first eight floors housed luxury rooms and suites, as well as conference space and banquet rooms.

The hotel was full this weekend, with one of the last business conferences taking place in the hotel before the holidays. I'd been in the elevator with many badged individuals over the past three days, and tonight when I'd gone down to grab a takeout salad from the hotel snack shop, I'd passed several men and women dressed in suits and cocktail dresses, heading toward their closing night cocktail party.

Seeing them had only made me feel more depressed. In addition to missing my mom, my two best female friends were in long-term relationships and while they often tried to include me, it was awkward to always be the fifth wheel, which was another reason I worked long hours, especially on Friday nights, when the looming weekend was almost too much to bear.

I'd just finished organizing my desk when the heat suddenly clicked off, leaving the office even more unnervingly quiet. Then I heard a loud thud and almost jumped out of my skin. No one else was on this floor. The crash must have come from somewhere else, but it still made me uneasy. I told myself to calm down. I was perfectly safe in one of the most secure buildings in the area. Located near the waterfront, the hotel was five-star luxury, and no one got upstairs without a keycard, especially not to the corporate offices.

Everything was fine. I needed to get my over-imaginative and weary self out of here. I shut down my computer, then headed out of my cubicle and down the hallway. I pushed the button for the elevator, and it dinged softly, immediately opening. When I stepped into the elevator, my eyes started to water, and I smelled smoke. Before I could jump out again, the elevator doors closed. I hit the button for the lobby, feeling my heart beginning to race.

Was there a fire somewhere?

The elevator started down, then stopped so abruptly I stumbled forward, hitting my hands against the silver doors. The overhead lights flickered as piercing alarms rang through the air.

There wasn't just smoke; there was a fire!

And I'd done the one thing you were never supposed to do—get in an elevator. If only the alarms had gone off thirty seconds earlier.

Panic shot through me as I jabbed the buttons, trying to get the elevator moving. Nothing happened. Taking several deep breaths, I tried to slow down my racing pulse and think. I didn't know why the elevator had stopped. Maybe it was some kind of backup security system for when the fire alarms went off, designed to keep me safe. But as the smoke grew stronger, my anxiety skyrocketed.

I hit the emergency button several times. Then the elevator suddenly jerked and started down again, stopping abruptly twenty seconds later. It looked like I'd made it to the ninth floor, one floor down from where I'd started. But the doors remained closed.

My options were limited, so I pushed the button for the doors to open—once, twice, then a third time, my desperation growing. Finally, they opened, but when they got halfway, they stopped. The ground was still two feet below me. Squeezing through the doors, I jumped, feeling immediately better to be off the elevator. But as the smoke thickened, clogging my lungs and burning my nose and throat, I wondered if I'd made the wrong decision.

The fire alarms were still piercing the air, but there was no one around. Maybe there was action on the lower floors. Management would be more concerned with getting the guests to safety, especially since they'd believe the office suites would be empty at this time of night.

I had to get to the stairwell. I knew it was nearby, but the smoke was making me lose my bearings. I had to concentrate. The stairs were only a short distance from the elevator. I started in what I hoped was the right direction, when a door next to me suddenly blew open, knocking me off my feet. My head hit the nearby wall and stars exploded behind my eyes as a loud ringing sound sent pain through my ears.

Dazed, I tried to make sense of what was happening. There were flames now blazing out of the room where the door had blown off. The heat was intense and the smoke so thick, I wasn't sure how far away from the stairs I was anymore. The situation was deteriorating rapidly, and that realization shocked me into awareness.

What if that was just the first of more explosions? I had to get out of here. But there was not only pain in my head but also in my leg, and I could see blood on my ankle. When I tried to stand up, the pain was so bad I fell back to my knees. I yelled for help, but I doubted anyone could hear me. Still, I screamed until my cries turned into gasping coughs.

And then a moment later, I saw him coming through the smoke —a man in a suit. He was tall and handsome, with blond hair and blue eyes. I had no idea who he was, but I was thrilled to see him.

"Help," I yelled again, my voice raspy with smoke. "Over here."

He paused as if he'd just heard me, his head swinging left then right, his gaze finally meeting mine.

"Are you hurt?" He came toward me, his voice cutting through the chaos in the scene, the ringing in my ears.

"Hit my head," I said, coughing through the words. "My ankle hurts, too."

"What's your name?"

"Lauren Gray."

"Okay, Lauren, we have to move."

Before he could pull me to my feet, another explosion sent huge chunks of ceiling down on top of us. He grabbed pieces of plaster and wood and threw them to the side, then tried to get me up, but I couldn't put any weight on my foot.

"I can't," I said, crying with pain and fear. "I can't walk. Go. Get help."

His jaw tightened, and his eyes grew darker with determination. "There's no time for that."

"I can't walk."

"Then I better carry you."

"You can't carry me down eight flights of stairs."

He smiled. "Challenge accepted."

"What? Are you crazy?"

"Maybe so. But I feel like being a hero tonight."

He grabbed under my arms and pulled me up until I was standing on one foot. Then he lifted me up and over his shoulder as if I was as light as a feather, and I was definitely not that light.

As he moved toward the stairs, I hung on for dear life, terrified he would drop me, that we would both fall, or another explosion would block our way. Hanging almost upside down made my head hurt even more, and I got so dizzy I couldn't help but close my eyes, praying that this man would somehow be able to save both our lives.

Finally, a rush of cold air washed over me, followed by my rescuer yelling for help.

A pair of firefighters grabbed me and carried me to a waiting ambulance. As they laid me on a gurney, I looked around for the man who had saved me. I wanted to thank him for not leaving me, like so many people had in the past. But he was gone, and I didn't even know his name.

CHAPTER ONE

Six months later...

His name was Andrew James Chadwick. And tomorrow I would be his wife. I would be Mrs. Andrew James Chadwick...No more single and solitary Lauren Gray.

I could hardly believe how much my life had changed since the fire, since I'd met Andrew, since I'd fallen in love with my rescuer. Now, we were getting married at the very resort I'd been writing marketing copy for six months earlier. Ironically, I was about to become the bride in the ad I'd created, the one I'd thought was impossibly perfect. I still couldn't quite believe it.

Nor could I believe that the Carrington Hospitality Group had decided to use my wedding as the launch for not only the marketing of our new resort on Catalina, the Carrington Coastal Retreat, but also the physical grand opening, which would happen on Wednesday, five days from now.

I'd not only met the man of my dreams; I was also getting the wedding of my dreams, thanks to the generosity of my employer, a family-run enterprise currently led by Victor Carrington, who had inherited the company from his father.

Victor's son Bennett was a vice president in the company, although that seemed to be more of a title than an actual job. But both Bennett and Victor had signed off on using me and Andrew as the wedding couple in the campaign, and Victor, in particular, had moved a significant amount of money into the team budget to make everything first-class.

In charge of the actual wedding events was Jeanette Bilson a forty-something whirlwind of energy, sophistication, and determination. She'd spent ten years directing weddings for Hilton, and she was determined that my wedding events would be absolutely perfect. Because the wedding and resort marketing were tied together, Jeanette worked closely with my boss, Megan Farris, who was the senior director of marketing for the Carrington Hospitality Group. That meant I not only had to impress as the bride; I also had to do my job and represent my employer to the best of my ability.

Megan and Jeanette had their heads together now, standing by the bar in the five-star restaurant known as Bella Mar, which was the site of my rehearsal dinner. The restaurant was stunning, with floor-to-ceiling windows, elegant lamps on the tables, and discreetly placed sconces on the walls, adding soft light to the beautiful ocean-inspired art. While Andrew and I had invited twenty of our friends and family to the rehearsal dinner and the wedding tomorrow, the rest of the group at tonight's event included resort employees and media. That had added another fifty people to the guest list, most of whom I didn't know.

But that didn't matter. The only person I needed to know in this room was the tall, blond, very attractive man who was laughing with his two groomsmen at the far end of the bar. Andrew was so handsome. My gut clenched every time I saw him. I could hardly believe he was going to be my husband. I'd never dated anyone so good-looking, open, and outgoing. He was always the life of the party, and because I was with him, I'd become a lot more popular, too.

If someone had told me six months ago, I'd be standing here

about to marry the man who had saved my life, I would have laughed and said they were crazy. Or maybe I would have cried because I'd been really sad before Andrew had rescued me. He hadn't just saved me from the fire; he'd saved me from my lonely, grief-ridden, workaholic life.

"He's just a man, Lauren," Harper said, coming up behind me. "Not a knight in shining armor."

I smiled at the knowing and cynical glint in my friend's hazel eyes. I'd met the tall, thin, very blonde, and very sarcastic Harper Miles on my first day of work at the Carrington Group a year and a half ago. While I was tasked with writing ad copy and developing art for marketing campaigns, Harper was an assistant director of guest experience, working with individual hotel managers to make sure there was consistency throughout the brand. Harper would be working with the on-site manager of guest experience at this new resort starting on Monday, but this weekend, she was one of my two bridesmaids.

My other bridesmaid, Jamie Trent, was also a coworker, but she was in the accounting department. Jamie and Harper had been friends long before they met me, but they'd included me in their lunches and after-work drinks, something I'd appreciated even more before I met Andrew.

"Seriously, Lauren, you're practically drooling," Harper added, rolling her eyes.

"Because I'm in love, and Andrew will always be my knight in shining armor. How could he not be? He saved my life."

"I know. I know." Harper gave a weary wave of her hand. "But that was months ago. What about when he leaves shoes on the bed or cuts his toenails while sitting on the couch watching football and drinking beer?" Harper challenged.

"He's not that kind of man."

"From my experience, they all turn into that kind of man at some point, Lauren."

"Not Andrew. He's different."

"Is he? You haven't known him that long."

"Time doesn't mean anything. You should know that better than anyone." My impulsive words landed hard, and I immediately felt bad. Harper's longtime boyfriend had turned out to be cheating on her after years of being together. That was three months ago, and Harper was still justifiably upset about it. "I'm sorry. I shouldn't have said that."

"No, you're right." Harper's lips tightened. "I knew Peter for two years, and it wasn't long enough."

I felt guilty that I'd reminded her of a painful time in her life. I'd just gotten a little tired of hearing about how fast I was moving. She'd been singing that song since I got engaged, and she wasn't the only one.

"I know you and Jamie are looking out for me," I said. "But you have to stop trying to make me nervous about getting married. I know what I'm doing. Andrew is my forever guy. He's the one." I almost added, *He has to be,* because I couldn't imagine how horrible it would feel if this ended, if I was alone again. But that sounded too desperate, too fearful, and I wasn't either of those things. Andrew and I were good together, and I wasn't going to second-guess my decision to marry him.

"Okay. I'll shut up. I want you to be happy, Lauren. You deserve it. I just feel protective of you. You went through such a difficult time after losing your mom. You were so sad and unhappy when we first met. I don't want to see that bleak look in your eyes ever again."

"You won't. And you like Andrew, remember?"

"I do like him. He's a hard man not to like. He's very charming. I promise to stop being a jealous brat and support you wholeheartedly."

"Good. Because I need you. This weekend is going to be a lot."

"It's definitely shaping up that way. I never thought your marketing idea would escalate into a two-day wedding weekend extravaganza. You're a lucky woman, Lauren."

"I know. I never could have afforded anything like this."

"None of us could. So is your family here?"

"I don't see them yet, but my Aunt Lydia texted me they'd gotten off the ferry around four, so they should be showing up soon."

My aunt and uncle, Lydia and Hugh Paulson, and their daughter Marian and her husband Travis, were my only family members that would be in attendance. I came from a very small family, and I wasn't even that close to them.

Lydia had been my mother's older sister by six years, and they'd never been that close, but Lydia had been nice enough to come, and I was happy to have some blood relatives at the event. Not for the first time, I felt a wave of sadness that my mom wasn't here to see me get married. But lingering on that thought was too painful, so I pushed it aside and looked back at Andrew, who had quickly become my stable buoy whenever my emotions threatened to overwhelm me.

"What's *he* doing here?" Harper suddenly murmured.

"Who?"

"Him."

I followed her gaze to the dark-haired man with piercing green eyes, wearing a black suit with a maroon tie. He was sipping a cocktail and perusing the group more like a predator than a guest.

But Ethan Stark wasn't a guest. At least, he hadn't been on my guest list. Victor had probably invited him. Ethan worked as an investigator for the insurance company that had insured the art in Victor's office, art that had been destroyed during the hotel fire. He had shown up in my hospital room the day after the fire to interview me, and then again at my apartment a week later, armed with detailed blueprints, security footage, and more questions.

He'd been particularly focused on my presence in the office so late, the elevator's malfunction, and Andrew appearing at exactly the right moment. I'd explained everything, but there was something unnerving about the way he relentlessly questioned me, the way he looked at me as if I were a puzzle piece he was trying to fit into a bigger picture.

Over the following months, he'd backed off, probably because he'd found no evidence to prove our stories weren't true. But now he was here at our wedding, and he was the last person I wanted to see.

"Did you know he was coming?" Harper asked, turning back to me.

"No. I thought the fire claims were settled months ago. And why would he be here on this island? The fire happened in Newport Beach."

"I heard Victor is moving some of his personal art collection to his villa here. Apparently, he's planning to spend more time on the island and less time in Beverly Hills."

"It is a beautiful location, but the Carringtons lead such busy lives, it's difficult to believe they'd be happy camping out on this island."

Harper shrugged. "They can afford to have as many homes as they want. And while Victor and Paula lead busy lives, they don't always seem to be living their lives in the same place. I'm not sure that marriage isn't in name only." Harper lifted her wine glass to take another drink, then realized it was empty. "I need a refill. Do you want something?"

"Not yet. I'm trying to pace myself."

"Why on earth would you want to do that? It's your wedding weekend. Have fun, go wild. It's your last chance."

"I don't care about going wild."

"Well, that's true. I sometimes wonder if Andrew knows you're not into partying as much as he is."

Andrew probably did like parties more than I did, but he was happy to leave when I was ready to go. And he always told me that being alone with me was all he really wanted or needed.

As Harper left to go to the bar, Ethan Stark appeared in front of me, carrying two glasses of champagne.

"Congratulations," he said, handing me a glass.

"Thank you," I said, avoiding his penetrating green gaze. There was something unnervingly perceptive about the way he watched people, as if he could see right through to their soul.

"I'm probably the last person you wanted to see at your rehearsal dinner," he said, a hint of a smile softening his hard jaw.

"You are," I admitted. "What are you doing on the island?"

"I'm overseeing the security for Victor's art collection, which is being delivered to his villa this week."

"That has nothing to do with my wedding or this rehearsal dinner."

"Victor told me the wedding events are open to everyone on staff."

"That's true," I said tightly. "I hope you enjoy yourself."

"No, you don't," he said with a wry smile. "But I get it. I'm not very popular with people I have to investigate."

"Well, clearly your investigation came up with nothing, or I would have heard from you before now."

"The insurance company paid off on the paintings that were allegedly destroyed," he said. "I'm still not convinced they weren't stolen and that the fire wasn't cover for the theft. Unfortunately, I can't prove that."

I was relieved to hear that the investigation was over. I didn't want anything to mar our wedding weekend.

"It's interesting how quickly you and Andrew went from a rescue to a wedding," Ethan continued. "It's only been six months since you met."

"When you know something is right, you know."

"Or you're not looking closely enough. Perfection is often an illusion."

"Andrew and I aren't perfect, but we are in love. And that is not an illusion," I said. "Do you come by your cynicism because of your job or because you haven't been lucky enough to find love?"

He gave me a small smile. "Both. Working fraud for the last

decade has definitely made me unwilling to take anything at face value. But I was also married for a short time until I found out my wife wanted the big fancy wedding far more than the marriage."

I couldn't say I was surprised he'd been married. He was very attractive in an intense, I'm going to know everything about you kind of way. Maybe that's why his wife had left him. But I kept that thought to myself, muttering, "I'm sorry."

"Love can be blinding."

Another not-so-subtle insinuation I was moving too fast. "I'm not blinded by love. I have my eyes wide open. Please don't judge my relationship by your own."

"Fine. How well do you know Allison McGuire?" he asked, changing the subject.

The random question startled me. "Who's Allison McGuire?"

"You don't know her? She's the redhead talking to Andrew."

I turned to see Andrew's trio had expanded to include a beautiful woman with dark red hair, wearing a form-fitting strapless dress, her shoulders bare, and a beautiful diamond necklace hanging around her neck. I had never seen her before, but Andrew was giving her a warm smile that suggested he knew her well.

"She must be one of Andrew's friends," I murmured.

"You haven't met her?"

"Not yet."

"Interesting. Did you know Allison had been staying in the room next to Andrew's for the three days prior to the hotel fire?"

"No. But he was there for a conference. I assume she was as well."

"She was registered for the conference."

"There you go."

"But they were more than friends back then, which makes me wonder why he'd invite his ex to his wedding, especially since you don't even know who she is."

My palms started to sweat. I felt like he'd just dropped a bomb, and he'd done it deliberately. He was looking for a reaction, and I really shouldn't give him one.

"How do you know they were more than friends?" I asked carefully. "Or is that another theory?"

He pulled out his phone, clicked on the screen, and turned it around to show me a photo of Andrew and Allison embracing outside the hotel. They were gazing into each other's eyes, and the hug definitely felt more intimate than friendly. The image hit me like a physical blow. Andrew had never mentioned he'd been at the conference with anyone he was involved with. But then, he hadn't really talked about his past at all. He'd told me he couldn't remember anyone he'd met before me, that everyone else had faded from his mind.

"Maybe you should ask him about Allison before you say I do," Ethan suggested.

"I don't need to do that. I trust Andrew completely. I don't care about his past relationships. He's with me now. Whatever happened before we met doesn't matter. And that photo was taken before the fire, which was before he met me."

"But isn't it odd that she's here at your wedding? Especially since he never mentioned her to you. It seems like you might want to ask yourself what else you don't know."

"Why are you trying to stir up trouble, Mr. Stark? You told me the investigation is closed."

"It's officially closed. Unofficially, I'm still looking for answers, and I'm going to find them."

"You won't find them here." I walked away. I couldn't listen to him for another second, but his words lingered in my mind. And somewhere beneath my anger was a whisper of doubt.

Why hadn't Andrew told me about Allison? He'd never even mentioned her name to me.

When I reached Andrew, Allison and his groomsmen had disappeared, and he was looking at something on his phone. As I joined him, he gave me a smile and put his phone into his pocket.

"I was just about to come looking for you, Lauren." He paused, his gaze running down my very expensive, form-fitting, navy-blue beaded cocktail dress that, according to the stylist, was the perfect shade for my dark-brown hair and light-blue eyes. "You look beautiful."

"Thanks. It took a village," I said lightly, still feeling like an imposter. I wasn't a sophisticated woman. I preferred jeans and sweaters, very little makeup, and barely running a brush through my shoulder-length wavy brown hair. But tonight, I looked like someone else, and maybe that was okay, because Andrew was looking at me with so much pleasure and longing that it made spending time in the makeup chair all the more worthwhile. "You look great, too. We clean up pretty well."

"We do." He gave me a speculative look. "Is everything okay? You seem...nervous."

"Ethan Stark is here."

"Really?" He turned his head, perusing the room, his gaze landing on Ethan, who was standing across the room, sipping his drink, and making no pretense of not watching us. "Did you talk to him?"

"Yes. He's still very suspicious of us. He can't seem to shake the idea we had something to do with starting the hotel fire and stealing Victor's paintings."

"He's never been able to prove that, and the investigation is over. I wouldn't worry about him, Lauren."

"He said the official investigation is completed, but he's still digging."

Andrew shrugged. "Well, he won't find anything, because there's nothing to find."

"I wish he wasn't here. He's very annoying."

"Don't let him get to you, Lauren."

"I don't like that he thinks we're thieves."

"Who cares what he thinks?" Andrew challenged. "We know

who we are. And since the Carringtons are paying for everything, they get to have whoever they want at our wedding. If they believed we were thieves, they wouldn't have put us in the marketing campaign. Ignore him."

"You're right. Obviously, he told Victor what he thought about us, and Victor didn't care."

"Exactly. It's all good. Look at this beautiful restaurant we're standing in. We're about to be served dinner by a Michelin-starred chef. This is a wedding most people could only dream about. You should be smiling."

His words brought a smile to my lips. "You're right. I'm just starting to feel like I'm getting married in front of strangers."

"You have friends and family here, too. Try to relax and enjoy yourself."

I felt bad for dragging down his good mood, because he seemed irritated by my comments.

"I'm going to do that," I promised, but as soon as I saw the woman he'd been speaking to earlier re-enter the room with Andrew's friend Colin, I felt my entire body stiffen. I had to say something, but I didn't want to sound accusatory. "Who's that woman?" I asked, trying not to act like I cared that much. "The one with Colin."

"Allison McGuire," he replied without a trace of emotion in his voice.

"Is she with Colin?"

"Not as his date. She's a mutual friend of ours."

"I don't think I've heard you mention her."

"She's an interior designer we work with. We've known each other for years. She's been traveling in Europe the past few months, so I wasn't sure she could make it here this weekend."

And because she'd been traveling, it was probably why I'd never met her. I felt stupid for having felt even an ounce of jealousy about her. "That makes sense."

He gave me a speculative look. "What do you mean?"

"Mr. Stark told me Allison is your ex-girlfriend, and that she was staying in the room next to yours in the hotel the night we met."

An angry light flickered in Andrew's eyes. "She's not my ex-girlfriend. But she was at the conference. She works with a lot of real-estate developers." He paused, giving me a pointed look. "I'm in love with you, Lauren. I can't believe you would let some investigator make you think otherwise."

"I didn't believe him. I'm just telling you what he said."

"Good. Because you and me—that's all that matters."

"It is," I agreed as he drew me in for a kiss, his warm lips reassuring me more than any words could.

He was right. We were the only two people who mattered.

And if he wasn't right...Well, it was probably too late to be wrong.

CHAPTER TWO

Thirty minutes later, as the waiters discreetly asked our guests to be seated for dinner, Andrew and I made our way to the front of the room, where a tall, silver-haired man with bright- blue eyes was waiting for us to join him at the microphone. Victor Carrington, the CEO and owner of the Carrington Hospitality Group, was in his mid-sixties and was a gregarious, handsome man who loved luxury and sophistication. He also liked adventure, which was why this new coastal retreat would offer guests hiking trips, kayaking, and boating adventures, as well as a five-star restaurant and spa.

I'd only met Victor three times in my life, once at my first company picnic six months after I'd started working at the company and twice during the past three months when Andrew and I had met with the executive team before being selected to be the couple featured in the marketing campaign.

While Andrew and Victor had hit it off immediately, I'd felt a little intimidated by him. But then, he was my boss, and I didn't want to do anything to jeopardize a job I loved. Andrew, on the other hand, had relished the opportunity to connect with Victor. Andrew was a real-estate developer, and while his small business was far from the scale of operations of the Carrington Group, Andrew had big ambitions and admired Victor immensely.

"Here's to our beautiful couple," Victor said, stepping up to the microphone, as he waved his hand toward us.

His gesture brought forth a wave of applause, and my nerves ratcheted up a notch as I looked out at the crowd. There were so many people I didn't know. So many people who didn't seem that supportive, like Ethan Stark and the beautiful redhead who was giving me a very speculative look. Or maybe that was only in my mind.

I'd never been good in groups. I felt more comfortable in the background. I liked my work to show how creative and interesting I was, but there was no work tonight. This was all personal, and yet it felt very impersonal, too. I wished Andrew and I had eloped. It wouldn't have been my dream wedding, but this dream wasn't turning out exactly as I'd imagined.

"Thank you all for coming," Victor said. "I'm honored to be hosting the wedding of Lauren and Andrew. This weekend is going to be very special, and my family is thrilled to be a part of it. My wife, Paula, will arrive tomorrow. But I have my son, Bennett, here." He waved his hand to the thirty-two-year-old brown-haired man standing off to the side.

Bennett nodded his head to the crowd as another round of applause rang out.

"At the Carrington Hospitality Group," Victor continued, "we've always believed our resorts should feel like a home away from home, and our fellow travelers and hosts should feel like family. So, this weekend, we're all going to be family. And we're going to celebrate the beautiful love story that Lauren and Andrew have found together. We want this new resort to be the site of many more happy weddings to come. We appreciate that Lauren and Andrew are giving us a chance to start with them. Now, Andrew, would you like to say a few words?"

I was happy Victor had called for Andrew instead of me.

Andrew let go of my hand to shake Victor's. Then he

moved to the microphone and sent his dazzling smile around the room. "Lauren and I are grateful and honored to be having our wedding at this beautiful new resort. As Victor mentioned, we truly feel like we're part of the Carrington family, and we want you to know how appreciative we are. To the resort staff and to the company employees who have helped create this magical time, you are all amazing, the best of the best. To our friends and family who have made the trek here, we can't tell you how lucky we feel to have you be a part of this."

He paused for a moment, turning to two women standing off to the side. "We want to give a special shout-out to Megan Farris and Jeanette Bilson, who have put in long hours before tonight, and I'm sure will put in many more long hours before this weekend is over. You are truly making this our dream wedding. Thank you."

As the crowd clapped once more, Andrew turned to me and held out his hand.

I stepped forward, feeling anxious, shaky, and more than a little relieved when his fingers tightened around mine.

"And to my beautiful bride," he said, gazing at me, "who is making me the happiest man on earth, I can't wait to see what our future brings."

He gave me a kiss as our guests cheered once more.

As he ended our kiss, he added, "We'll have more toasts later in the evening. But for now, please enjoy your meal."

The music ensemble in the corner of the room began to play quietly as Andrew ushered me to our table and pulled out my chair. He was always such a gentleman.

"You didn't want to say anything, Lauren?" Harper asked as I sat down next to her.

I shook my head. "I'm happy to let others do the talking. It was very nice of Victor to be here to welcome everyone."

"He's definitely taking a personal interest in this event," Harper commented as she sipped her wine. "But it's not surprising. He's invited a lot of industry media here, so he needs to be front and center."

The reminder of the media present sent another wave of anxiety through me. I dreaded the thought of the photos and interviews ahead, but I wasn't going to think about those now. Putting my napkin in my lap, I smiled at our friends.

Sitting next to Harper was my other bridesmaid, Jamie Trent, and her fiancé Brad Stevens. On the other side of Brad was Andrew's best man Colin McCallum, who was on his own this weekend. Filling out the table was Jay Hollingsworth, who was with a woman named Dana. Apparently, she was someone he'd just started dating, which was why I hadn't met her before tonight. Both Colin and Jay worked with Andrew at his real-estate development company.

"This wine is fantastic," Colin said as he held up his glass of red wine. "The Carringtons are pulling out all the stops for you two."

"They've been very generous," Andrew agreed. "It's probably because Lauren is one of their best employees."

"It's all about the marketing campaign," I said hastily. "That's why everything is so good. It's not about me."

"It's a little about you," Harper said dryly. "It's not like they offered Jamie the wedding of a lifetime. She's engaged, too. This could have been her dream wedding."

My gaze swung to Jamie, a short brunette who was far more easygoing and positive than Harper. But tonight, her smile looked forced.

"I already had my venue selected when this all started, and I'm having a much bigger guest list," Jamie said. "This is perfect for you, Lauren. I have no hard feelings about it. I wouldn't have felt comfortable getting married as part of a promotion, not that this isn't amazing. And I'm thrilled I can help make this weekend special for you both. I want it to be perfect."

"It will be perfect," Andrew interjected, putting his hand on my thigh, sensing I probably needed the comfort of his touch.

He was so good at reading my feelings. I didn't even have to say anything most of the time; he just knew what to do. And that's why it didn't matter that I didn't know half the people in this room, because I knew him. All I had to do was eat a delicious meal and enjoy myself. I really didn't need to worry about anything else.

The dinner was wonderful, as expected, and after dessert, there were fun toasts from Harper and Colin, both of which recapped our first meet and our whirlwind love affair. After that, Megan and Bennett introduced us to the media, both traditional industry press, as well as travel bloggers and influencers. Most of those conversations were brief, with promises of a longer chat over the next few days. Eventually, the room began to clear, and we were able to call it a night.

As Andrew and I left the restaurant and walked hand in hand through the lush grounds of the resort, I felt my stress ease. It was a beautiful starry night with a temp in the low sixties and the crashing ocean waves adding a reassuring and calming cadence.

"It's nice out here," I murmured.

"The weather gods want this weekend to be perfect, too," Andrew said lightly.

I gave him a smile. "I'm beginning to worry we've said *perfect* too many times. I don't want to jinx anything."

"That would be impossible." He paused, turning to look at me. "I wish I could help you feel more relaxed, Lauren."

"I wish you could, too," I said with a sigh. "I don't know why I feel so anxious. It's probably all the people we need to impress. It doesn't feel like this is about us starting a marriage. I know that's the trade-off we made for getting all this for free, but it doesn't feel the way I thought it would."

"I get it. But there are more positives than negatives, right?"

"Yes, that's true."

"But you don't look convinced," he said, giving me a knowing look.

"I just feel a little off. Harper and Jamie have been tense, too. I'm starting to think they both have some resentment toward me getting so much attention from the Carringtons. You heard what Harper said about Jamie not getting picked to be the bride."

"I also heard Jamie say her wedding will be much bigger. That was a factor, remember? We were the right couple because we had a good story and because we didn't want a big wedding."

I nodded in agreement.

"I've never been good at girl drama," he continued. "But I suspect Harper is feeling sorry for herself because she's single again. And maybe Jamie wishes she could have her rehearsal dinner in a five-star restaurant. But you're all good friends, and I'm sure they care more about you than about the rest of it."

"I hope they do. I've always thought we were close, but lately...I don't know. It has felt different ever since we got engaged. I wish..." My words fell away as I realized I didn't even know what I wished.

"What? What do you wish, Lauren?"

I gave him a helpless smile. "I don't know, Andrew."

"Yes, you do. I think your nervousness is because you're missing your mom. You don't want to think about the fact that she's not here. So you're getting annoyed by everyone else. Could that be why no one seems as supportive as you want them to be?"

He made a fair point. "Possibly. It is difficult to do this without her. I'm mostly okay, but now and then, I'm reminded of how much of my life she'll miss. She never even got to meet you. And she won't be able to see me get married or have kids." I blew out a breath. "I guess it is bothering me more than I thought."

"That's completely understandable. But from everything

you've told me about your mom, I'm sure she would want you to be happy on your wedding day."

"She would. She wanted me to be happy every day. We had some good talks before she died, but it's still hard."

"What can I do?"

"You're already doing it." I leaned in for a kiss, letting my mouth linger against his warm heat. "You're such a good man, Andrew. I love you so much."

"I love you, too."

"Maybe we don't need to sleep apart tonight," I suggested. We'd made the plan earlier, thinking it would make our wedding night more special, but we'd practically been inseparable the last few months, so I didn't really know what we were trying to prove.

He gave me a regretful smile. "It's tempting, but I think we should stick with our plan. It will make tomorrow even better. Everything is going to be fine, Lauren."

"I guess," I said with a little sigh.

He laughed. "Come on, let's go."

A few moments later, we entered the hotel lobby and headed to the elevators. I was staying in the bridal suite on the third floor while Andrew would be spending the night in a three-bedroom villa with Colin, Jay, and Dana.

"You don't have to walk me all the way to my room," I said as I pushed the button for the elevator. "I can make it from here."

"I'm going to see you safely to your suite."

"Our suite," I corrected. "It feels too big and extravagant for only me."

"Well, I'll enjoy it tomorrow night and for the rest of the week."

When we got off the elevator, Andrew used his keycard to open the door, and I was shocked to see Harper and Jamie sitting on the couch with a few other women from work.

"It's girl time," Harper declared. "No boys allowed, Andrew."

"I know. Have fun, ladies." He gave me a smile. "I told you everything would be fine. You should always believe me, Lauren."

"I do believe you. I'll see you tomorrow." I kissed him again and then turned back to my friends as he left.

"We couldn't let you spend this evening alone," Jamie said as she got up from the couch to hand me a glass of champagne. "It's your last night as a single woman."

"This is really special. I appreciate all of you so much," I added, my gaze sweeping the four women in the room, two of whom would be standing up with me tomorrow.

"We feel the same way about you," Jamie said, giving me a hug. "Sorry if I seemed off earlier. Brad was in a pissy mood. I'm not jealous of your wedding, but he's a little annoyed that we can't afford anything so grand. I was angry with him, not you."

"I understand, and we're good. Everything is good," I said, finally feeling the truth of that statement for the first time all day. I might not know everyone at my wedding, but I had the groom and my friends, and that was all that mattered.

"Change out of those clothes and get comfortable," Harper ordered.

"I'll just be a minute," I said, slipping through the living room into the bedroom, which was a white haven of romantic décor. I took off my dress and put on my comfy PJs. As I put on my slippers, I realized the door to the balcony was slightly ajar, which seemed odd. I must have left it open when I'd changed for dinner.

As I moved to close the door, I heard voices on the lawn, and one sounded like Andrew. When I stepped outside, I saw two people walking away from the building toward a thicket of trees. My heart skipped a beat when I realized it was Andrew, and the woman with him had red hair that glinted in the moonlight. He was with Allison McGuire.

I swallowed hard, my earlier doubts rushing back like a freight train intent on wiping me out. I told myself there was nothing to be concerned about. They weren't touching each other, although they were walking very close together, but they were friends. He'd invited her to the wedding. She was a coworker.

But as they disappeared behind the trees, a number of questions ran through my mind. *Was Allison the reason Andrew had been happy to spend the night apart? Why hadn't he told me about her before inviting her? And why hadn't he introduced us at some point tonight?* I'd seen her looking at us a few times, and Andrew had gazed in her direction as well, but they'd made no move to connect. *Had that been deliberate? Or was I making up problems that weren't there?*

I decided to go with the latter, but then a gust of cold breeze came off the ocean, sending another chill down my spine. I shook off the foreboding feeling and forced myself to go back inside. I closed the door and locked it, as if that would banish the worrying thoughts from my mind.

Andrew had told me Allison was just a friend, and I had no reason not to believe him. Once we had the pressure of the wedding behind us, our lives would go back to normal, and I was really looking forward to that, which probably wasn't the sentiment a bride should be having the night before the wedding.

I put a smile on my face and went to join my friends, because no one could know that I was anything less than thrilled.

CHAPTER THREE

My wedding day dawned with bright sunshine and a deep blue sky. It was absolutely perfect, and as I ran along a winding seaside path in the hills above the ocean a little before eight, I savored the warmth of the sun on my head, wanting to soak it in, wanting every step to take away the anxiety I'd gone to bed with and that was still haunting my thoughts.

While the fun night with my friends had distracted me for a while, my worries had returned the second I'd gone to bed, and after hours of restless tossing and turning, I'd gotten up with the sun and decided to do what I always did when my emotions were too much—run. I'd started running when I was a kid, when my mom worked late hours to keep a roof over our heads and I worried about money, or when I felt anxiety every time I had to draw a picture of my family and had only my mom and me to put in it.

I never knew my father. He'd died before my mom found out she was pregnant, and she'd only known him for a few weeks, so she knew next to nothing about him. She said I'd saved her life because she'd been sad after he died, and knowing she was going to have a baby was what kept her going. But her father, my grandfather, had not felt like I was a gift but rather a reminder of his daughter's shame. He'd disowned her and hadn't been around while I was growing up. Since my grandmother had died years earlier and my aunt and uncle lived on the other side of the country, it really was just me and my mom, and she had had to make a lot of sacrifices to raise me on her own.

She'd worked in the hotel business, too, starting as a front desk clerk and working her way up to supervisor and night manager. It was a job with often demanding hours and not great pay, but I'd loved hanging out in the back rooms of the hotel with her, sometimes getting to take a dip in the pool late in the evening when no one was around.

My mother had tried to steer me away from following in her footsteps. She'd insisted she wanted more for me: opportunities to grow, to be in charge, to make good money. So, I'd gone into marketing, and I'd stayed away from the hospitality industry until after she'd died. When the marketing job with the Carrington Group had come up, I'd decided to try for it, because it was a good-paying corporate job but also in a hotel and it felt like it would tie me to my mom in some small way.

That thought brought another wave of sadness, and I increased my pace, wondering why it felt like I was running away from something when it should feel like I was running toward something. I was about to enter a new chapter in my life, one that held promise, love, and excitement. That's what I should be thinking about. That's what I should be running toward.

So I turned around and headed back to the resort, adjusting my earbuds and changing my music to a more upbeat song. As I ran, my sneakers crunched softly against the gravel path that wound along the shoreline. I had a better view of the seashore going in this direction, and the sunlight now cast a warm, golden light over the water, which was mostly calm, just a few ripples now and then.

Catalina was different in the early hours. Quieter. The tourists hadn't yet descended onto the paths that led into the main town of Avalon, and the buzz of activity that usually filled the air later in the day was replaced by the soft sounds of waves and the distant cries of seabirds. The scent of saltwater and wildflowers drifted on the breeze, mingling with the earthy aroma of sun-warmed sand.

As I drew closer to the resort, I couldn't help but admire the grandeur of the Carrington Coastal Retreat. The hotel and villas with their white stucco walls and red-tiled roofs stood out against the rugged cliffs and hills rising up behind the main building where there were more villas currently under construction. Those wouldn't be opening for another three months, but Victor hadn't wanted to wait a second longer before bringing his new resort out into the world. And I had to admit this place was special.

The resort had been built in a previously unincorporated part of the island. While the main ferry stopped at the bigger harbor in Avalon, a mile away, there was also a private boat dock in front of the resort where Victor's large yacht was already bobbing in its slip along with several smaller boats, some with Carrington Coastal Retreat logos that would be used for sunset and sunrise cruises.

The pretty view drove all the worrying thoughts out of my mind. I had a beautiful day ahead of me. Not only would I marry the man of my dreams, but before that, I would be treated to a day of luxury and pampering, followed by a beautiful oceanfront ceremony on the great lawn and a spectacular reception in the indoor/outdoor banquet facility.

At the end of it all, I would be Andrew's wife, and that's what mattered most. I was going to build a new life with Andrew, and hopefully, we would have children one day. That was one thing we had talked about. We wanted our kids to have two parents to love them and care for them. Andrew had been raised by divorced parents who had hated each other and gone on to marry other people. Once he was of age, they'd had no time for him, and he hadn't talked to them in years. And with my mom gone, I was looking forward to building a new family with him.

Ethan Stark had told me his wife had wanted the wedding, not the marriage, but I definitely wanted the marriage more than the wedding. As if I'd conjured Ethan up with my thoughts, my steps slowed as I saw him standing by the railing in front of the dock. He was dressed more casually today in dark slacks and a short-sleeved black polo shirt. When he saw me, he straightened and moved down the path toward me, as if suspecting I was about to make an abrupt turn and dash through the trees, which was what I wanted to do. But that would make me look guilty of something, and I didn't want to give him the wrong impression.

"Morning," he said with a nod. "How was your run?"

"It was good."

"I didn't expect the bride to be out so early."

"The rest of the day will be busy."

"That's true. Weddings are a crazy time, so many things to worry about. But what you don't realize at the time is that place settings aren't what you should be worrying about."

"I'm not worrying about place settings. Jeanette is very good at her job."

"That's not exactly what I meant," he said dryly.

"I know what you meant, and I assume you're talking about your own experience again."

"I believe that the marriage should get more thought than the wedding, but that's not the way it usually goes. You spend days and weeks talking about color schemes, flowers, and wedding invitations, instead of discussing what's really important: fidelity, children, money, and work. You see red flags and hear warning bells, but you blow right past them because the wedding train has already left the station."

"Andrew and I are on the same page," I said confidently. "We know what we want. And there have been no red flags or warning bells."

"You don't think the red-haired Allison is a red flag?" he challenged.

I frowned at his question. "No. I asked Andrew about her,

and he told me they never had a relationship, that they're just friends, and they work together on occasion."

"Did you tell him about the photo I showed you?"

"No. But that photo was nothing. Two friends exchanging a hug. You're making something out of nothing."

"It's not the only picture of them together, Lauren."

"What are you talking about?"

"I went online last night. I checked out Allison's social media, and there are other photos of her and Andrew together."

My lips tightened. "Are those photos from the last six months? Because if they aren't, they don't matter to me."

"You're working very hard to convince yourself of that."

"I'm really not, and I don't understand why you're trying to start trouble. I'm marrying Andrew today, and there is nothing you can say or do that will stop that. I trust Andrew far more than I trust you. I don't even know you."

"I'm not sure you know him. I thought you did, that you were working together, but the more we talk, the less likely that seems."

"You're obsessed with trying to pin a crime on us, but you're wrong. And I'm not going to keep trying to defend myself or my soon-to-be husband."

"Has Andrew told you about his family?"

I sighed. "His parents are divorced and married to other people. He doesn't see them anymore. Are you going to tell me that's not true?"

Ethan gave me a long look. "Andrew's father, Frank Chadwick, died four years ago. He left Andrew fifty thousand dollars in his will. Shortly after that, Andrew opened his own real-estate development company."

My stomach churned. Andrew had never wanted to talk about his parents. In fact, he'd said they were dead to him because he'd been dead to them once they moved on with their new families. I probably should have asked more questions, but it was clearly a painful subject he hadn't wanted to discuss, and I'd chosen to respect that.

"Well, they were estranged long before he died. What does it matter to you, anyway? I don't understand what game you're playing."

His green gaze seared through mine, making me feel like he could see right through me.

"Maybe you don't understand the game at all," he murmured. "But I'm not the one who's playing it. That would be Andrew."

"That's not true. You've created some story in your head about Andrew and me because you want to pin an art theft on us, but you have no evidence. What does Mr. Carrington think about your suspicions? I can't believe he would have ever chosen us to be the faces of his grand launch and marketing campaign if he thought we were criminals."

"I've expressed my concerns to Mr. Carrington, but without proof, he didn't want to act on my suspicions. He likes both of you. He thinks I'm wrong."

I was relieved to hear that. "You are wrong, Ethan. You're chasing the wrong people. You need to move on."

"I can't do that. My employer is about to insure Victor's private collection. I need to protect those pieces and my employer's investment. I have to be suspicious of everyone and everything, especially when several people who were at the hotel fire are now also here. I'm not just talking about you and Andrew, but also about Allison McGuire, Colin McCallum, and Jay Hollingsworth, all three of whom were staying in the hotel that week."

"Because they were at the conference together. And I was working in the hotel," I said, exasperated by his stubbornness. "I have nothing more to say to you except this. It's Victor's collection, his art pieces, and if he's not worried about us, you shouldn't be, either."

"I'm paid to be worried, Lauren. And I don't work for Victor. I work for the insurance company, which is counting on me to protect their investment. I will make sure that the security at this resort and Victor's villa is impenetrable. There won't be another fire or another theft. Not on my watch. So, I'm going to keep a close eye on anyone I think is suspicious, and that includes you and your soon-to-be husband." He paused. "Look up Allison online. Look up Andrew's friends, his background. You have time to possibly save yourself a lot of heartache. You may believe I'm your enemy, but I might be your best friend. And remember, it's not too late to run. You're even wearing the right shoes for it."

"I'm not running away from Andrew; I'm running to him. I know who he is. You're as wrong about him as you are about me."

"I doubt that." His phone buzzed, and he pulled it out of his pocket. "I have to go."

"Good. Because we're done."

He turned and walked away without a response, and while I should have been happy about that, I felt uneasy. Despite my defense of Andrew, Ethan had put some doubts in my mind about Andrew's relationship with Allison, and the fact that I'd seen them together last night still stuck in my mind. I also wondered why Andrew wouldn't have told me his father was dead. *Why would that have been a secret?* We'd talked about my mother's death a lot. Maybe he hadn't wanted to speak about his father because he hadn't felt the same sadness and grief. That was probably the reason.

Sighing, I pushed the anxious thoughts out of my head and told myself to stop borrowing trouble. Nothing was going on with Andrew and Allison. What had happened with his dad was also in the past. It was time for me to get on with my day.

I headed up the path to the resort, pausing when I saw a moving van parked in front of Victor's three-story villa, which was as grand as the main building of the resort. There were at least four men unloading the truck, while Ethan stood nearby, talking to Bennett Carrington, Victor's son.

I was about to cut through the trees to avoid walking in front of the villa when, to my shock, Victor and Andrew came out of the house together. And right behind them was the beautiful redhead who seemed to be everywhere—Allison McGuire. She was chatting with an older blonde woman, who I quickly realized was Paula Carrington, Victor's wife. She must have arrived early this morning.

What on earth was Andrew doing with Allison, and why were they talking to Victor and Paula like they were all old friends?

When they reached the sidewalk, Andrew shook hands with Victor, Allison gave Paula a hug, and then Andrew and Allison walked away together. Fortunately for me, they weren't coming in my direction, because I suddenly realized how embarrassing it would have been to be caught staring at them.

I hurried through the trees, finding my way back to the main building. I jogged up the steps and bypassed the elevator to take more stairs to my room. I needed to burn off the anxiety that was rocketing through me again. When I hit my floor, I saw Harper knocking on my door.

"Oh, there you are," Harper said. "I was wondering if you were still asleep, but it looks like you've been running."

"Yes, I was."

"Is something wrong?" Her gaze narrowed on my face. "You look really red. Why did you run so hard the morning of your wedding?"

"I'm fine." I pulled out my key, avoiding her questioning gaze as I opened the door. "What are you doing here so early? Weren't we going to meet at eleven?"

"I thought you might want some company."

"Actually, what I want right now is a shower."

"What's going on, Lauren? You've been nothing but blissfully happy the last few months, but ever since we arrived on the island, you're tense. Are you having second thoughts?"

"No," I snapped. "And you promised you were going to support me."

"I am supporting you," she said, looking surprised by my words. "But you are clearly upset, and since I haven't said or done anything, I'm guessing it's not me you're bothered by. So, who's to blame for your mood?"

"No one. I just want this day to be over."

"You should want to savor every second of your wedding day. This is about Andrew, isn't it?"

"No, it's not about him," I said with exasperation, knowing Harper still wanted to be right about me moving too quickly into marriage. "I had another run-in with that insurance investigator. He's really annoying. And while I know we are completely innocent, I don't like to be the focus of his unfounded suspicions."

"You need to put him out of your head. You and Andrew are representing the company. Do you think the Carringtons would have paid for all this if they had any doubts about you?"

"Probably not."

"No *probably* about it. So stop being so nervous around the investigator." Harper cocked her head to one side, giving me a speculative look. "Or are your nerves more about the beautiful woman with the striking red hair who seems to be very friendly with Andrew?"

My body stiffened as I stared at her in surprise. "Why would you ask me about her?"

"I saw Andrew having what looked like an argument with her during the rehearsal dinner last night when I went out on the patio to get some air. It was right before dessert was served. You were at the table talking to Jamie. When Andrew saw me, he shut down their conversation and came inside, but I have to admit I was curious about her. Who is she?"

"A work friend. They were probably talking about something work related."

"What's her name?"

"Allison McGuire." I shivered as a sweaty chill ran down my body. "Anyway, there is nothing wrong. I just need to take a shower and focus on what's important, which is my wedding."

"You're right. Can I get you anything?"

"No." I offered her an apologetic smile. "And I'm sorry I snapped at you."

"You're entitled to have some big emotions today. I'll come back at eleven."

"Thanks."

As Harper left, I walked over to the small refrigerator in the kitchenette and pulled out a bottle of water. I took a sip and leaned against the counter, trying to calm my nerves. For a distraction, I took out my phone, but that was a bad idea because Ethan's words now rang through my head—*I didn't have to believe him; I could do my own research.*

Before I could think twice, I went on social media and searched for Allison McGuire. It took a few tries to find the woman I was looking for. I went through her accounts, searching her photos for some sign of Andrew, because clearly Ethan had found something when he'd investigated her.

It took several minutes for me to go far enough back in time, since Allison loved to post photos of every meal she ate, as well as design photos from her many jobs. I was about to quit looking at her annoying face, until I found what I hadn't wanted to find: a photo of the two of them together.

My stomach tensed as I saw Allison with her arms around Andrew's neck. His hands were on her waist. They were gazing into each other's eyes while standing on the balcony of some hotel, fireworks going off in the distance. The date was from the previous July, which was well before I'd met Andrew, so there really was no reason for me to be jealous, except that Andrew had claimed they'd never dated, that they were just friends. They looked like more than friends in this photo. There was an intimacy to their stance that suggested they knew each other on a much deeper level.

I felt sick as a dozen thoughts collided in my head, and I

blew out a shaky breath, trying to rid myself of the onrushing wave of doubt.

Did I have any right to be angry? The photo had been posted almost a year ago. Maybe I was reading into it. They could have been drinking and just had a moment, not a relationship.

But Andrew had been so definite when I'd asked him about her last night, when he'd said there'd been nothing between them. *If he'd lied about that...*

No! Stop!

This was all Ethan Stark's fault. He'd put the doubts in my head.

But he hadn't put this photo online. Nor had Ethan put Allison and Andrew together last night or a few minutes ago when I'd seen them with Victor and Paula.

Why had they been with the Carringtons?

Watching them say goodbye to Victor and Paula had made me feel like they were the couple, and I was the outsider. My pulse wouldn't slow down. Nor would my breath. I had so many questions and no answers.

My phone buzzed, and I jumped. I drew in a breath as I saw an incoming text from Andrew: *Morning, Beautiful. Can't wait to marry you. Love you.*

His words immediately eased the tightness in my chest.

What was I doing? Andrew was a good man. And it wasn't like I'd caught him cheating on me. I'd just found a photo of him from a year ago with a woman he was friends with. I needed to get a grip.

I read Andrew's message two more times, then texted back: *I love you, too. See you soon.*

I wasn't going to confront him, not today, not hours before our wedding. That would be pointless. But maybe there was someone else I could talk to. Someone who could fill in some blanks.

Moving back into the suite, I picked up the hotel phone and

asked for Allison McGuire's room. A moment later, a woman answered. My gut tightened.

"Allison?" I said.

"Yes. Who's this?"

I couldn't answer. I couldn't do this to Andrew. I couldn't go behind his back. I hung up the phone, my heart beating way too fast. I couldn't believe I'd just done that. *How stupid was I?*

I needed to take a shower. I needed to forget all about Allison and move on with the day, the happiest day of my life.

My cell phone suddenly buzzed, Andrew's name flashing across the screen with an incoming call. *Why was he calling me when we'd just texted?*

"Hello?" I said, trying to sound calm.

"Lauren? Is everything okay? Are you looking for me?"

"No. Why?"

"Allison said she thought you called her."

My heart almost leapt out of my chest. *Had Allison immediately called Andrew the second I'd hung up or had he been standing right next to her?*

"Lauren?" Andrew pressed. "What's going on?"

"Nothing. Sorry, I'm distracted. I was about to jump into the shower."

"Why did you call Allison?"

I could lie and say it wasn't me, but that might be easily disproven, and getting caught in a lie would be worse than saying I wanted to talk to her. But I needed a reason, a good reason. My mind spun. I had to come up with something fast.

Finally, I said, "The caterer told me that Allison hadn't marked down her entrée choice for steak or halibut. I said I'd find out. I didn't think the call went through. I didn't hear anything on the other end of the line. I was going to have you call her on her personal phone to find out what she wants to eat."

"Oh, okay. I can do that."

"Great. Can you text me the answer? I need to shower before the hair and makeup people arrive."

"No problem. You're sure there's nothing bothering you? Because I want this day to be perfect, and if anything is not perfect, you need to tell me."

My hand tightened on the phone. I was being stupid. Andrew loved me, and I loved him. Nothing and no one else mattered.

"I am happy. You're happy, too, right?"

"More than I ever thought I would be," he said with a sincerity that touched my heart. "I love you, Lauren. I can't wait to spend the rest of my life showing you that."

He always knew the right thing to say. "I can't wait for that, either."

I ended the call and vowed it would be the last time I let doubts about my wedding get into my head. I didn't want to look back at this day and wonder why I'd let an obsessed insurance investigator and an attractive redhead mess up my wedding.

CHAPTER FOUR

When Harper returned at eleven, along with Jamie, Jeanette Bilson, and Megan Farris, I was ready to go and determined not to get bogged down by unrelated problems on my wedding day. Andrew and I would have a lifetime to talk about everything and everyone in our lives—past, present, and future. And once Jeanette and Megan started going over my schedule for the day, I doubted there would be time to think at all.

While Jeanette would be acting as my day-of-wedding coordinator, Megan would be focused on directing the media team, which included two photographers, a videographer, and a social media expert, who would be posting throughout the day, beginning with the getting ready shots, to the first look, the actual wedding ceremony, and finally the reception.

Jeanette and Megan were both high-energy, driven women who were incredibly organized and determined to showcase their talents through a series of events that would be under the scrutiny of Victor, Bennett, and, even to some degree, Paula. While Paula didn't work in the company, her opinion might still matter to her husband and her son. And Bennett technically oversaw Megan's division, so she would definitely want to impress him.

I also wanted everything to go well and to do my part to the best of my ability. Because at the end of this, I still had a job I wanted to do well and a company I wanted to grow with.

As soon as Jeanette and Megan finished with the rundown, Taylor Castle and Carrie Ridgway arrived to set up for hair and makeup. Taylor and Carrie would be running the resort salon once it opened, but today they were responsible for making me and my bridesmaids look as good as possible.

"I think that's it for now," Jeanette said, drawing my attention back to her. "I've also scheduled room service to deliver healthy snacks and drinks for you and your bridal party. They should be arriving shortly."

"You've thought of everything," I said. "I really appreciate all the work you're both doing for me."

"This day will be perfect," Jeanette said. "You can count on that. If you have any questions, please contact me." She glanced at Megan, who had brought a photographer into the room and was discussing what photos should be taken. "Megan, do you need me for anything else right now? I need to talk to the banquet manager and the ceremony staging crew."

"I'm good," Megan replied. When Jeanette left, she turned back to me. "I'm going to the villa now to talk to Andrew and his groomsmen. My media crew will be back to take some photos at different points during the day. I've given them keycards so they can come and go. Do you have any questions, Lauren?"

"Not at the moment."

"Okay then. I can't stress enough how important all of this is. I know it's your wedding day, but the Carringtons have sunk a huge amount of money into this marketing campaign, and it has to work."

"I understand."

"I hope you do. The company has suffered some financial losses with the hotel fire in Newport, and also the storm damage at our properties in Florida. Victor wants everyone to see this new resort as our emergence from those issues, the new crown jewel in our collection. And there's a lot of pressure on the marketing team coming from him and also from Bennett, who has suddenly decided to actually work and doesn't seem to understand that the rest of us have been working all along."

I heard the irritation in her voice, and I knew it bothered her to report to Bennett, who knew next to nothing about the business and was only a vice president because he was Victor's son. "Do you think Bennett's interest will continue after this week?"

"Yes. I think he wants to take over the company, but Victor doesn't have a lot of respect for Bennett, so there's friction. But there's also blood. I'm sure Bennett will get everything at some point. It is a family business we work for."

"That's true."

"We just have to make sure Bennett doesn't mess anything up. He seems to be focused on new media—influencers and travel vloggers, so that should be an area he can't do too much damage in. Anyway, we have to accommodate him, even if some of his ideas are stupid. Don't tell him I said that."

"I'm on your team. I've got your back."

"Thanks," she said with a smile. "I'm trying to have your back, too, Lauren, but this wedding has taken on a life of its own. While I know you would like to keep parts of it personal and intimate, there's a lot at stake. This is a huge investment for the company, and it has to work."

"I understand."

"Good. I'll see you later."

As soon as Megan left, the temperature in the room warmed, and the atmosphere turned more fun as Harper put on some music, and we started talking about hair and makeup. The bridesmaids went first, which was fine with me. It was fun watching their makeovers. Around noon, room service arrived with bottles of champagne, sparkling water, and iced tea, as well as a magnificent charcuterie platter, fresh fruit, and tea sandwiches.

Harper decided we needed to open at least one bottle of

champagne to really get the party started and after filling our glasses, she said, "To you, Lauren. May today be the first of many fantastic and wonderful days ahead for you and Andrew. Jamie and I truly wish you only the best. You deserve that."

"Thank you," I said, seeing my friends for who I'd always thought they were before things had started to get muddled with wedding and marketing plans.

"Cheers," Jamie said as we clinked our glasses together.

"We'll be doing this for you soon," I told her.

She immediately shook her head. "Today is only about you, Lauren. I'll have my turn."

"And hopefully someday so will I," Harper said. "I think Andrew's groomsmen are kind of cute, especially Colin. Is he single?"

"As far as I know." I was reminded once again that I knew very little about anyone in Andrew's life.

"Interesting," Harper murmured, moving back into the makeup chair.

Once Harper and Jamie were done with hair and makeup, they were given manicures while my shoulder-length, dark-brown hair was swept up into soft tousled waves, strategically pulled back with sparkling embellished pins. My makeup turned me into someone I barely recognized, hiding the pesky freckles that often showed up on my nose, adding color to my lips, and the perfect shadow to my blue eyes, which were the one thing I'd inherited from my mother.

Shortly before two, the photographers arrived: Elisa Jacobs, an older woman with a lot of experience in wedding photography, her assistant, Tony Marino, who was also apparently her nephew, and a videographer, Owen Webb, who was in his thirties and came with more of a marketing-focused background.

Elisa directed the shoot, based on a list Megan had given her, starting with Harper and Jamie helping me get into my dress and adjusting my train and veil. I felt a little awkward changing in front of Tony and Owen, but they seemed completely dispassionate about anything except getting the right shots, and I didn't have time to care about modesty. Elisa never seemed particularly happy with my poses. I tried to be the best model I could be, but I was clearly falling short as they continued to shoot until my face was cramped from all the smiling.

Finally, after a stressful hour, we were done, and the team moved out of the suite and headed down to the villa to shoot Andrew and his groomsmen. Taylor and Carrie also disappeared, saying they'd be back to do touch-ups in an hour. Once it was just Harper, Jamie, and me, I slipped out of my dress so I could sit down without worrying about wrinkling my dress or spilling something on it. I put on the luxuriously soft hotel robe, feeling happy to have a few minutes before we had to do it all again.

"You're doing great," Jamie told me, giving me an encouraging smile, as she handed me another glass of champagne. "Maybe try to relax a little more. This is supposed to be fun."

"I'm trying," I muttered, taking a small sip of champagne. I'd lost count of how many glasses I'd started, and I didn't want to be drunk at my wedding, although maybe then I'd finally look relaxed.

"Have you heard from Andrew today?" Jamie asked.

"He texted me earlier to tell me he loves me, and he can't wait to be married." He'd also texted me with Allison's entrée choice, which I'd done nothing about since that whole fabrication had been a lie. I still felt stupid for having called her on the day of my wedding.

"Andrew is a good guy," Jamie said with a nod. "He always seems to know how you're feeling. When we've been out together, I've noticed how attentive he is. He's very aware of your mood, whether you're hot or cold, tired or happy, having no fun or too much fun."

"He takes good care of me. He knows I can be an introvert and a little shy, and he tries to make things easier."

"He almost seems too good to be true," Harper said.

"Don't start with the doubts," I warned, wagging my finger at her.

"I wasn't going to," she said quickly.

I wasn't sure I believed her, but I let it go, and when a knock came at our door, Harper got up to answer it.

The woman she let in was the last person I'd expected to see. I jumped to my feet as Paula Carrington walked into the room. In her early sixties, Paula was bone-thin with very fair skin that had aged from her long love affair with tanning. Her white-blonde hair was styled in a short, angled cut, with straight silky strands framing her face and accenting her brown eyes. Paula had been a model in her twenties and still carried herself like someone who was used to a catwalk and a lot of attention.

"I hope I'm not disturbing you," Paula said as we all stood somewhat awkwardly in the living room.

"Of course not. It's lovely to see you," I replied. "I really appreciate you coming to the wedding."

"I wouldn't have missed it for the world. This wedding and marketing campaign have consumed my husband's thoughts over the past several weeks. I've never seen him so invested in the grand opening of our resorts. But he became quite captivated with your fairy-tale love story."

"It doesn't feel like a story to me," I couldn't help saying. "It's very real."

"Oh, of course, I understand. People outside of a relationship always see it differently than those inside it."

There was a tension in her voice now that suggested she was not talking about my relationship but probably her own. "Is there anything I can help you with?" I asked.

"I wanted to speak to you for a moment...privately." Her gaze moved to Harper and Jamie.

"Of course," Harper said quickly. "We're going to go in the other room, and...do something."

As they quickly vanished, I felt a little nervous being alone with Paula. I couldn't imagine what she wanted to talk to me about, since the two of us had never had a personal conversation. And I'd probably only been in the same room with her twice before.

"I understand your mother passed away not too long ago," Paula said, surprising me with her words.

"Yes, she did. It's been about a year and a half, and I still miss her every day."

"I lost my mother when I was in my thirties, so I understand a little of what you're going through. But I had Victor's support when she passed. We were already married and had a baby, so I wasn't alone as you were. This day must be especially difficult for you."

"I've been trying not to think about it too much, but then I feel guilty."

"Why?" she asked curiously.

"Because I shouldn't be trying to keep her out of my thoughts. It's the only way she can be here with me, and we used to talk about me getting married. When she was sick, she worried about me being alone and finding the right person. I just wish she could see that I have."

"Maybe she can. I still like to believe my mother and father are watching over me."

"I like to believe that, too." I felt an unexpected bond with Paula.

"Did I hear that your mother worked in hotels as well?"

"Yes. She was at Hilton and then the Meridian for many years."

"You followed in her footsteps."

"She didn't want me to go into this industry. She worked the front desk and a lot of nights, a lot of weekends, but I grew up in hotels and I feel very comfortable in them."

"Well, from what I hear, we are lucky to have you. This whole marketing campaign was your idea, right?"

"The idea was mine originally, but at the time, I did not imagine that there would be a real wedding or that I would be the bride. I feel very lucky and grateful for everything your family and the company are doing for me. And I love this new resort. It's a beautiful property, truly special."

"That's certainly what Victor seems to think. He'd like to make this island our primary residence, but it feels too small to me."

A somewhat awkward silence followed her words. Finally, I said, "Is there anything I can do for you?"

"It's actually the opposite—what I can do for you." Paula opened her very expensive handbag. She took out a velvet box and handed it to me.

"What's this?"

"Take a look."

I opened the lid and pulled out a stunning gold necklace with a teardrop diamond. "Oh, wow! This is beautiful."

"It's for you to wear today if you're comfortable with it. Consider it your something borrowed."

"I don't know what to say. I've never worn anything as nice as this."

"May I help you put it on?"

I nodded, turning around as she fixed the clasp. And then I walked over to the mirror, shocked again by how beautiful it was, simple yet elegant. "It's perfect."

"Well, that's what this is all about, isn't it? Perfection? That's what Victor keeps telling me, that this resort will embody perfection in every way, especially for potential brides and grooms. This will be the ultimate in destination wedding locations. And you are our first bride, so you must look the part."

I turned away from the mirror, beginning to once again feel like an imposter in my own life.

"It looks good on you." Paula gave an approving nod as we faced each other. But the moisture in her eyes didn't match that approval.

"Is everything all right?" I asked as she dabbed at her eyes with her fingers.

"I was thinking about my wedding, how excited and optimistic I felt. Victor's mother put that necklace on me, and I also thought it was perfect. So perfect, but perfection is really just an illusion..." Her voice faded away. Then she immediately straightened and shook off whatever emotion had her in its grip. "Anyway, Victor said you needed a special piece of jewelry for the wedding photos, and he thought this might be the best choice, so I offered to lend it to you for the evening."

"It's very generous, but it feels like it's too much."

"Don't be ridiculous. Nothing is too much, not when it's representing my family."

"Then I'm honored to wear it. Thank you. I'll return it right after the ceremony."

"Tomorrow is fine. I hope you'll be very happy in your marriage, Lauren. I'll let you get back to your friends, and I'll see you at the wedding."

I walked her to the door. "Thank you again."

She paused once more as if she wanted to say something else, but in the end, she simply smiled and left.

As I closed the door, Harper and Jamie came out of the bedroom with questions in their eyes.

"What was that about?" Harper asked. "And what is that around your neck?"

"Mrs. Carrington is letting me wear one of her necklaces. In fact, it's the one she wore at her wedding."

"It's gorgeous," Jamie breathed as they both moved in to take a closer look. "This must be worth a lot of money."

"They thought I needed to wear a signature piece of jewelry for the photos."

"You're quite the Cinderella, aren't you?" Harper asked, a bitter edge to her voice. "I hope everything won't turn back to ashes at the stroke of midnight."

"This is all about the campaign; it's not about me. I'm representing the Carringtons. They probably thought any jewelry I would wear would look cheap, which it would, compared to this."

"It will go perfectly with your dress, which probably also cost a fortune," Jamie said, a wistful note in her voice. "And the necklace can be your something borrowed."

"That's what Mrs. Carrington said."

"And your something old," Jamie added. "It looks vintage."

"It belonged to her mother-in-law."

"Well, you still need something blue," Harper commented. "Is there a sapphire coming your way, too?"

"No. And remember how you told me you were going to be supportive? That's not happening right now, Harper."

"Sorry. What's your something blue?"

"The blue forget-me-nots in my bridal bouquet. They remind me of my mom. They were her favorite flower, and she always said they matched my eyes."

"That's sweet," Jamie said. "You better get your dress back on. The next round of photos starts in twenty minutes." She paused. "I know it's better to take all these photos before the wedding, but does it bother you that Andrew will see you in your dress before the ceremony? I hope it's not bad luck."

"Are you kidding?" Harper interjected. "Lauren cannot have any bad luck. The Carringtons wouldn't allow it."

An uneasy feeling shot down my spine...not only because of her snide remark, but also because everything was feeling too good to be true.

CHAPTER FIVE

I caught my first glimpse of Andrew, standing in a shrub-enclosed area, perched on a grassy bluff overlooking the ocean. He was surrounded by a natural frame of palm trees and windswept flowers. The sea stretched endlessly into the horizon as the colors in the sky began to move toward sunset. The light was golden, warm, and forgiving, the kind of light photographers dream of, and I knew it would make our first-look photos even better.

The sight of him dressed in a black tuxedo, the gold in his hair sparkling as bright as his eyes, made my breath hitch—especially when his gaze found mine. His reaction was everything I'd wanted it to be, his lips parting with admiration, his smile making me feel like I was the only person in the world.

"You look beautiful, Lauren." He took my hands in his, his voice low and intimate, as if the rest of the world had disappeared.

My throat tightened, my eyes moistening at his words. "I'm glad you like the dress."

His thumb brushed over the back of my hand. "I do like the dress, but I love the woman who's wearing it more."

"And I love you," I said, the truth of those words making me feel like everything was right in my world.

And then Megan and the media crew descended on us, directing us to repeat our first look—three times, from different angles. The clicks of cameras and low whir of video equipment invaded our bubble, breaking it apart piece by piece. By the time the wedding party joined us for more photos, I felt like a doll being posed, stiff and smiling on command.

The Carringtons arrived near the end of the session, sweeping in with their usual grace. Victor looked every inch the powerful patriarch in his black tuxedo, flanked by Bennett, whose darker mood contrasted with his polished appearance. Paula's champagne-colored gown shimmered with intricate beading, and Harper and Jamie's pale-gold dresses matched perfectly, elegant but not enough to outshine the bride.

We posed together endlessly—Andrew and me with Victor, with Paula, with Bennett, with all of them at once—until we were finally done with this location. Then the golf carts came to take our group through the resort, stopping at every photogenic corner: the stone terrace overlooking the ocean, the rose-covered arch near the reflecting pool, the twisting garden paths lined with bougainvillea.

Every scene was designed for romance, and every shot carefully staged for the resort's marketing campaign. Andrew played his role perfectly, his arm wrapped around my waist, his smile warm and constant.

When the last photo was taken, Andrew pressed a kiss to my cheek. "See you soon," he said, heading off with his groomsmen toward their villa. Harper, Jamie, and I returned to the bridal suite, where Taylor and Carrie hovered, ready to touch up hair and makeup. And then it was time for the ceremony.

Another golf cart took us from the hotel to the staging area, which was hidden behind a grove of trees. From there, we could see the crowd filling in the chairs set on a grassy bluff overlooking the ocean. We'd say our vows in front of an amazing arch of flowers, the sea in the background, and the sun sinking low enough in the sky to send streaks of pink, orange, and purple across the horizon.

Harper and Jamie disappeared almost immediately. Jamie wanted to check on her fiancé, and Harper said she wanted to mingle before the ceremony. So, I waited alone, with sweaty palms and a racing heart. Moving to the side, I was able to see some of the setup through the trees, and I smiled when I saw Andrew and Colin talking. But my smile faded when Allison McGuire joined them, giving each one of the men a hug, her embrace with Andrew lasting a lot longer than the one she'd given Colin.

They had definitely had more than a friendship. Jealousy and worry ran through me once more. But whatever they'd had together was over. He was marrying me, not her.

I just wished she wasn't here. And it puzzled me that Andrew hadn't considered how awkward it might be. Turning away, I saw Victor approaching me, and I put on my bride smile.

"Are you ready, Lauren?" he asked.

"As I'll ever be."

"My mother's necklace looks perfect." He gave me an approving nod. "I had a feeling it would be just the right finishing touch."

"It was generous of you and Mrs. Carrington to lend it to me."

"It wasn't a big deal. You make a beautiful bride, Lauren. I hope you and Andrew will be very happy. I know it may feel like we're losing sight of why we're all here, but I want you to know that I understand this is more than an event—it's your wedding. It's one of the biggest days of your life. I want you to enjoy every minute of it."

I was touched by his words. "I appreciate that. Thank you."

"You're more than welcome." He paused. "Andrew is a good man, isn't he?"

I was a little surprised by his question. "I wouldn't be marrying him otherwise."

"Of course. That's what I thought."

"It's time," Jeanette said, interrupting our conversation as Jamie and Harper joined us. Jeanette's assistant handed us our bouquets, and as I glanced down at the blue forget-me-nots, I wished again that my mother was here. But she wasn't, and all I could do was remember some of her last words to me. She'd wanted to make sure I would be okay. And she'd grabbed my hand with more strength than she'd had in weeks. *I do not want you to mourn me for long, my sweet girl. I want you to be happy and to live a full and long life. I want you to experience everything. You deserve nothing less than all of life's blessings. Promise me you won't stay inside, that you won't linger in sadness. I want you to remember me with a smile.*

I blinked away tears at the memory. I hadn't known at the time that those would be her last words, but I'd given her the promise she'd wanted. She'd passed away less than an hour later.

Despite my promise, I had mourned her. I had lingered in the sadness. But I really did want to be happy, and Andrew had shown me I could be, and I would be. I put a smile on my face as Victor offered me his arm, and we moved to the edge of the staging area as Harper and Jamie started their walk toward the petal-strewn white runway placed between the chairs.

And then it was our turn. I was happy to have Victor's steadying presence by my side as our every step was captured by a barrage of cameras, shooting over and over again as I tried to smile with the joy, love, and giddy excitement that the campaign demanded and also what my husband-to-be deserved.

I couldn't let the chaotic circus that was following us around get in the way of what was important, so when our gazes finally met, I looked only at him. And when we took each other's hands, everyone else faded away. I wasn't marrying them; I was marrying him. This man would be my husband, my future, and I was not turning back or looking back. Andrew had never let me down, and he was about to promise that he never would.

I'd thought it would feel different after we exchanged vows, but the ceremony, though perfect on the surface, felt like a blur. Sunset, picture-perfect kisses and endless flashes of cameras later, Andrew and I found ourselves taking more photos and charming our way through the cocktail hour.

At least the setting was beautiful. The terrace where the reception began was lined with flickering lanterns, and the ocean glowed under the final streaks of twilight. The salty breeze carried the hum of conversations and the gentle clink of champagne flutes, mingling with soft classical music from a string quartet.

We were introduced to dozens of people, including the influencers and traditional press, who'd been invited by either Bennett or Megan. The Carringtons had also invited friends and business associates, all of whom wanted to meet us. After the sixth or seventh person, I stopped trying to remember everyone's name or even what I'd said to them. Because this kind of social networking was not what I was good at.

Andrew, however, was flawless. He recounted our love story with such precision and emotion that it even tugged at my heart, and I'd lived it.

"The first time I saw her," he told one wide-eyed blogger, "was in the middle of a fire. I didn't think either of us would make it out alive. And then...I saw her again in the hospital the next morning. Fate had handed me a second chance." He squeezed my hand and smiled at me like I was the center of his world. "I knew then how important she was going to be to me. And here we are."

That blogger had eaten up the story, enchanted by our fairy-tale ending, and she wasn't alone. It certainly proved that almost everyone could be moved by a good love story.

By the time we sat down for dinner with our bridal party, I was grateful for the break. The long table was set with candlelight and flowers, the food artfully plated and delicious, but I barely touched it. Harper was seated on the other side of me next to Jamie and Brad, and none of them seemed particularly chatty. Andrew was having a bit more fun conversing with Colin, Jay, and Dana, but I didn't bother trying to get into their conversation. I was a little tired of talking, and I knew there was more to come so I might as well enjoy the momentary quiet.

The toasts that followed our meal were rehearsed and impersonal, carefully scripted by Megan's marketing team. Harper and Jamie delivered their remarks with little emotion, keeping things lighthearted and definitely staying on script.

Jay did add some improvisation, sharing an anecdote about Andrew declaring he was in love with me after our first date. Andrew squeezed my hand as Jay told that story, his thumb brushing over mine, and I felt the connection I'd been searching for off and on all day. Andrew was still here, still mine. And for now, that had to be enough.

Our first dance went off without a hitch. Andrew's hands were steady on my waist, his gaze focused entirely on me as we swayed to the soft strains of a jazz ballad. For those few minutes, it felt like we were the only two people in the world. But as the music shifted, the dance floor filled, and the whirlwind began again.

We changed partners often, mingling and spinning through a blur of family and friends. Harper danced with Colin, who passed her off to me, while Andrew laughed with Jamie. I lost track of time until my feet ached and my smile felt stuck in place. And then, when I finally paused to catch my breath, I saw them.

Andrew and Allison.

They were dancing to a slow song, and they were close. Her hand lingered on his shoulder, her eyes locked on his, and the way she smiled at him reminded me of the photo I'd seen of them—proof that there had been something between them. Perhaps something that still lingered now, if only on her side.

I turned away, the sight bothering me more than I cared to admit. The room suddenly felt too warm, too crowded. I slipped quietly out of the reception and down the hallway to the private restroom reserved for me and the bridesmaids, my heels clicking softly against the polished floor.

Harper was standing in front of the mirror reapplying her makeup.

As our gazes met, she raised a brow. "Everything okay, Lauren?"

"Yes. I'm just hot. I couldn't get off the dance floor."

"It's a fun party," she said as she dabbed at her face. "You might want to put on some lip gloss. Jeanette put our things in that closet."

I walked over to the closet and found my makeup bag on a shelf. I brought it back in front of the mirror and added some color to my lips.

"That's better," Harper said, giving me a thoughtful look.

"It is."

"What can you tell me about Colin, Lauren? Do you know anything about him?"

"Not much. Andrew said they met in college, and Colin joined him in his firm last year. According to Andrew, Colin is a very good salesman."

"I'm almost sold," Harper said with a laugh. "Although, he gives off serious serial-dater vibes. Not that I necessarily want anything more than a good time. My bruised heart wouldn't mind a little break."

"I'll see if I can get more information from Andrew."

"Don't worry about it. I'll figure it out. He asked me if I

wanted to get together tomorrow. Apparently, he's staying on the island until Tuesday."

I was a little surprised Colin was staying that long, since Andrew and I would be on our honeymoon, and Jay was with his girlfriend. But maybe the three of them just wanted to explore the island. However, it now looked like Harper would join them. And it definitely seemed like she was in a better mood now, so I was okay with whatever was going on.

Harper checked her reflection one last time, satisfied. "Are you heading back now?"

"In a minute."

"See you out there."

After she left, I stared at my reflection in the mirror. My lips were glossy, my hair perfect, my dress impeccable. And yet, I couldn't shake the feeling that something was off.

But it wasn't off with me; it was off with Andrew. Or more specifically, Andrew and Allison. She shouldn't be here at my wedding, and she definitely shouldn't have been dancing to a love song with my husband.

More importantly, he shouldn't have been dancing with her, smiling at another woman the way he smiled at me.

Jealousy clawed at my chest, making my breath come short and fast. It was an emotion I had never experienced before. I'd never even seen Andrew glance at another woman. And none of my previous relationships had stumbled because of another woman. It had always been something else. So this was a new feeling, and one I shouldn't be experiencing on the night of my wedding, and I kind of blamed Andrew for putting me in this position.

But I didn't want to get in a fight with him, and I wouldn't. There were far too many eyes on us. I also didn't want to give Allison the satisfaction of thinking I was at all bothered by her presence. I had to act like everything was fine. And I needed to do that because I couldn't hide out in the restroom all night. I returned my bag to the closet and left the room.

I was about to return to the reception, but a cool breeze blowing through an open door tempted me to take a little longer break. The thought of walking back into the crowd of people and facing the cameras and the endless questions made my skin itch. I slipped outside and followed the path toward the beach.

The farther I moved from the reception, the lighter I felt. The air was cooler here, tinged with the sharp tang of the ocean, and the sound of waves crashing in the distance softened the noise still echoing in my head. Shadowy darkness wrapped around me as the tall trees along the path swayed gently in the breeze. For the first time all day, I wasn't performing for anyone, wasn't smiling for cameras, or answering questions about how in love I was.

Then I heard voices. They were close, two people arguing just ahead. I froze, my pulse kicking up as I recognized one of them—Allison. The second voice, low and controlled, belonged to a man. At first, I thought it might be Andrew, but as I moved closer, staying behind the trees, I saw Colin.

"This is not your business, Colin," Allison said sharply, her voice carrying through the still night.

"You're pushing too hard," Colin shot back. "You're going to ruin everything. You need to stop."

"I'll stop when I want to stop," she replied, her tone icy. "No one tells me what to do, Colin."

"What are you even doing here?"

"Same as you. Celebrating Andrew's wedding."

"Exactly. He's married, Allison. *Married!* You know what that means, right?"

"I know, Colin. I saw. I heard. And I don't care."

"You should care. You're playing with fire. And you know it."

"I know what I'm doing, Colin. In fact, I know a lot more than you do. Your best friend isn't being completely honest with you."

"What does that mean?" Colin demanded.

"Andrew didn't have to do this. He didn't have to take things this far. You must be concerned about all this, too. How could you not be?"

"Because I trust Andrew."

I stiffened as a branch cracked behind me. My stomach dropped, and I whipped around to find Ethan a few feet away, his expression unreadable. As he opened his mouth, I pressed a finger to my lips, motioning for him to stay quiet.

Then I heard Allison say, "Is someone there? Hello?"

Oh God! This was worse than hanging up on the woman. Now I was standing in the woods spying on her. Panic flared in my chest.

"Is that Allison?" Ethan whispered. "Is Andrew with her?"

"Colin," I murmured, hearing them move in our direction. There was no way to escape before they came through the trees.

"Yell at me," Ethan ordered. "Make it look like we're arguing."

"I..." Licking my lips as they got closer, I said, "How dare you come to my wedding and try to cause trouble? You need to leave, Mr. Stark."

He gave me a nod of encouragement, then said, "I'm not leaving until you answer my questions. You didn't want to talk inside, so here we are. There's no one around. Tell me what you know about the fire."

"I don't know anything about it. I've said that a million times."

"I don't believe you."

"I don't care what you believe. I'm going inside. My husband is waiting."

"Your husband is a liar," Ethan said coldly.

His words made my heart lurch. For a moment, I'd forgotten we were pretending, and my fury flared to life. "He's not a liar. I trust him completely. Who I don't trust is you."

"Hey," Colin said sharply as he approached, his expression hard and wary. "What's going on out here? Are you all right, Lauren?"

I swallowed the knot in my throat and forced a smile. "I'm

fine," I said, wondering where Allison had gone. "Mr. Stark was just leaving, and I was about to go back to the reception. Maybe you could walk with me?"

"Of course." His tone was calm, but his eyes flicked to Ethan with a hint of suspicion. "Let's go."

As I moved away from Ethan, I couldn't help wondering if I wasn't trading one suspicious person for another. While I knew what Ethan had doubts about, I had no idea why Colin had been arguing with Allison in the woods or what he'd meant when he'd told Allison she was going to ruin everything. *What was everything?*

And Allison had told Colin that there were things he didn't know, and that Andrew hadn't had to take things this far.

What things? Had she been talking about my marriage to Andrew?

Colin had told her he trusted Andrew, so it didn't sound like he had as many doubts as she did. But then, he was Andrew's friend, and I didn't really know who the hell she was.

"That's the insurance investigator, right?" Colin asked, interrupting my thoughts. "What were you doing with him, Lauren?"

"He started to ask me questions inside, and I didn't want the cameras to capture any of our conversation, so I came out here with him."

Colin shot me a look. "Questions about what?"

"The hotel fire six months ago. He's been suspicious of both me and Andrew because we were the only people in the area at the time, but you know the story."

"I do. And I know both you and Andrew have talked to Mr. Stark several times about that night. What is he hoping you're going to tell him now?"

"I have no idea."

As we neared the party, I slowed my steps, wondering if I dared to ask Colin anything about Allison, but that seemed way too risky. "Thanks for saving me," I said.

"No problem. I'm actually glad we have a minute alone. I haven't had the chance to tell you that you're making Andrew a very happy man. In fact, I don't believe I've ever seen him so content."

"Really? I mean, I feel that way, too, but a lot of my friends think our relationship happened too fast."

"It's what you and Andrew think that matters. I've known him a long time, and when he knows what he wants, he goes for it. So far, I've never seen him make a bad decision."

His words struck me as a little odd, as if I was some prize that Andrew had wanted to win, but I was so on edge, I couldn't trust that I was interpreting anything the right way. "Well, thanks."

"Sure. Hey, your friend, Harper. She's single, right?"

"Very single. And really great, in case you were wondering."

"Good to know," he said as he ushered me inside the reception.

The dance floor was still packed, couples swaying together to yet another love song, but I didn't see Andrew or Allison, and that made me both happy and worried about where they might be. But then I saw Andrew cutting through the crowd to reach me, a smile lighting up his face when our gazes met.

"There you are," Andrew said, coming across the room. "I was about to come looking for you. Where have you been?"

"Just taking a break from the crowd."

"Anyone need a drink?" Colin asked.

"I would love some champagne," I told him.

"I'm on it," Colin said, heading toward the bar.

Andrew slipped his hands around my waist, pulling me closer. His lips brushed my cheek before he whispered, "You okay? You seem...distracted."

"I'm fine. It's been a long day."

He tilted his head, studying me with a thoughtful expression. "I know, but we're almost done. We're cutting the cake in thirty minutes, then it's the bouquet and garter toss. After that, we're free."

"Free," I echoed, the word catching in my throat. "That sounds...good."

His smile turned slightly wicked, his grip tightening on my waist. "And then it's just us. No cameras, no distractions."

"I can't wait."

"Me, either. But before all that, I need to run down to my villa for a minute. Dana isn't feeling well. I told Jay I have some Advil, but they can't find it. Will you be okay on your own?"

"Sure, but do you want me to come with you?"

"It will only take a few minutes. Stay here. Enjoy yourself."

I nodded, watching as he disappeared into the crowd. A moment later, Colin returned with my champagne.

"Alone again?" he asked, handing me the glass. "Where did Andrew go?"

"Jay's date isn't feeling well. He went to get her some Advil from his villa."

"Ah. That's too bad," he said, pausing as Harper joined us.

"I'm looking for a dance partner," she said, giving him a pointed look.

"You've found one," Colin replied, a charming grin sliding into place as he offered her his hand.

I watched them disappear onto the dance floor, Harper laughing as Colin spun her into the crowd. It felt like everyone else was moving forward—laughing, dancing, drinking—while I stood still, tethered by a weight I couldn't quite name.

When I saw the photographer heading in my direction, I bolted, slipping out onto the patio. The air was cooler here, but I wasn't alone.

Ethan leaned against the railing, his silhouette sharp in the moonlight, a whiskey glass in his hand.

"Really? You're here, too?" I said, my frustration spilling over. "Why are you everywhere I am?"

"I was here first, Lauren. And by the way, you're welcome," he added, his tone dry.

"For what?"

"For saving you back there. Allison would've caught you spying if I hadn't stepped in."

"I wasn't spying," I said quickly, too quickly. "I was just...walking."

"What did you walk into?"

"I'm not sure. It sounded like Colin wasn't happy Allison was here. He said she was going to ruin everything. Allison didn't care. She said no one tells her what to do."

"Colin said she was going to ruin everything?" Ethan echoed, his eyes narrowing. "What do you think he meant by that?"

"I think he thought Allison's presence might cause problems for Andrew and me."

"Or he could have been referring to something else."

"Maybe. I don't know," I murmured. Allison had told Colin there was something he didn't know, something Andrew was keeping from him, which bothered me, but that could be anything, and I didn't want to give Ethan any more ammunition against Andrew.

"Did you know Andrew and Allison were with the Carringtons this morning?" Ethan asked, his tone shifting slightly.

"I...yes. I saw them coming out of Victor's villa when I was walking back to the hotel."

"What were they doing there?"

"I have no idea. You were there, too. Why didn't you ask them?"

"I didn't get the chance. But it seems odd, don't you think? Andrew, Allison, and the Carringtons, all in the same villa hours before the wedding?"

"Allison is an interior designer. Maybe Victor wants to hire her for something."

"And that conversation had to happen on the morning of Andrew's wedding?" Ethan's skepticism was plain, and it fed into the tiny doubts I was trying so hard to ignore.

"You need to stop asking me questions I can't answer. If you want to know what they were doing there, ask them, or ask Victor. I'm sure someone will tell you what you want to know."

"Where did Andrew just go?" Ethan asked. "Or is that another question you can't answer?"

"His friend's date isn't feeling well. He went to get her some medication."

"Interesting."

"It's not at all interesting, but you seem fascinated by Andrew's every move, so I'll leave you to your obsession. I'm going inside. Please, don't follow me."

"Don't worry, I won't," he returned. "I have somewhere else to go."

Ethan walked past me before I could ask him where he was going, although I had a feeling I already knew. He wanted to see if Andrew was where I'd said he was. I hoped he was there. Because I secretly admitted that it did seem a little odd Jay and Dana needed Andrew's help to find a bottle of ibuprofen.

CHAPTER SIX

As soon as I entered the reception, Jeanette Bilson descended on me with irritation written across her face. "Where on earth have you been, Lauren, and where is Andrew?" Jeanette asked.

"He's checking on his friend's girlfriend, who isn't feeling well. He'll be back soon."

"I hope so. Because we still have a lot to do. And where are your bridesmaids?"

"Uh, I don't know. Aren't they in here? Colin was dancing with Harper when I left."

"They're not on the dance floor now." Jeanette let out a weary sigh. "Could you try to find them? Honestly, I feel like I'm herding cats. We have one hour to go, in which we will cut the cake, throw the bouquet and the garter, and then do a champagne toast before you and Andrew call it a night. Can we get all that done?"

"Yes, we will get that done," I promised.

As Jeanette left, I walked further into the room, my gaze sweeping the dance floor. I didn't see Jamie or Harper, although Jamie's fiancé, Brad, was sitting in a corner, studying his phone, while he drummed his fingers on the tablecloth. Jamie was probably in the ladies' room, maybe with Harper. Although, I didn't see Colin, either, so it was possible the two of them had gone somewhere together. The other person noticeably absent was Allison, and I really didn't want to think about where she might be, because when I'd last seen her, she'd been very close to the villa where Colin, Jay and Dana were staying.

"Lauren?"

I turned my head to see my aunt and uncle approaching. "Hi," I said, feeling bad I hadn't spent any time with them. "Aunt Lydia, Uncle Hugh, I'm sorry we haven't had a chance to talk. Are you having fun?"

"It's been a beautiful wedding," my aunt replied. "Fancier than anything we've ever been to, isn't that right, Hugh?"

"Never seen so many silverware choices on a table," Hugh muttered. "First-class all the way."

"The Carringtons made sure of that."

"I'm just sorry your mother wasn't here to see you walk down the aisle or to meet Andrew," Lydia said, giving me a sad look. "Sarah would have been over the moon to see you being treated so well. She used to tell me how guilty she felt for not giving you a dad, a two-parent family. But I always told her she gave you all the love you needed."

"She did," I said feeling a lump grow in my throat at her words.

"And look at you, getting so far ahead of where she got in the hotel business. She never made it away from the front desk."

"I know. She sacrificed a lot for me."

"She was happy to do that. She loved you. Anyway, we're a little tired. Marian and Travis already left to take a walk down by the beach, so we're going to head to our room."

"We're about to cut the cake, if you want to wait a few minutes."

Lydia put her hand on her stomach. "I couldn't eat another bite. Thanks for including us, Lauren. I know we haven't been close. Let's try to do better."

"That sounds good." I suspected there wasn't any real intent behind her words. Lydia had barely made time for my mother; I couldn't see her making time for me. But it didn't matter. I had Andrew, and we would build our own family unit. I just wished he'd come back so we could wrap our arms around each other and let everyone else fade away.

I wandered around the room for the next ten minutes, smiling and chatting and trying not to wonder about where Andrew was, but the longer he was gone, the more anxious I got. I was about to go get my phone out of my bag in the lounge when Harper and Jamie joined me. At least they were back.

"Jeanette says it's time to cut the cake," Jamie said. "Are you going to smash it in each other's faces, or will the two of you be polite?"

"Polite. The last thing I need for the photos and video is cake on my face."

"It might make the video more fun," Harper suggested. "And real. But I guess we're not that interested in *real*."

"No, we're not. It's about the dream," Jamie said. "And Lauren is right. The cake cutting and first bite should be perfect, because dreams aren't supposed to be messy."

"Oh, you two are no fun," Harper said with a roll of her eyes. "Sometimes you have to let loose and live a little."

"Is that what you're doing with Colin?" Jamie gave Harper a pointed look.

A somewhat secretive smile crossed Harper's lips. "That's between me and Colin."

"Since when do you not want to talk about private stuff?" Jamie asked curiously.

Harper shrugged. "This isn't the time or the place. I will say that I'm intrigued. Colin is more interesting than I thought he would be."

"How so?" I asked curiously.

"He's very well-read, for one thing. He brought a book on art history on his vacation. He loves jazz, and he played the saxophone growing up. I've never gone out with anyone who was interested in art and jazz. It's cool."

As Harper continued to talk about the apparently amazing Colin, my brain got stuck on what she'd first said. "Wait a second," I interrupted. "How do you know he has a book on art history?"

"I saw it on his nightstand."

"Were you in his villa just now? Was Andrew there?"

"I didn't see Andrew. Jay and Dana were settling in to watch a movie."

I wondered if Harper had just missed Andrew or if he hadn't gone there at all. "I thought Dana wasn't feeling well."

"She said something about having a headache."

"Why were you even there?" I asked.

"Colin wanted to check on Dana." Harper gave me an irritated look. "Just because I'm your bridesmaid doesn't mean I owe you every second of my time. I can have some fun, too, can't I?"

"Of course," I said, frowning as I wondered once again why Harper and I were continually at odds.

"Where is Andrew?" Jamie asked, cutting through the tension between Harper and me. "I haven't seen him in a while."

Fortunately, I finally had an answer to that question as Andrew walked over to us, with Jeanette right on his heels.

"He's here," I said with relief.

"Good, you're all together," Jeanette said as they reached us. "Except for my groomsmen. Where are my guys, Andrew?"

"Jay isn't going to make it for the rest of the reception. He's with his girlfriend who isn't feeling well. I told him to stay with her. I'm not sure where Colin is."

"I'm here," Colin said, coming up behind Harper. "What are we doing now? Is it time for cake?"

I couldn't help noticing that Colin looked a bit flushed, his hair windblown, as if he'd run in from somewhere. But there was no time to linger in that questioning thought as Jeanette turned to Andrew with annoyance.

"We really need Jay. The photos won't be balanced without him." She paused as Megan joined the group. "We're missing a groomsman," Jeanette told Megan.

"What? That's a problem," Megan said, distress in her eyes. "We need to get him in here, Andrew. He committed to all the photos."

"Well, he's not coming," Andrew snapped, for the first time losing some of his patience. "We need to make it work without him. We're just cutting a cake. It's not that big of a deal, is it?"

It was nice to have someone else tell Jeanette and Megan to make it work, because I was exhausted with trying to keep up with their demands.

Megan's lips tightened, and she shot me a dark look as if I was the problem and not Andrew. That was probably because I reported to her and Andrew didn't.

"Fine," Megan said. "We'll do a group shot around the cake." She paused. "Actually, why don't we lose one of the girls? Let's do you two," she added, pointing to Harper and Colin. "You look good together."

Jamie's expression darkened as Jeanette paired Harper and Colin together.

"I could bring my fiancé into the shot," Jamie suggested.

"He's not wearing a matching tuxedo," Jeanette replied with a dismissive wave of her hand. "That won't work."

"Fine," Jamie said. "I'm over this anyway."

"Uh, she doesn't seem happy," Andrew muttered, his gaze following Jamie's abrupt departure.

I couldn't help but agree. In fact, Jamie seemed unusually pissed. But since she was gone, and I wanted to get this over with, I said, "It's fine. I'm sure she doesn't care that much."

"She doesn't care," Harper agreed. "She told me a few minutes ago she couldn't wait for this to be over."

Harper's words made me feel sad my wedding was such a

chore for my friends. But it had been a long day, and I probably would have felt the same if I were in their shoes.

The four of us moved across the room to the cake table while the media team set up for the photos and video. Then Jeanette took over the microphone by the band, encouraging everyone to watch the cutting of the cake. As the crowd gathered in front of us with more lights and cameras whirring, Andrew and I picked up the knife, his warm hand covering mine. Then we slid the blade through the sponge cake.

After placing a piece of cake on a pretty china plate, we fed each other pieces of cake without smearing any icing on our faces. Although for a split second, I was oddly tempted to do just that. Everything felt so orchestrated and formal, so very unlike me. Andrew probably would have laughed, too. But in the end, I couldn't do it. I knew how important this campaign was and how costly it would be to reshoot anything, so I did my job, because that's what this whole wedding was about.

Once we were done, the catering staff took the cake into the kitchen to slice up individual pieces for our guests, and Jeanette announced the traditional garter and bouquet toss.

We made a big production of Andrew taking the garter off my leg. Then he turned around and launched it over his head like a slingshot. Colin jumped to catch it, looking triumphant, as if he had caught the winning touchdown in the Super Bowl.

Then it was my turn to toss my bouquet to one of the single women at the party. Jamie was sitting this out as she was officially engaged, but Harper was in the front row, so I wanted to toss it in her direction and hope she caught it.

As the band played a drum roll, I threw the bouquet as hard as I could, then whirled around, realizing that I'd actually tossed it to the back of the group, and it had landed in the hands of Allison McGuire.

Damn! What were the odds of that happening?

My gut tightened as she walked over to us. "I finally get a chance to officially meet the bride," she said, giving me a smug look. "I'm Allison McGuire. I'm a good friend of Andrew's." She sent Andrew a challenging look, as if she were daring him to refute that.

"Nice catch," Andrew said.

"Well, I have been thinking about moving forward in my personal life, so maybe this bouquet will bring me luck and love."

As they exchanged another look, I felt like a third wheel. Every word they spoke, every glance between them, seemed like it held some hidden meaning.

But then Megan asked the four of us to stand together, with Colin and Allison on one side and Andrew and me next to them. He put his arm around my shoulders, and my tension eased. I told myself it didn't matter if Allison still had a thing for Andrew. He was with me. He was my husband. And if he'd wanted to be with her, he would have been.

After a dozen more shots, Megan said it was a wrap, and I had never been so relieved to hear those words. We took the next twenty minutes saying goodbyes, ending with Victor and Paula Carrington.

"Thank you again," I told them. "This has all been amazing, better than I could have ever imagined my wedding being. I really appreciate all of it."

"I'm glad you enjoyed it," Victor said. "And thank you both for giving us so much great material to use in our campaign."

"You two are very photogenic," Paula commented. "Or maybe it's love that gives you that glow."

I didn't feel like I was glowing right now. I felt exhausted and wrung out, but apparently my makeup was still giving off the shine it was supposed to.

"We'll see you tomorrow for brunch," Victor added. "Some of our friends from the media are looking forward to speaking to you both at greater length."

I'd almost forgotten our duties would continue tomorrow. The events would be smaller and less formal, but they still required our attendance.

"We're looking forward to it," Andrew said, shaking Victor's hand.

Victor opened his arms to me, and I gave him a hug, and then shared a quick and very light embrace with Paula. Andrew did the same, and then it was time to leave.

We didn't have to say anything further to the crowd. We just waved goodbye as we left the banquet room. We were followed down the steps by some of our guests and the photographers and videographer, who captured us getting into the horse-drawn carriage waiting to take us on a starlit ride through the resort and then up to the hotel. It was all very romantic.

When we finally pulled away and the bright lights and cameras were gone, I looked at Andrew in the moonlight and felt a wave of relief.

He cupped my face and gave me a kiss, then said, "We did it, Mrs. Chadwick."

I couldn't help but feel a little thrilled with my new name. "I can't believe it's over."

"I hope you had some fun today."

"The best part was when we said our vows and now," I said as we exchanged another hot kiss in the cool night air.

"I agree. It's back to you and me, Lauren."

"I never thought we'd get here. My head is still spinning from all the people I had to talk to, all the smiles I had to give. My face is actually aching from those forced smiles."

"I hope they weren't all forced," he said, a questioning gleam in his eyes.

"They were never forced when I was looking at you, Andrew."

"Good."

"I just wish we didn't have to do brunch tomorrow, and I've heard talk of other events, too. I thought we were going to be on our own for the next few days, but it doesn't look like that will happen."

"I can guarantee you it won't. Bennett told me he has a

horseback riding session planned for tomorrow afternoon with some of his favorite influencers. We'll be doing that after brunch."

I sat up straighter. "Seriously? Horseback riding?"

"Yes. What's the problem?"

"I've only ridden a horse once, and I didn't like it."

"It will be fun, Lauren. A slow, picturesque ride through the hills. We won't be racing or anything."

"I'd still like to get out of it."

"You want to tell Bennett that? It's part of the campaign. It's what we signed on to do."

He was right. I really had no choice, and I definitely couldn't tell my boss's son that I was unwilling to participate in what he probably thought was a fun marketing event.

"Let's not worry about tomorrow," Andrew added. "It's the first night of our future together. That's something to celebrate."

I smiled, feeling like an idiot for not appreciating how fortunate I was to have met Andrew, fallen in love, and married him in a spectacular wedding ceremony. I was the luckiest woman in the world, and now I would get to be his wife, which was what I wanted most.

"Looks like we've arrived," he said as our horse-drawn carriage stopped in front of the building.

Andrew helped me get down from the carriage. Then we said goodnight to the driver and hurried into the hotel. Privacy was seconds away, and I couldn't wait.

Andrew must have shared the same thought as he started kissing me the moment we got on the elevator, and when the doors opened, he swept me up off my feet and carried me down the hall to the bridal suite.

Then he gave me a sheepish smile as his gaze met mine. "I don't have the key."

"I thought everyone had a key," I said with a laugh. "Mine is in my bag. You're going to have to let me down."

"Damn. This was going to be so romantic," he said as he set me on my feet.

I dug through my bag, pulled out the keycard, and then opened the door.

"Wait. Let's try this again," he said, before I could move inside. He picked me up once more and carried me over the threshold.

As Andrew set me down on my feet, his gaze narrowed as it moved past me. "What the hell?"

I turned around to see what he was looking at, and my jaw dropped in shock.

Our beautiful bridal suite had been completely trashed: the sofa cushions thrown around on the floor, and the champagne glasses from our earlier drinks smashed on the floor. The snacks had been tossed against the wall with smears of dressing still dripping down the mirror.

Andrew suddenly moved, striding toward the bedroom. I ran after him to see even more chaos and horror: the bed ripped apart, the pillows tossed on the floor. Chocolates smashed on the sheets. And another broken champagne bottle with sparkly liquid still spreading across the hardwood floor.

Even worse than the destruction were the words written on the wall by the bed:

You'll be sorry...

CHAPTER SEVEN

"Sorry?" I looked at Andrew in bewilderment. "Sorry about what?"

His lips tightened, his jaw and gaze harder than I'd ever seen them. "Who would do this?" he demanded.

"Someone who doesn't like us."

"Who doesn't like us?" he asked in bemusement.

I thought about all the people who'd given me a bad vibe the past two days and that included Harper and Jamie, who both had keys to the suite. But so did a lot of other people.

Jeanette had a key, Taylor and Carrie, the photographers and videographer, Megan...

Who knew who else had come and gone from this suite during the day? I hadn't been here in hours, not since we'd left for the ceremony.

"Lauren? Is something going on I don't know about?" Andrew asked, as if I were keeping some secret from him.

My eyes widened at his question. "You're asking me that?"

"Well, yeah. I don't know anyone who's pissed off at me. Is someone angry with you?"

I thought about that. "I can't imagine anyone doing this."

"What about Harper or Jamie? They seem like they've been

needling you the last two days. I get that Harper is naturally sarcastic, but she's been even sharper than usual."

"They wouldn't have trashed my bridal suite. They're my friends. They might be a little jealous of all the attention I've been getting, but they've been supporting me the past two days." I paused. "However, there is someone who doesn't seem happy about our marriage, and that's your friend, Allison." I hadn't wanted to talk about her tonight. I'd wanted us to have the perfect intimate wedding night, but that dream was dead now.

"That's ridiculous." He sent me an irritated look. "I told you. Allison and I are friends. We work together."

"But you dated her, didn't you? You weren't always just friends."

"We didn't date," he said, running an angry hand through his golden-blond hair. "We hooked up twice. It was over a year ago, and it didn't mean anything."

My heart sank as he finally told me the truth. "Maybe Allison thought it meant something. Why did you invite her to our wedding if the two of you have a past? It's inappropriate."

"It was a long time ago, and she's a valuable work associate. I didn't feel it was right to leave her out."

"You were with her earlier today at Victor's villa. What were you doing there together?"

"Were you spying on me?" he asked in surprise.

"No. I was coming back from my run. I saw you walk out of the villa with Allison, Victor, and Paula. It seemed very odd that the two of you would have been with the Carringtons and that you never mentioned it to me."

"I haven't had two minutes alone with you all day to talk about anything. Allison wanted to pitch her design services for the villas that are still being constructed on the hillside. She asked me to introduce her to Victor, and that's what I did. It wasn't a big deal."

"Is she going to get the job?"

"Victor is interested in her work. She's going to stay a few days and work up some sketches for him. He said he'd take a look."

I frowned at the thought of Allison staying longer on the island. "I don't get it. Carrington Resorts works with established designers, and the company that has been decorating this resort has done excellent work. Why would Victor want to bring in someone new for the last few villas?"

"He wants each villa to be unique, and having a different designer might accomplish that. Look, I don't know why this bothers you, Lauren, but we have more pressing things to worry about. I'm going to call the front desk and get security up here."

"Andrew, wait."

"What?"

At his demanding look, I found myself not sure what I wanted to say. I felt confused by everything that was happening, including our conversation about Allison, which didn't feel at all resolved. But he was right. We did have bigger problems to worry about. "Nothing. Just call security."

He moved to the phone by the bed and picked it up. I walked toward the dresser and felt my heart sink as I saw the lid on the small jewelry box my mother had given me had been ripped off.

"I can't believe they broke this," I muttered, picking up the lid and remembering my twenty-first birthday when my mother had given me the small opal ring I wore on my right-hand ring finger. It had come in this small jewelry box, and it had been the most expensive present she'd ever given me.

Tears filled my eyes, and I tried to blink them away. I hadn't cried in a long time, and I didn't want to start now. This was my wedding night, and I couldn't let someone's destructive anger ruin it. But I felt very alone, and that was the scariest feeling, because I hadn't felt this alone since I'd met Andrew. He had driven all that hollow emptiness away. Now it was back.

That made me angry. It shouldn't be back. I was married. This was supposed to be the best day of my life.

Andrew came up behind me and put his hands on my shoulders. "Is that your jewelry box?"

I nodded, still too choked up to speak.

"I'm sorry, Lauren. I know how much that means to you. We'll get it repaired. And they didn't get the ring, so that's good."

"I guess." I set the broken box down on the dresser as he turned me around to face him.

"We'll figure out who did this," he assured me.

"Does it even matter?" I asked wearily.

"Of course it matters."

"I doubt they stole anything. This was about ruining our wedding night."

"Or ruining the best suite in the resort," he suggested. "Maybe there was damage done to other rooms that we don't know about."

"Did security tell you that?"

"No, but they're sending up the director of security, Martin Demora."

I knew Martin. He'd worked at the hotel in Newport Beach for the past year before being assigned here. He was a smart man, and he had years of experience in hotel security, having worked for other chains before coming to the Carrington Group. "Even if he figures out who did this, it won't change what happened. We can't get this night back."

"This night isn't over. We'll talk to Martin and then we'll move to another suite. There are plenty of open rooms. We'll catch our breath and regroup. It doesn't have to be ruined, Lauren."

I usually appreciated his positive outlook, but I was too exhausted to buy into it now. "It is ruined, Andrew. And whoever did this was probably hoping that would be the result."

"Well, we can choose to not let them win."

"What are you talking about? We've already lost."

"With that attitude, yes."

"Sorry if you don't like my attitude, but it is what it is. And I still think this looks like the work of a scorned woman."

He frowned but before he could say anything, the doorbell rang. I followed him into the living room. He opened the door to Martin Demora, a stocky, weathered Italian man in his late forties. To my surprise, Martin was followed into the suite by Ethan Stark.

"This is Mr. Stark," Martin said. "He's overseeing the security of Victor's personal property, and he was with me when you called, so I thought he might help."

"Whatever works," Andrew said. "Let me show you the bedroom."

As Andrew took Martin into the bedroom, Ethan gave the room a long look and then turned to me. I crossed my arms in front of me, always feeling defensive around Ethan, even when I was the victim, which I was now. Just like I'd been in the fire.

"Any idea who might have done this?" Ethan asked.

"Not a clue."

"Someone was angry. They wanted to make a point. Martin said there's a message on the wall of the bedroom."

"You can look at it yourself. But all it says is *You'll be sorry*."

"Sorry for what?"

"I have no idea."

"It could be referencing your wedding. In fact, it looks like it could be the work of a scorned ex-girlfriend."

"Andrew doesn't believe Allison is upset about our wedding. He says they are friends, and they work together, and whatever was between them was over a year ago."

"You talked to him about it?"

"Yes. I talked to him," I snapped. "He's my husband."

"Hell of a thing to happen on your wedding night."

"There must be security footage in the hallway, on the elevator, right?"

"The security system was being worked on before the grand

opening. Martin doesn't believe any of the cameras in this area were online."

"Great. So there might not be any footage?"

"We'll find out. I'm going to check the bedroom."

"You don't really need to be here, do you?"

I blew out a breath as he left and hugged my arms around my body, feeling cold and in shock, my anxiety deepening as I took in every horrible, destructive detail in the room. I could feel the anger behind the vandalism, and that was more than a little disturbing.

Who could do this hateful thing?

That question was still running around my head when the men returned to the living room.

"Andrew told me that quite a few people had keys to the suite today," Martin said. "I've asked the front desk clerk to bring you a key to another suite. She should be here any—" He paused as a knock came at the door. "That's probably her." He opened the door to a young woman in her twenties, whom I'd met earlier. "Gabby, thanks for coming so quickly."

"Oh, wow." Gabby's eyes widened when she saw the condition of the suite. "This is bad."

"Yes," Martin said crisply. "Which is why we need to move Mr. and Mrs. Chadwick into another suite."

"I have the key for one of our executive suites upstairs. We only had one room ready to go. I hope it will work." She handed Andrew two keycards.

"I'm sure the room will be fine," Andrew said.

"Greg is going to come up and help you with your luggage," Gabby added. "What else can we do? Do you want any food, snacks, or chocolates sent up?"

I shook my head at her question. "No food, but I'd love some bottled water."

"The fridge in the suite is stocked with non-alcoholic drinks," she replied.

"Do you two need any more help?" Martin asked. "If not, I'll start investigating what happened here."

"Please do," Andrew said. "We'll grab our things and head upstairs."

"If you have any further issues, please call me personally," Martin added. "You have my card. Otherwise, we'll touch base in the morning. Good night."

"Good night," I muttered as Martin and Ethan left.

Andrew turned to me. "I don't have anything to move. My suitcases are in the villa I stayed in last night. I was going to get them tomorrow." He gave me a somewhat sad smile. "I wasn't thinking I needed my clothes tonight."

I tried to smile but I fell short, and I didn't have the energy to try again. Instead, I said, "My bags were unpacked earlier. Everything is in the closet."

"I'll help you pack and then we can get out of here."

I wished I could just walk out the door, but I didn't want to leave my things here, not knowing if whoever had the key might come back, although that was unlikely. They'd done what they wanted to do. And if they had wanted to steal something, that would have already happened. Not that I had much to steal. I was wearing the ring my mother had given me, and the necklace Paula had loaned me for the wedding was still around my neck. Those were the only pieces of jewelry worth stealing.

But this hadn't been about theft. I just didn't know what the true motive was.

It took us about fifteen minutes to pack. While we were gathering my clothes together, I changed out of my dress and heels into leggings, a sweater, and sneakers. It wasn't the sexy lingerie I'd bought for my wedding night, but I felt more like myself again.

Andrew tried to lighten the mood with a few dark jokes, but I couldn't drum up a laugh, so he stopped trying. When we were done packing, the bellman helped us take my bags up to the new suite, which was on the floor above us and in a different wing.

It was also a lovely one-bedroom, but far more neutral and minimalistic in décor. Definitely not the romantic, dreamy decadent luxury of the bridal suite, but it was clean, and everything was in its place, which eased my stress.

After the bellman left, I hung my wedding dress in the closet, put the necklace Paula had lent me back in its velvet box, and placed it in the drawer next to the bed. I'd return that to her tomorrow.

"So," Andrew said as he came around the bed and put his hands on my waist. "Should we start over?"

"Where would that be?" I asked with a heavy sigh.

"How about when I picked you up and carried you over the threshold? We could do it again."

I shook my head. "I don't think so, Andrew."

"We can salvage tonight, Lauren. We just have to try."

"You mean I have to try."

"Well...yes," he said, gazing into my eyes. "There's nothing we can do about what happened downstairs."

"I feel so violated. Someone wanted to hurt us, to scare us. Doesn't that bother you?"

"I'm not going to be scared by some message written on a wall. I don't think you should be, either. Whoever trashed our room was a coward. And letting them ruin our wedding night only means they win. I don't want to be sorry. I want them to be sorry their actions didn't work."

He had a point, but I was so damn tired. "I can't blow it off the way you can. I feel bad. And I'm emotionally and physically exhausted. It's been a crazy long day. I've tried to be whatever someone wanted me to be since we arrived on this island, and I can't do it anymore. I can't pretend I'm not upset."

"You're right. I'm asking too much."

"It's not you. I'm not mad at you, Andrew. You know that, right?" I needed him to understand that. "It's the whole situation."

He nodded. "I get it. I just don't want you to look back on our wedding day and night and think about this."

The memories of this day and night were never going to be a highlight, but I couldn't tell him that, because, clearly, he'd had a lot more fun than I had. And I didn't want to ruin his memories. None of this was his fault.

At least, I hoped it wasn't his fault.

I did still wonder about Allison. *Had she been the one to sneak into the suite and trash it? But how would she have gotten the key?*

Although, Andrew didn't seem to have his key. He said it was in the villa he'd stayed at last night. Allison had probably been in that villa since she was friends with all of them.

"Lauren?" he asked, a question in his gaze. "What are you thinking about?"

"Allison," I admitted.

He blew out a frustrated breath. "You need to stop worrying about her, Lauren. Allison had nothing to do with what happened."

"You don't know that for sure."

"Neither do you."

"It makes the most sense."

"How on earth does it make sense?" A mix of anger and incredulity ran through his eyes.

"Because you two were involved before you and I got together. She might still have feelings for you, and whoever destroyed our bridal suite did it out of anger. Since I didn't invite any of my exes to our wedding, she's the best suspect."

His lips tightened. "She wouldn't do this."

"Well, I don't know her, because you've never told me anything about her. And you should have told me you were inviting someone to our wedding with whom you'd had an...intimate relationship."

He let out a heavy sigh. "It wasn't a relationship. I honestly didn't think it mattered. And if you had wanted to invite an ex, I would have trusted your decision. Why don't you trust mine?"

"Because it feels like you kept a secret from me."

"I didn't consider it to be a secret. We've been together constantly the last six months. We've barely spent a night apart. Do you really believe I was having something with Allison while we've been together?"

"Well, no, but you still should have told me."

"Maybe I should have. But putting that aside, Harper is a better suspect than Allison. She's been bitching all weekend about one thing or another. And what about Jamie? She was pissed off when Jeanette kicked her out of the cake-cutting photo, and she stormed off. Who knows where she went?"

"She was back for the bouquet toss. There wasn't enough time for her to vandalize the suite."

"Maybe. Maybe not. We can speculate all night, but we're not going to get to an answer. Let's wait and see what Martin can find on the security cameras."

"It didn't sound like they were operational."

"Maybe some of them were. Hopefully, they can narrow it down to who might have come into the building during the hours in question. Whether we get an answer or not, it's over."

"Is it over? They said *you'll be sorry*. There could be something else coming."

"They just wanted to scare you." He paused, his lips tightening. "You know who we haven't talked about..."

I met his gaze. "Who?"

"Ethan Stark. Colin told me that you were yelling at him earlier. What did he say to you?"

"The same things he's been saying all along...that we're thieves, that he doesn't trust us."

"Us or me?"

"Both of us. But I have to admit he's suggested lately that I don't know everything about you. He was the one who told me about you and Allison. I hate that I had to find out she was your ex from a man who's trying to make us out to be criminals. It gave him an advantage."

"There's no advantage. Allison didn't stay with me at the conference. She had her own room, and, yes, we hugged outside one night when we said goodbye. It didn't mean anything. Ethan is trying to work you. Maybe he trashed the suite because he knew the cameras were off. Then he was quick to show up and blame Allison, giving you another reason not to trust her or me. Don't let him play you."

He had a point, and I didn't want to fight with him about Ethan. "I'd rather not talk to him at all, but he keeps showing up."

"I get it. Let's put all this aside. There's nothing more we can do tonight. There's a spa tub in the bathroom big enough for two. Why don't we fill it up and try to relax?"

He was trying to make the best of a bad situation, and his positive attitude was one of the things I loved most about him. I just didn't feel like being cheered up. Nor did I feel like taking a bath.

"I'm sorry, Andrew. I know you're doing everything you can to make this right, but I want to go to bed. Will you hate me if I ask if we can start over tomorrow?"

"Of course we can start over tomorrow, and I could never hate you. I love you. We've got the rest of our lives ahead of us, Lauren. This is a little blip."

"I'll feel better after I get some sleep."

"Why don't you get into bed then? I'm going to take a shower." He gave me a kiss, then went into the bathroom.

As I pulled back the covers and got into bed, I let out a sigh of relief as the soft mattress and pillows enveloped me. I felt a little guilty that I'd rebuffed Andrew's every effort to salvage our wedding night, but I was too exhausted to turn that thought into some sort of action.

I'd make it up to him tomorrow and the day after that. As he'd said, we had the rest of our lives. And in the morning, we could get back to being us.

CHAPTER EIGHT

Sunday morning came way too soon. Despite my unsettled emotions, I must have fallen asleep fast, because I couldn't even remember hearing Andrew come to bed. Now the sun was blazing through the parted curtains in the bedroom, and the clock on the nightstand said it was half-past nine. Andrew wasn't in bed with me, but I could hear his voice in the living room. He must be on the phone.

I got up, used the bathroom, put some water on my face and ran a brush through my tangled hair, then headed into the living room. Andrew was standing out on the balcony now, his back to me, his voice muffled. His bags were by the front door, one suitcase opened on the couch. And I could see that he'd changed into a pair of gray slacks and a blue polo shirt.

As I moved toward the patio, I saw him wave an angry hand in the air as he said, "I can't keep having this conversation with you. I told you what's happening. Deal with it." He paused, turning his head, his smile coming a second too late to cover up the anger in his eyes. Then he said, "We'll talk later." As he ended the call, he said, "Good morning, beautiful."

Despite his words, I could see the tension in his face. "Who were you talking to? You seem angry."

He hesitated, then said, "That was someone from security who works with Martin. They haven't found any camera footage that might be helpful to us."

"That's too bad but also not surprising."

He walked over and gave me a hug. "Well, as I said last night, it doesn't matter, and I'm not going to let it ruin our honeymoon. I also spoke to Victor this morning. He wanted to make sure we were all right and that we would still be coming to brunch. He thinks it's important that we meet his media guests, although he would prefer that we didn't discuss what happened to the bridal suite last night."

"He wouldn't want that to get any press coverage days before the grand opening." I paused. "I see you changed your clothes. Did you have to go down to the villa to get your bags?"

"No. Colin packed them up and brought them over earlier so I could change."

"I must have been in a deep sleep. I didn't hear you come to bed or get up this morning."

"You were definitely out," he said, giving me a kiss. "I was tempted to wake you, but I thought you needed the rest."

"I did. I feel better now."

"Good." He glanced at his watch. "You need to get ready for brunch."

"I will. Did you tell Colin what happened last night?"

"Yes. He was upset that our night was ruined."

"Did he say anything about Allison as a possible suspect?"

Andrew frowned. "No. Why would he? She's his friend, too. We both know her, Lauren. We know she wouldn't do something like that."

"He might be her friend, but Colin was upset with Allison last night. I heard them arguing outside the reception. He asked her why she'd come to the wedding. She didn't seem to care that he was bothered by her attendance."

Andrew's gaze narrowed. "You didn't mention that last night."

"There was a lot going on."

"Colin didn't think it was a great idea for her to come, but he understood why I invited her. She's a valuable business associate, and she wanted to have an opportunity to pitch to Victor."

"Now you're saying you invited her so she could pitch to Victor? And not because she was a friend?"

His lips tightened. "I really don't understand why you're jealous, Lauren. But I won't keep defending myself, because there's nothing to defend. Are we going to spend our day fighting about someone who doesn't matter?"

His anger was suddenly very real, and I couldn't remember him ever being mad at me. Maybe I was pushing too hard. He'd told me why he'd invited Allison. He obviously didn't think I had a reason to be bothered by her presence, and I was either going to spend my honeymoon fighting about her, or I was going to have to drop it and move on. Since we had a busy schedule ahead of us, I opted for the latter. And I decided to start with an apology.

"I'm sorry, Andrew. And, no, I don't want to spend the day fighting with you."

"Then trust me, Lauren. I'm being one hundred percent honest with you when I tell you that I don't care about Allison. She is not a threat to you or to our marriage. If I made a mistake by inviting her, then I apologize, too."

"Okay. Thank you for saying that. I'll go get changed for brunch."

"Good. And, Lauren, I know you're still shaken by what happened in the suite. But I don't want you to be scared. I'm going to protect you. I'm going to protect us. You don't have to worry. I love you."

His words touched me deeply. It had been a long time since anyone had stated so firmly and so directly that they would protect me. I blinked the moisture out of my eyes as I gave him an emotion-filled smile. "I love you, too." It felt good to be back on the same page. I just hoped we could stay there.

Victor and Paula's villa was as magnificent as I'd expected, yet it still overwhelmed me. The entryway alone was a statement of wealth: towering twenty-foot ceilings, marble floors that gleamed so brightly I could see the reflection of the massive crystal chandelier hanging above, and walls lined with intricate molding and adorned with original oil paintings. The air smelled faintly of lemon polish and something floral, like lilies or roses, as if even the scent of the house had been curated.

The middle-aged woman who greeted us was dressed in black, her sharp heels clicking as she led us past arched doorways into a grand living room. The space was as polished as the entryway, with silk-upholstered furniture in soft creams and golds, and an ornate stone fireplace that stretched almost to the ceiling. Above the mantel hung a painting I didn't recognize, but it radiated the kind of importance that made me nervous. I didn't belong in a house like this, but here I was.

Victor and Paula stood in front of the fireplace, chatting with a small group. Victor's dark suit was perfectly tailored, and Paula's light-blue, form-fitting sheath dress shimmered under the light. They were magnetic, a study in power and elegance. Around them were Mitchum Conroy, a silver-haired editor with an air of self-importance; Olivia Maxwell, a glamorous travel reporter whose sharp eyes missed nothing; and Leah Bradford, a striking blonde who looked more like a model than a wedding planner.

"There they are—the couple of the hour," Victor said as we entered, spreading his arms in welcome. "Andrew, Lauren, you've met Mitchum and Olivia, I believe?"

"Yes, " Andrew said smoothly, exchanging handshakes. "It's a pleasure to see you both again."

"And this is Leah Bradford, " Victor continued. "She's one of the best wedding planners in the business. Works with all the stars."

"Nice to meet you, " I said, trying not to sound intimidated.

"That must be a fun job," Andrew added.

"Stressful more than fun, but I enjoy the challenge. Yesterday's wedding was stunning, by the way. Truly flawless. You have found yourself a prime wedding venue, Victor. "

Victor inclined his head, pleased. "We aim to impress. "

"Shall we sit? " Paula interrupted. "Brunch is ready."

As the group moved toward the dining room, I fell into step with Paula. "I have your necklace in my bag," I said. "Shall I give it to you now?"

"After brunch will be fine," Paula returned.

"All right. This villa is beautiful."

"Yes, well, it's very grand, as my husband wanted it to be."

Paula didn't sound as enamored with her island home as I was, which seemed surprising, because it really was amazing.

I was about to head into the dining room when Paula put a hand on my arm, holding me back. "Maybe I'll have you give me the necklace now," she said.

"Whatever you like." I reached for my bag.

"Not here. One second." Paula moved into the dining room and said, "Lauren and I have to run upstairs for a moment. We'll be right back."

"Can it wait?" Victor asked as he took his seat at the head of the table.

"We won't be long." Paula led me up the stairs to the third floor and through a pair of floor-to-ceiling double doors.

Paula's suite was a world apart from the rest of the villa. It was softer, warmer, with creamy walls and gold accents. Everything—from the delicate curtains framing the balcony doors to the lace pillows on the bed and the chaise lounge by the window—seemed chosen with care. Unlike the imposing style of the rest of the villa, this room felt personal, like it belonged to Paula and no one else. It certainly didn't feel like Victor stayed in here. He must have his own room.

Paula closed the door behind us and held out her hand.

I retrieved the velvet box from my bag and passed it to her. She opened it, lifting the necklace with an odd expression on her face. Clearly, the piece of jewelry meant something to her, but I couldn't tell if it brought her joy or some other emotion. She was a difficult woman to read.

"It suited you," she said quietly, running her fingers along the stone. "But it's back where it belongs now."

Her words carried a weight I didn't understand, but I nodded anyway. "I appreciate you lending it to me."

Paula walked to her dresser and placed the now-boxed necklace inside the top drawer. Then she turned back to me, her expression sharpening. "There's something else I wanted to discuss with you, Lauren."

I stiffened, unsure of what was coming. "What's that?"

"Your husband's friend, Allison McGuire. Is she single?"

"I believe so." The question caught me off guard.

"What else do you know about her?"

"Not much," I admitted. "She's an interior designer who's worked with Andrew on a few projects. Why?"

"Victor wants to hire her for the hillside villas. But I'm concerned about her motives. My husband has a weakness for a certain type of woman. Allison wouldn't be the first one to take advantage of that. I won't let that happen."

I blinked. "I see."

"Do you?" Paula stepped closer. "I have to admit that I was a bit puzzled by Victor's interest in using you and Andrew for the marketing campaign. I've never seen him get so involved in that end of the business before. Now that I've met you both, I have fewer concerns, or I did until Allison McGuire showed up. You need to know that I will do anything to protect my family."

"I understand," I said quickly, feeling intimidated by her threatening words. "Andrew and I want what's best for you and Victor, as well as the resort. If you have concerns about Allison, speak to Andrew. He can give you more information than I can."

Paula studied me for a moment. "You don't know her that well, do you?"

"I don't. She works with Andrew. And she's been traveling during the time we've been together, so we haven't talked much."

"Interesting," she murmured. "All right. I thought I'd mention it to you first—woman to woman. But I will speak to Andrew about my concerns when it's appropriate. Until then, why don't we keep this conversation to ourselves? There's a lot going on this week, and we're doing a great deal to give you and Andrew the best possible experience, so I'd appreciate your discretion."

"Okay." As I followed her downstairs, I realized I'd just agreed to lie to my husband. That damn Allison McGuire was causing me problems every time I turned around. I really hoped she'd be gone soon.

I could probably get Andrew to send her away if I told him Paula didn't like Allison, but then I'd be breaking my promise to Paula, who had recently reminded me of how much I owed them. I needed to stay out of it and let whatever was going to happen...happen.

When we returned to the dining room table, I noticed that Bennett had joined the group and was sitting directly across from me. While everyone was nibbling on their salads, Victor was telling a lively story about his most recent trip to Cairo.

Andrew gave me a side glance, a question in his eyes. I shrugged, happy I didn't actually have to answer that question yet.

Brunch was as delicious as I had known it would be. Everything with the Carringtons was first-class, and it was quite an experience to sit at their table, as if I were one of them, as if I were on the same level with these very influential people. Mitchum was a legend and wielded enormous power when it came to the hotel resort business. A few good words in his magazine or spoken to his counterparts could triple our business.

But as the conversation flowed around the table, I wondered how Mitchum really felt about the resort. He seemed a bit more reticent in his praise than the others, and I wondered why. It wasn't until we got to dessert that his attitude made more sense.

"What about the rumors, Victor?" Mitchum asked.

"I never discuss rumors," Victor said, a new edge to his voice.

"I heard you may be selling off some of your properties to offset the losses in Newport Beach and Florida," Mitchum said, ignoring Victor's comment. "Is that true?"

"Of course it's not true," Bennett interjected before his father could answer. "We would never sell our properties to anyone outside the family."

Mitchum's gaze stayed on Victor. "Is that correct, Victor? Is it a rumor?"

"Yes," Victor said. "Which is why I don't discuss rumors, Mitchum. Now, we've talked enough business. I thought you all might enjoy seeing some of my private collection. It hasn't all arrived yet, but I do have a few pieces I think you might enjoy."

"I would love to see your collection," Olivia said. "And while I know you don't like to discuss rumors...I heard you might have acquired the Heart of Eternity."

"What's that?" I asked.

"It's a legendary blue diamond in the shape of an unbreakable heart," Olivia said. "It went missing during the French Revolution and was lost for centuries. But rumors have been flying that it was discovered at a very old French estate, and it was sold to a private owner. I would very much like to see it."

Victor's smile was both smug and secretive. "That is quite a rumor, Olivia. I would very much like to see that, too. But today, I'll be showing you a very old manuscript, a painting by Ferdinand Bol, and other treasures that are quite impressive."

"Speaking of diamonds," Leah said. "I wanted to discuss an idea that I ran by Megan earlier. I was wondering if you might consider offering a signature diamond ring for couples who want to get married at a Carrington resort. Since you are a well-known collector of art and gems, it could be an interesting tie-in. We could partner with a jeweler of your choosing. It would add something extra special to potential brides. It doesn't have to be a ring. It could be a pendant or a bracelet with a special clasp, something to remember the day by. Of course, if this incredible blue diamond that Olivia just mentioned did come to be in your possession, we could do an offshoot of that."

"It's an interesting idea," Victor said. "What do you think, Paula?"

Paula gave her husband a sharp look, something passing between them. Then she said, "I like the idea of a signature piece. Since Lauren wore the teardrop diamond from your mother during her wedding and it was featured in all the photos and videos, we should tie into that. We can also tell your mother's story, which will give it even more of a Carrington feel."

"I like that, too," Megan said. "But I'm also intrigued by the Heart of Eternity. The Unbreakable Heart would make a hell of a slogan for the campaign. Or maybe we could do more than one piece. We could have a bridal jewelry collection, pieces offered exclusively to brides who hold their weddings at one of our resorts."

"That would sell like crazy," Leah agreed.

"All excellent ideas," Victor said. "Definitely something to consider."

"We should do more than consider it," Bennett interjected. "We should make it happen. Why don't I run with that idea?"

"We'll talk about it later," Victor told his son. "If we do it, I want to do it right."

"I wouldn't do it any other way," Bennett snapped.

"Why don't we go upstairs?" Paula suggested, cutting into the sudden tension in the room. "We may not have a famous diamond to show you, but Victor has some other beautiful pieces in the gallery."

As the group got up from the table, Andrew took my hand, holding me back as the others left the dining room. "What did Paula want to talk to you about?"

"We can talk about it later," I replied.

Andrew didn't look happy with my response, but I didn't want to talk about Allison again, especially not right now. We headed up the stairs to the second floor, where a man in a suit stood outside an open door. He looked like private security, reminding me that this collection was probably similar to something I might find in a museum, and it was strange to think it was in someone's vacation home.

But as soon as I stepped into the gallery, I left the vacation villa behind as I entered what felt like another world. The room was cool and pristine, the air carefully controlled to protect the treasures it housed. Glass display cases lined the walls...some empty, others filled with artifacts so exquisite they seemed almost unreal: A ceremonial mask carved from ivory. An illuminated manuscript that looked like it belonged in a cathedral. A jeweled box that could have been plucked from a queen's boudoir.

Victor's voice was rich with enthusiasm as he described each piece. It was clear that Victor had an understanding and appreciation for art and history that had driven his desire to possess these incredible artifacts.

Andrew seemed captivated as well, asking detailed questions that surprised me a little. I hadn't seen this side of him before. I'd had no idea he also knew a lot about history and art. It was interesting but also unsettling—another reminder of how little I truly knew about my husband. But it was fine if we were still getting to know each other. Life was a series of discoveries, and we would grow together through our marriage.

As Victor talked about the manuscript on display in one of the cases, my glance moved across the room. Ethan Stark came through another door, a tablet in hand, speaking quietly with someone whose uniform implied he was a security tech. When their conversation was over, Ethan moved toward our group.

"Making progress, Ethan?" Victor asked.

"Yes. The atmospheric controls are stable now."

"Good." Victor turned to our group. "This is Ethan Stark. His firm insures the artwork and collections both here and within the entire resort. The premiums are astronomical, but then, so are the security requirements."

"Only the best for the best," Ethan said. "Excuse me."

As Victor moved us toward a painting on the wall and began to talk about its history, I was distracted by Ethan's movements around the gallery. He seemed to be checking camera angles while appearing to only casually observe us, but I had a feeling that he wasn't missing anything, and that it wasn't an accident he was here while Andrew and I were here. He probably wondered how two people he thought were thieves had found their way into Victor's private art gallery months after being the last people to escape from a fire at Victor's hotel. If I didn't know us, I'd be suspicious, too.

As I grew bored with Victor's story, I wandered toward another glass case displaying a ceremonial mask. It was very ornate, making me wonder what it had been used for, but not enough that I wanted to ask about it.

"Not your thing?" Bennett asked as he joined me. "You look as bored as I feel."

"I'm just tired. I'm really impressed by all this. I've never seen these kinds of treasures in someone's home."

"Lucky you. All the houses I've lived in have felt more like museums than homes."

"I guess you didn't inherit your father's love of history."

"Not even a little. I don't care about the past; I'm interested in the future. I liked the idea of a signature diamond bracelet with an unbreakable heart. We could sell the hell out of that."

"I agree."

"Good. Tell my father that."

"I'm sure he would listen to you over me."

"I'm the last person he listens to," Bennett said, disgust lacing his voice. "Have you heard that rumor about him selling off some of our properties?"

I could see the anger in his eyes, and I didn't want to feed that fire. "Your father said it's not true, so I would believe him over anyone else."

"Maybe. But my father is good at keeping secrets. He doesn't show his cards unless he has to."

"That's probably why he's so successful."

"That's the problem; he isn't that successful anymore. That's why there are rumors. He's stuck in the past, entertaining traditional media instead of the people who are actually influencing customer behavior. But I'm going to show him that there is a new path forward, and I'm leading the way." He paused. "Which is why I'm going to need you and Andrew to sell your story this afternoon on the trail ride."

"Right. I'm not a big fan of horses."

"I don't care," he said. "We just threw you the wedding of the century. This is part of your job. I have three influencers who are avid horse riders and want to see more of the property. They also want to get to know you and Andrew better. They don't just care about the resort; they're buying into the love story because they know it will add to their content."

"We'll be there, and we'll do our best to entertain."

"Do better than that. We got a lot of great shots and video from the wedding, but there were also a ton of photos with you looking like you were about to go to the dentist and have a root canal. I don't want anyone to think there's trouble in paradise." He paused, his gaze narrowing. "There isn't any trouble, is there?"

"No. Why would you ask that? We just got married yesterday."

"I saw Andrew several times yesterday with a very attractive woman who was not you."

I let out a sigh. *Would I never escape Allison?*

"She's a friend of his and an interior designer, who wants to work on the hillside villas," I said.

"So I heard. My mother isn't happy about that. You might want to tell Andrew to stop pushing attractive women into my father's path. That doesn't usually end well for my mother." He blew out an irritated breath. "I need a drink."

As he left the room, I wandered around, pausing in front of an empty display case. I wondered what was going to go on the small shelf in the middle of the case.

Ethan suddenly appeared at my side. "You know you're looking at nothing, right?" he asked dryly.

"What's going in this case?"

"I can't say."

I looked at him in surprise. "Really? Why not?"

"Security."

"You still don't trust me," I said with a sigh.

"I don't trust anyone, which is why I'm good at my job. I never take anything at face value."

"Some people don't have secrets."

"Everyone has a secret," he contradicted.

"I don't."

"Then you'd be the first person I've ever met who doesn't."

"Then I'm the first person," I said defiantly. Pausing, I added, "You must have investigated me. Did you find any dirt?"

"No. I found very little of interest on you, Lauren. But sometimes that's a red flag. Can someone's life really be that normal, that boring..."

I bristled at his words. "My life has not been boring." Despite my quick defense, I couldn't really argue that it had been that exciting, either, at least not before Andrew had shown up. "My mom was sick for almost three years. The last six months I had to quit my job to look after her. I was happy to do that. I don't regret it for a second. But it was a dark period in my life, and that darkness disappeared when I met Andrew."

"Exactly. Everything changed when you met Andrew."

I frowned at the implication in his words. "Because he's a wonderful guy, and he treats me better than anyone I've ever gone out with." I could see the cynicism in his eyes. "I don't know why I keep talking to you."

For the first time, he smiled. "Sometimes, I don't know why you do, either." He paused as Andrew walked over to us.

"What are you two discussing?" he asked.

"I was asking Mr. Stark what's going in this display case," I replied. "But he said he can't tell me."

"I'm sure it will be something amazing, like the rest of Victor's collection," Andrew said.

"Excuse me," Ethan said, tipping his head to me before he left.

"Was that really all you were talking about?" Andrew asked, giving me a speculative look.

"Mostly. I asked him if he'd been investigating me, and he said that he had, but my life was very boring."

Andrew smiled. "I don't find you at all boring, Lauren."

"Because everything changed when we met. I was a shadow of myself the year after my mom died. But that fire woke me up. Coming that close to death, then meeting you, finding a love I never expected, it was like my life turned upside down, but in a really good way."

"My life changed that night, too."

"Did it?" I questioned. "I mean, I know we fell in love, but you couldn't possibly have been as boring as I was."

"You were a workaholic back then, and I was, too. It was always about business for me. No real time or interest in love relationships. But then I met you, and, well, let's just say you knocked me off my feet."

It wasn't the first time he'd said that or the first time I'd felt dazzled by his complimentary words and his brilliant smile. A tiny voice inside wondered if maybe Andrew did sometimes lay it on a bit too thick. But I had no reason to believe he was being anything but sincere.

"I love you, Lauren," he said as if he knew I needed to hear that. "I feel like it's been too long since I said that."

"It's probably only been a couple of hours," I said with a laugh. "But it's our honeymoon, so I'm going to keep saying it, too." I paused at the sound of someone clearing their throat and realized Victor was right next to me.

He gave us a somewhat awkward smile. "I don't mean to interrupt, but we're going downstairs now. And I need everyone to leave at the same time. I hope you enjoyed seeing some of my collections."

"We did," Andrew said. "I hope you'll invite us back when the rest of these display cases are filled."

"Definitely. By the way..." Victor paused, looking toward the door as his wife ushered the others out of the room, and it was just the three of us. Ethan had disappeared and the other security guard had stepped into the hall. "I wanted to let you know that our security systems are back online in the main building, and our team will be on higher alert as we move forward. I'm sorry we weren't able to find the person who vandalized your suite, but Martin will continue investigating and interviewing our hotel staff. We pride ourselves on providing a safe as well as luxurious five-star experience, so any news to the contrary would be damaging to our reputation."

"We understand," Andrew said. "We won't say a word."

"I'm glad to hear I can count on you both." Victor hesitated, as if he wanted to say something else.

"Do you have a question?" I asked as the silence between us went on a little long.

"My investigator, Mr. Stark, has always had questions about your story the night of the fire," Victor said.

My gut tightened. We were suddenly going to talk about the elephant in the room.

"We're aware of that," Andrew said. "We've given him our

answers, but he seems determined to find something that isn't there. And it was my understanding that the investigation ended months ago."

"It did, and I told Ethan to back off, but as he reminded me, he doesn't work for me. One of the few people around here that doesn't," Victor added, an edge to his voice. "At any rate, I have to work with him to ensure the safety and insurability of my collection, so he'll be here, and he'll be assessing security on every level. I understand that his questions might make you uncomfortable, but it is what it is. He's part of the security team, and he's looking out for my best interests."

"We have nothing to hide," Andrew said with such clarity of purpose in his voice that I was reassured as much as Victor was. "In fact, if there's anything we can do to help, we will. Both Lauren and I are extremely grateful for everything you've done for us, Victor."

"Well, you're doing a lot for me, too. I know you have a busy afternoon ahead, so we should go downstairs. I hope you'll enjoy your trail ride. There are some spectacular views from the hills above the resort."

"I know we will," Andrew assured him, squeezing my hand.

I put on my fake happy smile and followed them both out of the room.

CHAPTER NINE

"What did Paula talk to you about when she took you upstairs?" Andrew asked as soon as we left the villa.

"She doesn't like that Allison is an attractive woman cozying up to her husband to get a job. Paula wanted to know why you were pushing Allison on Victor."

He frowned at my words. "I wasn't pushing Allison. I made an introduction. That was it."

"Well, Paula doesn't like her. She says that Victor has a weakness when it comes to beautiful young women, and she won't have him taken advantage of. By the way, Bennett told me the same thing. He said that attractive young women working with his father doesn't usually work out well for his mother."

"Good God!" Andrew said. "Allison is trying to get ahead in business. She's not after Victor personally. She's a pretty woman, yes, but she's not some supervillain adulteress. I don't know why everyone is getting so worked up about her."

His defense was far too passionate for my liking. "You asked me what Paula said, and I told you. And I wasn't the one who brought Allison up to Paula or Bennett. They asked me about her because she's your friend, and she's on this island at your invitation."

His jaw tightened. "All right. I get it. I'll talk to Allison."

"I could go with you. I'd like to get to know her better."

"You can get to know her another time. You have a lot of feelings about her, Lauren, and I don't want any more drama."

I frowned at the sharpness of his words. "She's the one causing drama, not me, Andrew."

"We don't know that she has done anything." He paused. "You need to trust me, Lauren. I don't know why it seems like you don't anymore."

"Maybe because it feels like you're not being completely honest."

"I've told you everything you need to know about Allison."

I thought his choice of words was telling. Everything I *needed* to know, not necessarily what I *wanted* to know. But I was tired of arguing about her. "I'll meet you back at the room. I could use some time to myself before I have to get on a horse, which I am not looking forward to doing."

"You'll be fine. I'm sure there will be a nice calm horse for you to ride."

"I hope so." I gave him a pleading look. "I don't want Allison to come between us, Andrew."

"Then don't let her. Believe me when I say she isn't important."

"Okay, I believe you. I'll see you in a bit." I kissed him and then headed up the path.

When I got back to our suite, I felt some trepidation upon opening the door, but the suite was just as I'd left it. I got a bottle of water from the fridge and took it out to the balcony, taking a few moments to enjoy the view. It was nice to be on my own, no one asking me questions or telling me to smile. But my peaceful moment was interrupted by the ring of the doorbell.

Letting out a sigh, I went back inside. After checking the peephole, I saw Ethan Stark in the corridor. I debated pretending I wasn't there when I heard his voice.

"I know you're in there, Lauren," Ethan said. "I saw you go in on the security camera."

I opened the door. "Now the camera is working?"

"Yes," he said, brushing past me.

I shut the door behind him. "What do you want? Didn't we just have a conversation?"

"We did, but I didn't want to talk to you about this in front of Andrew. I saw that you came up here alone."

"Great. Now you're spying on me?"

"I wasn't, but since I had the opportunity to speak to you alone, I decided to take it. Where is Andrew, anyway?"

"Talking to his friends."

"Does that include Allison?"

I shrugged. "Possibly. But Andrew and I have spoken about her quite a bit today, and I believe him when he says they're just friends, and there's nothing for me to worry about."

"I researched Allison's movements the last few months. Then I cross-referenced her travel with Andrew's to see if any of their trips overlapped. They did. Six weeks ago, they were in Paris at the same time. Did you know that?"

I stared at him in surprise. "Andrew didn't go to Paris six weeks ago. He hasn't been outside the country since we got together."

"He was there March twenty-second to the twenty-sixth."

I thought back to March. Andrew had taken a couple of trips that month, but he'd gone to New York and Chicago. "You're wrong. He wasn't in Paris. He went to New York."

Ethan took out his phone to show me a photo. I really didn't want to look at it, but I couldn't stop myself. It was a receipt from a hotel in Paris, and Andrew's name was on it. But that was impossible. He wouldn't have gone to Paris without telling me.

"Allison was staying in the same hotel," Ethan added. "Different room, though, if that makes you feel better."

"None of this makes me feel good. But even if they were in Paris together, so what?"

"I have a confidential informant who works as a fence in Paris. Someone approached him about the painting by Juan Martine that was allegedly destroyed during the hotel fire. He didn't like the offer, so he turned it down."

"Who are you talking about?"

"The offer was made through a third party; he didn't know the seller."

"But you think the seller was Andrew?"

"Or maybe Allison," he said. "The timing fits. They were both there."

I shook my head in confusion. "I don't know what you want me to say. I don't even know what a fence is."

"It's a person who facilitates the buying and selling of stolen art. The fact that a painting that was allegedly destroyed in a fire is now being offered for sale backs up my theory that it was stolen and not turned to ash. Andrew was in Paris at the time my contact met with a third-party seller offering that same painting. It feels like more than a coincidence."

"Why don't you track down the third-party seller and find out who hired him?"

"I'm in the process of doing that."

"Then I don't know why you're talking to me."

"I was curious if Andrew told you he was going to Paris. Clearly, he did not. Why do you think he didn't?"

That was a question I couldn't answer. I had never grilled Andrew about his work. When we were together, we didn't talk about our jobs. We'd both wanted to separate our business and personal lives, because before we'd met, we'd spent far too many hours concentrating solely on work. I'd thought it was great we were on the same page. I wasn't that interested in his job, and he wasn't that interested in mine, but we were both supportive and encouraging of each other. That was what mattered.

Now, I was reminded once again that my husband had not been completely forthcoming with me, and it was embarrassing to keep learning details about Andrew from a man who was trying to determine if my husband was a thief.

I told myself there was probably a perfectly good reason why Andrew hadn't mentioned Paris. It could have been a spur-of-the-moment business trip, and he hadn't wanted to tell me he was going to Paris without me, because I'd often told him how much I wanted to go there. He could have been protecting my feelings.

Or I could be making up excuses for another lie of omission.

But were they lies? Or had I not asked enough questions?

"Lauren? You're not going to answer me, are you?" Ethan asked.

"I don't have an answer. But thanks for once again trying to create drama and distrust in my life. Does that make you happy? Do you get off on it?" I challenged.

"If you're innocent in all this, I want you to see what's going on. I'm trying to help you, Lauren."

"You're trying to help yourself."

"Maybe working together is how we help each other."

"I don't want to help you. I'm married to Andrew. My loyalty is to him."

"What if he's a criminal?"

A wave of uneasiness ran through me at that suggestion. But Andrew wasn't a criminal. I knew what had happened the night of the fire. I'd been there. Andrew had risked his life to save mine. Then there was all the rest, all the time we'd spent together the last six months. Maybe we hadn't talked about everything, but we had talked about a lot. *Hadn't we? Damn! Why did Ethan's questions always bring more questions?*

Because that's what he was trying to do. He was trying to divide Andrew and me and find a weak spot, but I couldn't be the weak link in the chain between us. I had to be loyal and defend my husband.

"Andrew did tell me he might have to go to Paris," I said slowly.

"You're lying, Lauren."

"I'm not. I just forgot. I was busy at work. He was already in New York, so we weren't going to be together that week, anyway."

"You just remembered that?" Ethan asked, a doubtful look in his piercing green eyes. "That's convenient."

He could see right through me, and I didn't like it. "Is there anything else? Or maybe you'd like to wait here and ask Andrew your questions?"

"I'll talk to Andrew another time."

"Because you have nothing, and you know he won't let you get to him the way you get to me."

His gaze narrowed as it met mine. "I understand that it's difficult to lose trust in someone. You don't want to do it. You want to fight for the person you think they are. But this isn't only about trust or fidelity...it's about high-stakes crime, past and possibly present. Be careful, Lauren. You are right smack in the middle of whatever is going on, even if you don't want to believe it."

His words sent a chill down my spine. "The middle of what?"

"I don't know, but I'm going to follow the facts wherever they lead, and I hope, for your sake, they don't lead to you or your husband. But if they do, don't say I didn't warn you."

On that note, he left, and I let out a breath as the door closed behind him, my mind racing, my nerves tingling with fear, uncertainty, and anxiety.

Was Andrew up to something? Was I unwittingly part of it?

It seemed impossible to believe. But all the little things Ethan was coming up with couldn't be ignored.

When I had confronted Andrew about his relationship with Allison, he'd finally admitted they'd slept together after first claiming they were just friends. *Would he admit to Paris, too, if I asked him about it?*

But even if he had an explanation, would I be able to believe it? Because what had happened before we met was much easier to forgive than not telling me about a trip to Paris six weeks ago, after we were in love, after we were engaged, and after we'd started planning a future together.

I was still debating what to do when Andrew entered the suite.

He gave me a funny look. "Everything okay?"

"Yes," I said, realizing I probably looked as confused as I felt. I decided to go with an easy question, something I was already supposed to know. "Did you find Allison?"

"I did." He tossed his keycard on the table and walked over to the fridge to pull out a beer. He opened the bottle and took a swig before continuing, "Allison was working on ideas to show Victor tomorrow. That's all she wanted to talk about. She's desperate to get this job, and she doesn't give a crap about anything else. She's certainly not trying to seduce Victor. She just wants to work for him. I told her she needs to smooth things out with Paula, and she said she'll reassure her she only wants a job. I believe her, Lauren. Allison is not the horrible, conniving person you seem to think she is. She didn't trash our suite, and she's not looking for revenge because I married you."

I wondered if he'd actually asked Allison about the suite, but he wanted my trust, and I wanted to trust him. My wedding vows were still fresh in my mind. "Okay."

"You believe me?"

"I said okay. I'm glad she's just here to work."

Relief ran through his gaze, and his unusually serious mood lightened. "That's all it is. I'm sorry things got off track. I should have told you about her when I invited her to the wedding. I extended the invitation because she asked me for an introduction to Victor. I should have been up front with you about that, but I didn't think her presence would mean anything to you or anyone else. I had no idea Ethan Stark was looking into my relationship with Allison because we happened to be at the same conference. Or that he would come to you and try to turn it into something it wasn't."

I debated asking him about Paris, but before I could say anything, his phone buzzed.

Andrew pulled it out of his pocket and read a text. "I need to make a quick call for work. You should get ready for our ride. We need to be at the stables in twenty minutes." He gave me a smile. "It will be nice to get out on the trail and have some fun."

I had my doubts about that, but at this point, I was willing to risk getting on a horse to find some fun, because so far, my honeymoon was a dud.

CHAPTER TEN

At two o'clock, we met up with Bennett Carrington at the stables, which were nestled in a grove of eucalyptus trees just beyond the edge of the resort, the scent of horse feed and fresh hay mingling with the salty ocean breeze. A long, whitewashed barn with neatly painted blue shutters gleamed under the midday sun. Horses stood in outdoor pens, their ears twitching as stable hands moved between them, saddling and brushing the sleek animals.

The air was alive with movement and sound: the soft nickers of the horses, the rhythmic scrape of brushes, and the distant crash of waves against the shoreline. Bennett Carrington, now dressed in a casual button-down shirt, well-worn jeans, and boots, introduced us to the three influencers coming on the ride.

Talia Berensky was a pony-tailed brunette in her mid-twenties, wearing skin-tight jeans and knee-high boots. Her social media channels focused on wedding venues—the best and craziest places to hold a ceremony. Kat Lewis, a thirty-something former model with flawless makeup, wore her long blonde hair in a thick braid that fell halfway down her back, and her white jeans and gauzy top were probably more appropriate for a cocktail party than a trail ride. Her channels focused on budget-friendly luxury travel deals for honeymooners. And, finally, there was Tyler Reed, an attractive brown-haired man in his late twenties, who wore faded, ripped jeans, a T-shirt, and a baseball cap. He had a camera hanging on a strap around his neck and a phone in his hand, more than prepared to capture the entire experience for his social media, which focused on active, adventure travel ideas.

It was clear why Bennett wanted them here. They were worlds apart from the media professionals we'd mingled with at Victor's villa—these influencers were dynamic, creative, and perfectly attuned to their followers' desires. If Bennett's vision was to modernize the Carrington brand and attract a new generation of travelers, this was how he'd do it.

"We're excited to see what you've planned for us," Talia said, her polished voice cutting through the ambient noise of the stables. "I'm already thinking about weddings on horseback. Luxury meets the Wild West."

"Exactly," Bennett said. "I like that line a lot." He tipped his head to me. "You should remember that, Lauren."

"I will," I said. "It's a great hook. I hope everyone will have a good time, and Andrew and I are happy to help you capture whatever mood or scene you think will be good for your posts."

"Let's get everyone saddled up," Bennett said, leading his group toward the horses.

"Looks like a good crew," Andrew commented.

"I'll say. Three of the biggest influencers in the travel and wedding industry. Bennett is actually pulling his weight for a change."

"I wouldn't say that to him," Andrew said dryly.

"Oh, trust me, I won't. I try to talk to him as little as possible. Luckily, Megan is the one who has to deal with him. He's not the easiest person to work with. He's very entitled, and he hasn't had a lot of practical marketing experience, which is why I'm surprised he pulled this together. But Megan said he's starting to sound more committed to actually working for the company instead of just waiting to inherit it, so I guess that's a good thing." I paused, surprised when I saw Harper and Colin walking toward us.

"Oh, good, we're not too late," Harper said.

"I didn't realize you were coming."

"Andrew invited us," Harper said. "It's okay, isn't it?"

"It's fine," Andrew said. "I texted Bennett. He said the more, the merrier."

"Great. Because I love to ride," Harper said.

"Let's check out the horses," Andrew told Colin. "And don't worry, ladies, we will get the slowest horse we can find for Lauren and the fastest horse we can find for you, Harper."

"Perfect," Harper said. "I like a wilder ride."

Both Colin and Andrew laughed at her words, and I couldn't help but smile. Harper was far better at flirting and having a provocative personality than I was, which meant she'd be good to have on the trail ride. She was friendly and outgoing and a good representative for the hotel. Colin was also charming and a good talker. Add Andrew into that mix, and I might not have to say much at all, which would be good since I'd probably be hanging onto the reins and praying that I didn't fall off the horse.

"Don't you hate horseback riding?" Harper asked when we were alone. "I've tried to get you to go with me several times, and you've always told me you'd rather jump off a cliff than get on a horse."

"I didn't have a choice," I said with a sigh. "I'm trying not to get too worked up about it."

"You shouldn't. It will be fun."

"It looks like you and Colin are getting along well."

"Very well," Harper said, sending me a happy smile. "My slump with men might be over."

"That's good to hear."

"Colin is going to spend the week here, so we'll have some time to get to know each other."

"I thought he was leaving on Tuesday with Jay."

"Jay is staying, too, but the woman he brought with him left this morning. Jay didn't seem unhappy to see her go. In fact, I think he might have a little crush on Allison. They were huddled together for a while before Andrew arrived."

I frowned. "You were with Allison? I thought she was working on designs for the hillside villas."

"She mentioned something about that. I think she's going up there this afternoon to look at one of the units. She asked Andrew if he wanted to come, but he said he was tied up here, and that's when he invited Colin and me to come along. You know I love horses. And I thought you might like a friend."

"Are we back to being friends?" I couldn't help asking.

She gave me a sheepish look. "If I didn't completely blow it yesterday. I don't know what was wrong with me. Everything about the wedding bugged me. I felt so envious, and I couldn't seem to shake it. I was a bad bridesmaid, and I am sorry about that. I wouldn't blame you if you didn't forgive me."

Harper's apology seemed sincere and heartfelt. And it wasn't like she'd done anything that terrible beyond a few snippy comments here and there. I didn't believe she'd vandalized the suite, not just because she wouldn't do that, but also because she'd been more interested in getting to know Colin than ruining my wedding night.

"We're good," I said.

"Great." She blew out a breath of relief. "I want us to be friends, especially since Colin and I are getting closer. I think I could really like him, Lauren."

I was happy to see the light back in her eyes, but inwardly, I felt a little wary of their relationship because of Colin's close friendship with Andrew. I didn't want anything to get messy between the four of us. But I could hardly deny her a chance at love when she'd supported me—well, tried to support me, anyway.

"Are you okay with that?" Harper asked, reading my silence with some concern.

"Sure. Absolutely. If you're happy, I'm happy."

"Well, it's only been a day, so we'll see how happy I can be. But Colin is very cool. He likes to travel, and he has been to so many places. I love listening to his stories. When he goes to a new city, he said he always tries to find a hidden gem of a restaurant, something off the beaten path where no tourists go. He told me about this amazing place in Paris that he discovered a few months ago. He said he had a crepe to die for. He painted such a picture of that trip; I felt like booking a plane ticket when he was done."

As Harper rambled on about Colin and crepes, my mind kept running one word back and forth—*Paris*. "Did Colin go to Paris with friends?" I asked when she finally took a breath.

"He said Allison was there. I don't know who else. Why?"

"No reason."

"You don't like her, do you?" Harper asked, giving me a knowing look. "She's a little too pretty and too friendly with Andrew."

"I don't want to talk about her, and it looks like our horses might be ready to go."

As Andrew waved to us, we walked toward the barn. He gave me a confident smile when we joined him and Colin. "I have the perfect horse for you, Lauren. Her name is Sally, and she's that beautiful gray mare who, according to the stable hand, is very calm, easygoing, and will not be difficult to ride. If anything, she'll go too slow."

"Slow is good," I said as Andrew led me over to the horse.

I gave the horse's nose an awkward pat as Andrew suggested I say hello. Then he helped me into the saddle. When I was set, he got onto his horse, and I tried to take several deep, relaxing breaths as I waited for Harper, who was taking her seat on a horse that was already prancing and dancing, but Harper seemed incredibly comfortable with the energy. I wished I could feel that confident and relaxed, but I was too caught up in praying that I wouldn't fall off. Sally wasn't doing a damn thing but patiently waiting to go, but I could still feel the power of her body beneath me, and the slightest sway made me grip the reins tighter.

Finally, we were off, with one stable hand named Kyle leading the group from the front, another guy named Reece at the back. Andrew, Harper, and Colin were behind me, Bennett and the influencers in front of me. My horse fell into line with the others, and as a few uneventful minutes passed, I tried to breathe deeper and enjoy the scenery.

The trail wound its way up into the hills above the resort. We passed by the villas under construction, and I wondered if Allison was working in the model, but everything seemed very quiet in that area since it was Sunday and there were no workers around.

As we moved beyond the villas, we took a path flanked by golden grass and scattered wildflowers. Eucalyptus trees arched overhead, their leaves whispering in the breeze, and the salty tang of the ocean grew sharper as the trail climbed higher. Below, the resort spread out like a postcard, its white buildings nestled against the deep blue of the sea.

Andrew rode beside me whenever the trail allowed, his easy smile and encouraging words helping me feel slightly less like I was about to fall off. "You're doing great," he kept repeating, and I was starting to think he might be right.

I was touched by how attentive he was. It was one of the reasons I'd fallen in love with him, and maybe I needed to focus on who he'd always been to me instead of the mystery man Ethan was trying to make him out to be. Although that thought reminded me that Harper had mentioned a trip to Paris, too... not that she'd said Andrew was on it, but Colin had been with Allison, and according to the receipt Ethan had shown me, Andrew had been there, too.

I didn't want to think about that now. I was on my honeymoon. I had married the man of my dreams, and everything would work itself out. Once Andrew and I got past some of these events, we'd have more time to talk, and he'd have an explanation for that trip. I knew he would.

About ten minutes later, we came to a halt at a beautiful vista point. The clearing opened onto a stunning view of the coastline, the ocean sparkling in the afternoon sun. Avalon's harbor was visible in the distance, dotted with boats, while the rooftops of the town added a splash of color against the rolling hills. Almost everyone dismounted to take photos, including Andrew. He wanted to help me down, but I'd just started getting comfortable, so I decided to stay on my horse rather than get on and off. We were only going to be there for a few minutes anyway, and then we'd be heading back.

As the breeze picked up, Sally moved around a bit, and I started to feel uneasy, realizing that aside from our group leader, who was about ten feet away from me, I was the only other person still astride. The others were roaming around the trees and the enormous boulders, trying to find the perfect shots, especially the influencers.

Tyler seemed to be shooting video of everything and everyone, including me, while Kat was climbing up on a boulder that hung perilously close to the edge of the bluff. In fact, Reece was trying to get her to come down when I heard a sharp whizzing sound slice through the air near my ear.

Sally suddenly reared without warning, her powerful body launching upward as she whinnied in panic. I screamed, grabbing at the reins, but it was too late—she bolted down the trail, her hooves pounding against the dirt as I clung to the saddle for dear life.

Branches whipped at my arms and face, the world a blur of motion and sound. "Whoa, Sally! Stop!" I yelled, but it was no use. She was out of control, her body taut with panic as she tore through the trees with me along for the ride.

I heard shouts behind me, but Sally was running so fast I didn't know if I was hearing actual voices or the pounding of my own heart. Eventually, she'd have to stop, I told myself. But as the path got steeper and more uneven, I worried about when that might be and what might happen.

I'd no sooner had that panicked thought when the trail came to an end, the ground sloping sharply downward. Sally put on the brakes as she tried to pull up, but it was too fast, too sudden. She reared up again, and this time I couldn't hang on. The reins slipped from my hands as I flew through the air, landing hard on the rocky ground.

The impact knocked the breath out of me, pain exploding in my hip. For a moment, I couldn’t move, the world spinning around me. Sally thrashed nearby, her eyes wild with fear, but Kyle suddenly appeared, jumping off his horse to grab Sally's bridle.

Andrew appeared a moment later, his hair windblown, his eyes wide with fear, as he jumped to the ground and fell to his knees beside me.

"Lauren!" he said, his voice sharp with panic. "Are you all right?"

I stared at him in shock. "I—I don't know."

He put his hand on my shoulder. "Where does it hurt?"

"My hip, my side," I mumbled.

"What about your legs? Your neck? Your head?" he bit out, his gaze running down my body.

"I think I'm okay," I said, not aware of any other pain. "Can you help me up?" Even though Sally had calmed down, I wanted to get a little further away from the horse.

Andrew helped me to my feet. "What happened?" he asked.

"I don't know. The horse just took off."

"She never bolts like that," the young man holding the horse said. "She's the calmest horse we have."

I shook my head in confusion. "One minute I was sitting there, and then she reared up and took off." I paused. "I think I heard something whiz by my ear."

"She might have gotten stung by a bee," Kyle put in.

"Had to be something like that," Andrew agreed. "I'm so sorry, Lauren. I promised you'd be all right."

I saw the guilt in his eyes. "It wasn't your fault. I should have gotten off the horse when I had the chance."

"Sally is calm now," the stable hand said. "If you want to ride her back."

I gave him an incredulous look. "Not a chance. I'm not getting back on that horse. Do you think I'm crazy?"

"You can ride with me," Andrew said.

I didn't like that idea, either, but we were probably a few miles away from the resort, and I didn't feel up to walking. Still, I hesitated. "I don't know. Your horse looks even bigger than Sally. Maybe we could call for someone to bring a golf cart up here."

"A cart won't be able to make it up here," the stable hand said. "It's either ride with your husband or walk."

"I won't let anything happen to you," Andrew promised.

He'd told me that earlier. Not that it was his fault, but it was difficult to trust his words now.

"Dammit," I swore, knowing I had no choice. "Okay, fine, I'll ride with you, but I want to go straight back to the stables."

"Of course."

"Where is everyone else?"

"They're already headed back to the stable," the guide said, glancing down at his phone. "My manager wants to know if you need a doctor to meet you there."

"I don't think so," I said.

"Well, if you change your mind, let me know."

"I'm going to help you up, and then I'm going to get up behind you," Andrew said, giving me another warm, reassuring smile.

"All right." It took every ounce of courage I had to climb into Andrew's saddle, my body tense with pain and fear. His hands were strong and steady as he helped me up, then swung up behind me with practiced ease. His arms caged me in as he took the reins, his warmth pressing against my back.

"You're safe now," he murmured, his voice low in my ear.

I didn't feel safe. My skin prickled with unease, my mind replaying the moment Sally had bolted. *What had made my horse take off like that?* Something had definitely spooked her. Maybe it had been a bee. Just a freaky, bad-luck moment.

As we descended the trail, I could see the others in a pack far ahead of us, their laughter and chatter so carefree, so different from the way I felt. The scenery blurred past us: golden hillsides dotted with wildflowers, the ocean glinting in the late afternoon sun. But I couldn't focus on the beauty. My thoughts were a tangled mess of pain and unanswered questions.

When we got back to the stables, everyone was waiting for us, their expressions filled with concern. Andrew got off first and then helped me down. When I put my weight on my left leg, I winced, biting back a gasp of pain.

"Lauren! Are you okay?" Bennett asked, striding forward with both worry and annoyance in his gaze.

I had a feeling he was more concerned with what was going to be written about this event by the influencers than how I was actually feeling. But he was trying to act like he cared. And I needed to be cognizant of my reaction and the photos that were currently being snapped by Talia, Kat, and Tyler.

"I'll be fine," I said, forcing a smile. "Just bruised."

"Bruised?" Bennett echoed. "Did you fall off?"

"I didn't fall—I was thrown," I corrected. The memory made my stomach tighten.

Bennett shook his head, seemingly bewildered. "I don't understand what happened. Sally is such a calm mare. I rode her yesterday, and she was too slow for me."

"Well, she wasn't slow today when she took off like a rocket," I snapped, frustration bubbling to the surface. "Something spooked her. I heard it."

"What did you hear?" Bennett pressed.

I hesitated, glancing at the group. Harper, Colin, and the influencers stood nearby, avidly listening to our exchange.

"I don't know...it was a hissing sound."

"Or maybe a buzzing," Andrew suggested. "It could have been a bee that stung Sally and sent her running."

"That was probably it," Bennett said with a nod, happy to have a reasonable explanation.

"I'm going to take Lauren back to our room so she can catch her breath," Andrew said.

"Good idea," Bennett agreed.

My gaze moved to the influencers. "I'm sorry to cut our time short. I hope you enjoyed yourselves."

"We did," Kat said. "Just sorry you had such a rough time, Lauren."

The others murmured their agreement.

"Thanks. I hope I'll see you again before you leave the island."

"We'll be here through the grand opening," Tyler replied. "I actually caught some of your flight on my camera if you want to see it. I was shooting you sitting on the horse, looking like a queen, right before Sally bolted. Do you want me to show it to you?"

"I don't think she needs to see it. She just lived it," Andrew said.

"I will pass," I agreed.

"We've got a cart to take you back to the lodge," Bennett said, tipping his head to the young female driver waiting in the golf cart.

"Thanks."

"Our resort medical staff hasn't arrived yet, but there's a small medical center in town if you'd rather go there and get checked out," he added.

"I don't need a doctor. I'll be fine."

Andrew helped me to the cart, and it was a quick ride back to the resort. But even sitting for that long intensified the pain in my hip. Hopefully, it wasn't anything serious. Because I really didn't want to have to deal with a bigger injury.

As we entered the room, Andrew said, "I think you're lying about how hurt you are, Lauren. You're walking like you're in a lot of pain."

"I just need some ibuprofen and maybe a bath."

"Let's start with ice. See if we can't get the swelling reduced." He paused. "I think I left the ibuprofen with Jay."

"I have some in my bathroom bag," I told him as I headed into the bedroom. I stretched out on the bed on my good side and closed my eyes as I fought against the pain. Andrew returned a moment later with a glass of water and pain medication. I swallowed three tablets and then settled back into the comfortable mattress.

"I'm going to get you some ice," he said. "I'll be right back."

"Thanks."

As he left, my phone started vibrating in my jean jacket pocket, and I pulled it out. I'd taken it along to take photos on the ride, but, of course, I'd been too afraid to take my hands off the reins to make that happen.

A notification from my social media channel revealed I'd been tagged in a video posted by Tyler. I had a feeling I knew what it was, and while I didn't want to relive the nightmare, I was curious to see what it had looked like.

Of course, Tyler had added some fun text to the post, but I was more interested in the actual video. One second, I was sitting on my horse looking beautiful against a magnificent tree-covered hillside, and then I suddenly screamed as Sally jumped about a foot in the air. I clutched wildly at the reins before the horse took off.

Frowning, I played the video back again a few more times, pausing it right before the horse jumped. Andrew had thought Sally had been stung by a bee, but it seemed like something was moving through the air. The video was too grainy to really tell what it was, but it kind of looked like a rock.

My pulse leapt. Maybe the horse had been hit by a rock and not stung by a bee.

I played the video again, looking more closely at the first few frames where I could see people behind me: Harper, Colin, Andrew, and Bennett were all there.

If a rock had come from that direction...

My breath came fast as ridiculous thoughts filled my head. There was no way one of them would have thrown a rock at me or the horse. And maybe it wasn't even a rock.

As I heard the suite door open and close, I turned the phone face down on the bed. I didn't know why I didn't immediately show it to Andrew, why I didn't let him tell me I was imagining things. Before I could think too long about it, he entered the room, setting a bag of ice on the bedside table.

He gave me a sympathetic smile. "Let's get you out of those jeans and see what's bruised."

It made sense to look, but it hurt to move, and I was still thinking about what I'd seen. "I'll look later."

"We'll look now," he said forcefully.

"It's going to hurt."

"I'll help you, Lauren. We need to see what the damage is in case we need to get you to the doctor."

He helped me take off my jeans, and I winced as the denim moved past my hips.

"Damn," he muttered as he pulled them all the way off and tossed them on the end of the bed. "You have a hell of a bruise."

I twisted my head to see swelling around my hip bone and a large red and purple bruise developing. No wonder I was in pain.

"You might need to get this checked out."

"I don't think I broke anything and there's nothing anyone can do for a bruise. I just want to rest, Andrew."

He frowned, then got up and retrieved a hand towel from the bathroom. He draped it over my hip and gently set the ice bag on top of it. Even that small amount of pressure sent a stabbing pain from my hip to my toes, but I hoped the cold would help ease that.

He pulled a throw blanket off the chaise lounge next to the bed and put it over me with soft and kind hands. "What else do you need?" he asked.

"Nothing. Thank you."

He met my gaze and gave a regretful shake of his head. "This is not the honeymoon I wanted, Lauren."

"Me, either. But it can only get better, right?"

"I can't imagine it getting worse. What happened was such a freak accident. That a bee would sting your horse. What are the odds of that?"

"What are the odds?" I echoed, my gut telling me it had not been a bee.

But thinking about what it might have been would only make me feel worse, and my pain threshold was maxed out.

"You should rest. Hopefully, you'll feel better in a few hours. We have that bonfire tonight on the beach."

I sighed at the reminder. That was another one of the events Megan wanted to highlight for the campaign. "I don't think I can do it. I need to text Megan and let her know. She won't be happy."

"She'll have to understand."

"You should go without me."

"I don't think she wants photos of me by myself," he said dryly.

"Your friends will be there. Maybe she can take group shots, and we don't have to be the featured couple." I reached for my phone. "I can ask her."

"Put that down. I'll talk to Megan. You don't need to worry about it."

"What are you going to do now?"

"I have some work emails to answer. I also might run down and talk to the guys for a while if you don't need anything else."

"I'll be fine, Andrew."

"Okay." He pulled the curtains shut and turned off the light before leaving the bedroom, gently closing the door behind him.

Once he was gone, I picked up my phone and watched the video again. I didn't know if I was imagining things or seeing an actual rock hitting my horse. If that had happened, who had thrown that rock and why?

Were they trying to spook me, hurt me?

The words written on my wall last night suddenly rang through my head once more: *You'll be sorry.*

I was beginning to think they were going to be right.

CHAPTER ELEVEN

After taking a long nap and another dose of ibuprofen, by seven thirty that night, I was feeling marginally better. Andrew had gone to the restaurant around six and brought back pasta, salad, and garlic bread, which had also helped improve my mood. I'd even managed to put on a pair of soft sweatpants and make my way into the living room to eat.

After dinner, I convinced Andrew to go to the bonfire on his own. I wasn't up to answering questions about the trail ride or faking a smile. Andrew had spoken to Megan while I was napping, who had sent me a nice text telling me to take the night off and get ready for tomorrow...a subtle warning that I could skip the bonfire but nothing else. While Andrew had made a somewhat weak argument for staying with me, in the end, we'd both agreed that he should spend time with his friends since I wouldn't be up for anything more than lying around. And when he finally left, I was happy to see him go. I needed time and space to think about what had happened on the trail ride. I also wanted to look at the video again.

Maybe I'd just imagined seeing a rock hit my horse. But if I hadn't imagined it, then who would have thrown the rock? The only people visible in the video that were behind me were

Andrew, Harper, Colin, and Bennett. Out of those four, the only one who seemed even possibly likely was Colin, but I couldn't imagine why he'd have a motive to hurt me.

It could have been Harper, I supposed. I hadn't been able to rule out her involvement in trashing the bridal suite, but she had apologized for her behavior at the wedding, and she was having fun with Colin now. She'd seemed happy on the trail ride, too. Happier than I'd seen her in a long time. It didn't make sense she would have thrown a rock at me or my horse out of some jealous rage. And if she had, wouldn't Colin or Andrew have seen her?

The one person I couldn't blame for this was Allison. She hadn't been on the ride. Although I had no idea where she had been. She was supposed to be working on designs for the new villas on the hillside, and we had passed those villas on our ride. She could have seen us all together and gotten pissed off again. But she would have had to follow us up the trail, and that didn't seem likely, either.

With a sigh, I stretched out on the couch, putting my weight on my good side, and looked at the video again. I still wasn't sure what I was looking at. I needed someone to confide in, someone to tell me if I was going down a dark path, and that someone should be my husband. But Andrew was one of the people in the video, and any accusation I made would have made him angry, ready to defend himself and his best friend. I couldn't drive yet another wedge between us without anything more than a bad feeling and a grainy video.

As I was pondering what to do, an impulse took hold. I scrolled through my messages, finding one I'd gotten a long time ago from Ethan Stark. I asked myself what the hell I was thinking. Before I could come up with an answer, I was calling him.

"Stark," he said a moment later.

"It's Lauren."

"What's wrong?"

"I—I don't know." My hand tightened on the phone as second thoughts about having this conversation ran through me.

"I heard you fell off your horse on the trail ride."

His comment angered me, as if I'd somehow been clumsy enough to fall off a horse. "I was thrown from my horse after it tore down the path because someone threw a rock at her or at me," I said.

"I did not hear that. What can I do?"

"I'm not sure. Maybe nothing. But I think someone deliberately tried to spook my horse, to injure me or worse. There's a video that one of the influencers took. I've been staring at it for hours, and I'm not sure if I'm imagining something or if there's really a clue there."

"Where are you?"

"In my suite."

"And Andrew?"

"He's at the bonfire."

"I'll be there in five minutes."

Ethan ended the call before I could say he didn't need to come over, but maybe he did. He could look at the video and tell me there was nothing there. That would be the best scenario.

A few moments later, a knock came at my door. I got off the couch and limped my way across the room to let Ethan in. He wore jeans and a dark-green sweater tonight, and I had to admit he was a very good-looking man, something I tried not to notice because he usually made me nervous every time he showed up, and I couldn't wait to get away from him. But tonight, I was inviting him into my suite, which still seemed ridiculously risky.

"This was probably a bad idea," I said as he shut the door behind him.

"We can figure that out later." His gaze narrowed. "You look very pale."

"I'm in some pain from my fall. I landed on my hip, and it's pretty bruised."

"Why don't we sit down, and you can show me the video."

I nodded and made my way back to the couch. I gingerly sat down, then opened my phone to the video and handed it to him.

He took my phone and sat down in the chair next to the couch, while I stretched out once more. It was easier to lie on my side than to sit upright.

He watched the video several times in silence.

"Well, what do you think?" I asked impatiently. "Do you see something heading toward my horse right before she bolts?"

He nodded as his gaze moved from the phone to me. "I do. It looks like a rock. The only people visible in this video who would have been able to throw that rock are your husband, his best man, your bridesmaid, and your boss's son."

"I know. There are no good choices in that group."

"Is there anyone else who was there who isn't in the frame?"

"Only Kyle, who was the stable hand leading the ride. He was on a horse not far from me. The influencers were in front of me taking photos. And Reece, the other stable hand was actually trying to get Kat to come down from a precarious perch as she was taking a photo."

"Then it had to be one of the four behind you."

"They don't look like they're doing anything."

He glanced down at the phone. "Andrew and Colin are talking to each other. Bennett is looking at his phone, and Harper is off to the side."

"She's only a few feet from the others. She couldn't have thrown a rock without anyone seeing her do that."

Ethan nodded, his gaze meeting mine. "The story Bennett told was that you were a very nervous rider, and they believe your horse might have gotten stung by a bee and reared up. You yanked on the reins too hard, which escalated the situation, and the horse bolted. At the end of the ride, you fell off."

"I don't know why everyone keeps making a distinction between falling off the horse and being thrown off," I grumbled. "Either way, I ended up on the ground, and it wasn't my fault. I did nothing to make that horse freak out like she did. Once Sally was running, there was nothing I could do except try to hang on, which by some miracle I did, until the very end when she reared up again. I think she was as tired of me as I was of her."

"Well, I'm sure Bennett was eager to downplay what happened to you with the grand opening only days away. He doesn't want anyone to think the trail ride is dangerous or the horses are unreliable."

"I understand why he'd downplay it, why no one else would ever think something more malicious occurred than a random bee sting, but after what happened to the bridal suite, and the threat written on the wall, I'm not so sure it was an accident at all." I paused, not quite able to believe what I was about to ask, but this man, this needling investigator, seemed like the only person who might tell me the truth. "What do you think, Ethan?"

He met my gaze. "Someone deliberately spooked your horse."

I felt both relieved that he understood where I was coming from and upset to think someone had thrown a rock at me. "Do you think they were trying to scare me or hurt me?"

"Maybe both. The message scrawled on the wall of the suite said *you'll be sorry*. This seems like the next step. So we get back to the central question. Who would want you to be sorry?"

"I know you want me to say Allison McGuire, and she's the first one who comes to my mind, too. She's definitely jealous of me and Andrew. Her conversation with Colin last night implied she had some sort of plan for being here. Andrew claims her plan is to get business from Victor and has nothing to do with him. He can't believe that I'm turning her into some sort of supervillain, but it's not just me. Paula told me she was concerned about Allison's efforts to get into business with her husband, so I'm not the only one who isn't thrilled that the woman is here. But all that aside, Allison wasn't with us. She wasn't on the trail ride."

"I wonder where she was."

"Harper had told me that Allison was going to go up to the

model villa on the hillside, the one that's almost finished with construction, so she could pin down her design ideas. Apparently, she's planning to show them to Victor this week in the hopes that he'll let her design those villas. He wants each one to be unique, so having a different designer than the ones who did the other buildings is something he's interested in."

"Those villas are near the stables," Ethan commented.

"They are, and we passed them on our ride. I didn't see anyone around that area, though. It was quiet. If she was there, she was inside."

"She might have seen you all ride by."

"She probably didn't even have to see us. She knew we were going on the trail ride. But we were at the vista point, which was probably a mile or two from the stables, when my horse spooked. I don't know how easy it would have been for her to follow us and stay out of sight."

"Those hills are dense with trees and brush. You might have felt like you were farther away than you were."

"Possibly. When Andrew rode back with me on his horse, it didn't feel as long as the trip out." I winced as I shifted my weight.

"You need something?" he asked.

"I've already iced and taken ibuprofen. I just have to live through this."

"Hell of a honeymoon, huh?"

"Tell me about it," I breathed. "I keep thinking it can't get worse, but maybe it can."

I wanted him to reassure me this was probably rock bottom, but he wasn't about to tell me something he didn't believe. Something I didn't believe, either. Because I didn't think anything was over.

"I honestly don't know what I want from you or why I even called you," I added. "You think I'm a thief."

"I don't believe that anymore, Lauren."

"Well, I guess that's something. Why did you change your mind?" I asked curiously.

"Because you're too open, too anxious. You don't lie very well. You also seem to be a target of someone's anger, which leads me to believe you're just a player in whatever game is happening. But you're not the one running it."

"I hope you're not going to tell me you think that person is Andrew. Because he came to my rescue. And he's been incredibly kind to me ever since we got back. He doesn't hate me. He doesn't want to hurt me. We just got married. If he didn't want me in his life, why would he have made vows to me?"

"I don't know," Ethan said. "But I think the reason might be more complicated than you think."

"Not just love, huh? Thanks a lot. You're always so good for my ego."

"I'm not going to lie to you, Lauren. Andrew is too slick and too perfect. His background feels carefully crafted. And there are no people in his life now that were in his past. The only people I can connect him with are the people he works with. His company was created less than two years ago. They've made a couple of decent deals, but nothing huge, nothing that would seem to support the three salaries going to Andrew, Colin, and Jay, not to mention their support staff, which appears to be a woman named Sonia Waters."

"I don't know a lot about his business, but he's just getting it off the ground. He said he made good money working for his previous company, and he had enough in savings to go out on his own."

"The owner of his previous company went to jail for fraud."

"I do know that," I said, happy I knew at least one thing about my husband. "Andrew said that was more of a marital dispute than anything else."

"Your husband always has a good answer."

"I don't know about that, but that's what he told me."

"Did you ask him about his trip to Paris?"

"Not yet. I haven't had the chance. And he was already annoyed with me for asking questions about Allison. I couldn't keep fighting with him when we have to put on a united, loving front." I let out a sigh. "I shouldn't be talking to you about him. You're trying to pin something on him, and I feel like I'm helping you when I should be helping him."

"You're talking to me because you need an ally."

"That shouldn't be you. I have a husband. I have friends."

"And your husband and your friends have each done something to diminish your trust in them. That's why I'm here, right?"

He was right, but I hated to admit that.

"What do you think is going on?" I asked.

He thought for a moment. "It feels like there are competing forces at play. Andrew, Colin, and Jay seem to be on one page, but Allison's presence seems to have thrown something off-balance. She's getting into the middle of things. She's gotten Andrew to introduce her to the Carringtons, which might be to help her business or might be for another reason."

"What other reason could there be?"

"Are you sure you want to know? You won't like my theory, Lauren."

For a moment, I wasn't sure I wanted to know, but considering how much pain I was in, maybe I needed to know. "Just say it."

"I'm debating how much I should trust you."

"Me?" I asked in astonishment. "Look at me. I'm the victim here."

"Yes, but you're also in love, and if I tell you what I think, you might go running to Andrew. In fact, maybe you're playing me right now, Lauren, pretending to be confused so I'll give you inside information."

I sat up, ignoring the pain that swept through me at that movement. "That's crazy, Ethan."

"Not if this is a con, which I think it is."

"What is a con?" I asked.

"Everything. Your rescue. Your whirlwind love story. The wedding. The marketing scheme. I think it's all part of a plan to steal something or many things from Victor's gallery—a place, by the way, you were all able to access today because of everything I just said."

"Not only us. The media reps were there, too," I argued.

"But they weren't there to get an inside look at our security system."

"And you think Andrew was?"

"It was a great opportunity."

"If he's a thief, which I don't believe he is, our love story isn't a scheme. We met by accident. The elevator stalled. I had to get out on the ninth floor. That wasn't by design."

"Maybe it was. Or maybe it was all about opportunity. And the con started after the rescue."

"Andrew never tried to con me. We fell in love with each other. That had nothing to do with the Carringtons. The marketing plan, featuring a love story and a honeymoon couple, was a concept I came up with before I met Andrew. It's just that when our love affair took off, my boss thought Andrew and I should be in the campaign. That's how it happened. I didn't orchestrate anything, and Andrew certainly did not have the ability to do that."

"Andrew had nothing to do with you and him being selected as the faces of love at Carrington Resorts?" Ethan challenged.

I hesitated as an image of Megan having drinks with me and Andrew flashed through my head. "Well, Andrew did mention the idea to Megan at the St. Patrick's Day party that the company threw in March. He told her how he'd fallen in love with me at first sight and that our love was born out of fire, and she really liked the way he told the tale." I frowned. "But that was all by chance. It wasn't like he came up with the idea. He inspired it."

"I had a feeling he was in there somewhere," Ethan said.

"And look where you are now. Six months after you met, you're married, and you're representing the Carrington brand. You're having brunch with Victor and his family and being invited into Victor's private gallery. Despite my strong recommendations that Victor put some distance between his collection and you and Andrew, you were front and center earlier today."

"That's something you should ask Victor about."

"Oh, I have. I've challenged his continued belief in the two of you after relating my suspicions to him. He thinks I'm off base about both of you."

"Well, at least he believes in us."

"Which is odd, because you two were nobody to him when I first mentioned my suspicions. You were a mid-level employee, and Andrew was a guy at the conference who happened to rescue you. Why wouldn't Victor listen to me?"

I studied his face, seeing the gleam in his eyes. "It feels like you have another theory you're about to share."

"There's something about Victor's behavior in regard to the fire, to the allegedly destroyed paintings, and his reluctance to hear my concerns about Andrew and you, that leads me to wonder if he doesn't want me to find those paintings or the thief who stole them."

"Are you suggesting the fire was an inside job, done at Victor's request? Because that really sounds crazy. That fire could have taken down the whole hotel, and even though it did not do that, the repairs and remodel have cost a tremendous amount of money. I have to believe that's more money than those paintings were worth."

"True. But there's still something off, and I have to figure out what it is."

"I'm more interested in figuring out what's happening now to me and not what happened six months ago," I said with a sigh.

"It may all be tied together."

"I doubt it. You have a big imagination, Ethan. Maybe you should be writing crime novels."

He smiled. "I'm not much of a writer."

"How did you get into doing what you do?" I asked curiously. "Were you a police officer, FBI, an art fanatic? Or were you on the dark side yourself—a former thief or a conman?"

"Now who has a big imagination? My background is not that exciting."

"What is your background?"

"My mother was a sculptor, and my father was a museum curator for many years. However, his dream was to open his own gallery, and he finally did that." Ethan's gaze darkened, his voice turning rough as he added, "But two years after that opening, he was killed when he walked into the middle of a robbery."

"Oh, my God! I'm so sorry." I could see the pain in his eyes, even though he was telling the story in a very pragmatic way. "That must have been devastating for your family."

"I was nineteen when it happened, and in my second year of college. Before he was killed, my plan was to go into archaeology. I liked studying the past and digging things up, finding traces of lost civilizations, but after what happened, I decided to go into law enforcement. I had a dream of finding my father's killer and making him pay. I became a police officer, but I soon discovered I didn't have the resources, time, or opportunity to dig into that one case. After six years on the force, with no forward progress on my father's killer, an insurance company that had worked with my dad had an opening for an investigator, and I decided to take it. I had the investigative skills, and I'd grown up in the art world. That was seven years ago."

"Did you ever find your father's killer?"

He slowly nodded. "I didn't find him, but he was arrested after another robbery, and he confessed to killing my dad. The sad thing was that he had been hired by someone my father knew to rob the gallery that night. He wasn't supposed to kill my dad, but he panicked and pulled the trigger. The murder wasn't pre-planned, but the robbery was. And that plan was created by one of my father's friends, someone he had trusted enough to allow into his gallery, to see his security. It was a personal betrayal that led to his death."

"That's terrible. I hope both of those people are still in jail."

"They are. And it was good to finally have justice." He paused. "That case made me realize that I wasn't paying close enough attention to the people around the thefts my company was investigating. I was looking at the object as the purpose, but it was the motivation of the people that drove the crime."

"What do you mean? Isn't the motivation always money?"

"Not in the art world. Money is usually somewhere in the mix, but the motivation can be any number of things. There are thieves who just want the victory, the thrill of lifting something right out from under the most sophisticated security system. There are collectors who will pay anything to get something priceless, even if it was stolen. There are people who want something priceless just because they want it. They want to look at a piece of art and know it's theirs, even if no one else knows. And there are thieves who do it to prove they can."

"I don't know how you could have ever believed I'd be any of those people. I've always had to work. I didn't grow up rich. I don't even know what good art is. And looking around Victor's gallery today didn't feel that exciting to me. I'm sure everything was worth a fortune, but..." I shrugged. "I don't care about that kind of stuff."

"Andrew was enjoying the tour today."

"He did like being included, being part of that world," I admitted. "To be honest, I was a little surprised by the depth of his interest."

"Maybe you don't know him as well as you think you do."

"That seems to be a common accusation. But you know what else is interesting? Harper told me Colin has a book of art history on his bedside table. Andrew isn't the only one interested in art. Maybe Colin is your thief. He was at the hotel that night, too, right?"

"Yes, but he was nowhere near the fire. Video showed him

out on the street, one of the first to evacuate the hotel, and he had a drink in his hand. There was a cocktail party for the conference going on in the downstairs banquet room. But you make a good point, and it's possible Colin was still involved in some part of it. I have to admit I have also wondered why Andrew's friends are hanging around now that the wedding is over. It couldn't have been to spend time with Andrew, because they would have believed that Andrew would be tied up with you."

I shrugged. "They wanted some time off, I think. And now that Harper and Colin are hanging out together, Colin doesn't want to leave. She said something about him extending his stay."

"Well, she gives him a nice cover to do that," Ethan commented. "I think whatever is happening involves Andrew and his friends: Colin, Jay, and maybe Allison."

"And what is it that's happening?" I asked.

He gave me a long look, then said, "I think there's going to be a robbery attempt at Victor's villa. Or another arson event to cover a robbery. I am doing my best to make sure the villa and the collection are protected and secure. I wish I had more cooperation from Victor in that regard. I didn't want him to give you and the others a tour today, but he keeps telling me that he doesn't have a collection just for himself. It's for him to share with others."

"What about the empty case? You said you couldn't tell me what's going in it, but I heard something about an amazing and legendary diamond at brunch, and Victor was very cagey about whether he'd acquired it."

"I can't confirm or deny that."

"Well, it looked like you have a lot of security measures in place, so how much safer could it be?"

"I keep asking myself that question," he admitted. "The security is good, but I don't want to underestimate anyone, and, frankly, if you and Andrew weren't part of this weekend, I wouldn't be nearly as worried. I don't like coincidences. You and

Andrew were the closest people to that fire and now you're getting very close to Victor's private collection."

"Maybe that is a coincidence. Anyway, you should go. I don't know how long Andrew will be gone."

"You can always tell him I came by on my own." Ethan stood up. "I'm going to investigate what's been happening to you, Lauren, not just on the trail ride but also to your bridal suite. You might not like what I find out."

"I'll deal with whatever you have to say as long as it's the hard truth and not another theory," I said as I slowly got to my feet.

"The hard truth might bring you even more pain. I hope you're prepared for that."

A shiver ran down my spine. I wasn't sure I could handle any more pain, but I didn't say anything. I just watched him walk out the door. Then I sat down again and wondered if I'd made a terrible mistake. But the mistake might not be in telling Ethan but in trusting Andrew, because I was starting to see the coincidences, too, and they were somewhat alarming. I didn't want my life to be part of a con, but what if it was?

CHAPTER TWELVE

Monday morning, I woke up with pain shooting down my left leg from my hip to my toes. My lower back and butt were also achy, and it was hard to feel anything but weariness. This was definitely not how I'd envisioned my honeymoon. I had yet to put on my wedding lingerie. I had yet to have sex with my husband. I'd gone to bed before he'd come back from the bonfire, and while I'd sort of heard him moving around and felt him kiss my cheek, I hadn't found the energy to open my eyes. I hadn't wanted to talk to him. I was in too much pain, and I was also too confused about everything going on in my life.

But I would have to talk to him today. It wasn't fair to be talking to Ethan behind Andrew's back. I needed to find a way to trust my husband, and to rebuild that trust, we needed to have a longer discussion.

As I turned onto my back, I put out my hand, thinking Andrew was sleeping beside me, but my fingers landed on the mattress. I rolled over onto my bad side, surprised to see that the other side of the bed was empty, and the sheets were cool. I didn't know where Andrew had gone so early. Although, as I looked at the clock, I realized it was after nine. I was usually up and running by seven. But I wouldn't be running anywhere any time soon.

My phone buzzed on the nightstand, and I reached for it, seeing a call from Andrew.

"Hello?"

"Morning, beautiful," he said, his warm greeting reminding me that I really did love this man, and I needed to get things back on track.

"Where are you? I just woke up and realized you weren't here."

"I met Colin and Jay for breakfast. You were sleeping so soundly I didn't want to wake you. How are you feeling?"

"Like I got thrown from a horse."

"Still in pain?"

"Yes. Quite a bit, actually."

"I'm sorry to hear that. Are you taking the ibuprofen?"

"I haven't yet, but I will."

"You might need something stronger, Lauren."

"Hopefully the pain will ease with a hot shower. How was the bonfire last night?"

"It was good. But you didn't miss anything that exciting."

"Who was there?"

"There were probably about thirty people," he replied. "Megan had me take some photos with the guests, but she wasn't too pushy about it. She knew I wasn't the big draw on my own."

"I'm sure you were still popular. You're always the life of the party." I paused, knowing I probably shouldn't ask, but I couldn't seem to stop myself. "Was Allison there?"

"Yes," he said. "Along with Jay, Colin, and Harper. Jamie and Brad were there, too. She said to tell you she was thinking of you and hoped you were feeling better."

I'd gotten texts from both Harper and Jamie last night, but I hadn't had the energy to answer either of them. I needed to do that today.

"What are you doing now?" I asked.

"I thought I'd walk into town with the guys, if you don't mind. I figured you might want to rest before our lunch cruise this afternoon."

I sighed, once again reminded of my obligations. But a luxury cruise on a mega yacht really wasn't a hardship, so I needed to change my attitude.

"I can come back to the suite, if you don't want to be on your own," Andrew continued.

"No," I said quickly. "You're right. I'd rather rest up for later today. Is it just the guys, or is Allison going, too?"

"Oh, my God, Lauren. Why are you so stuck on her?" Andrew asked with irritation.

"I'm stuck on her because I keep finding out things about her you haven't told me."

"What are you talking about?"

"A trip to Paris six weeks ago. You said you were going to New York that week, but you went to Paris with Allison."

"I didn't go with her. She just happened to be there. And I wasn't alone; I was with Colin."

"Harper mentioned that Colin had been there. Apparently, he wasn't keeping that as a secret. Why were you?"

Silence followed my accusation, and it felt like Andrew was either trying to come up with a plausible explanation for not telling me about the trip, or he was trying not to yell at me. It really could be either. Finally, he said, "It was a last-minute trip. I was in New York, but Colin got us a meeting with a potential investor in Paris. It was too important to pass up, so we jumped on a plane. Allison was in Paris on her own business, completely unrelated to ours. But we did have dinner one night together—all three of us."

"I get why you didn't tell me before, but we talked almost every night. Why wouldn't you say, guess what, I had to make a quick trip to Paris? Or why wouldn't you tell me when you got back?"

"I felt bad going without you. We'd talked about making that our first trip together, and I thought you would be disappointed that I'd gone without you."

"Were you ever going to tell me?" I asked. "Or were you going to pretend you'd never been there with your friends?"

"I was going to tell you. It just didn't come up. When I got back, we were in crazy, hectic wedding planning and I didn't think about it."

He seemed sincere, but there were starting to be too many moments where he'd thought something wasn't important enough to tell me about, which made me wonder what else I didn't know.

"Who told you about Paris?" Andrew asked. "Harper?"

"No. She told me Colin was there. She didn't know if you were there, too. Although, she thought Allison was."

"Then who told you I was there? Or should I guess—Ethan Stark?"

"Yes, it was him. He stopped by last night to talk to me about the incident on the trail." That wasn't exactly how it happened, but I didn't feel like getting into the various conversations I'd had with Ethan.

"The incident?" Andrew queried. "Why do you say it like that?"

"Because it doesn't look like my horse was stung by a bee. It looks like someone threw a rock and spooked Sally."

"What are you talking about?"

"The video Tyler posted online. You can see something hitting the horse. It was deliberate, Andrew. Someone threw a rock on purpose. I don't know whether it was to scare me or to hurt me, but I don't think it was a bee."

"Why didn't you tell me this?"

"I saw the video after you left last night."

"And you talked to Stark about it? What's he going to do?"

"Look into it, along with hotel security, I don't know. He's still suspicious of us, Andrew. He thinks it's odd how the two people who barely escaped the hotel fire are now in Victor's inner circle, invited into his private gallery to see his personal collection."

"That's because you work for the company and we're featured in the marketing campaign," Andrew said. "You need to start avoiding this guy. Every time you talk to him you get all worked up about nothing. I don't understand why he makes you doubt everyone else in your life, how he makes you doubt me. For God's sake, we just got married. Didn't your vows mean anything to you? Because they meant something to me. If someone was accusing you of something, I'd be the first one to defend you."

"I have defended you," I said, shocked by his fiery words. "And it's not just you he doubts; it's me, too." That wasn't completely true, but it felt better to say it that way. "I hate that he keeps revealing small details about you that I don't know. I don't want to doubt you. I love you. And I have defended you to Ethan, and then he reveals a detail about you that I didn't know, and it weakens my defense because it makes me look like I don't know you."

"You know me, Lauren. You know what's important. The rest is noise."

"Maybe you need to stop deciding what's important for me to know and be more open."

"Maybe so," he said tightly. "I have to go now. Everyone is waiting for me. I'll see you later."

He was gone before I could say goodbye. I set the phone back on the table. Then I shifted my position on the mattress, ending up on my back, looking at the ceiling, my thoughts a jumbled mess, my emotions all over the place, and the pain in my hip and leg didn't help. It almost felt worse today than it had yesterday. So bad it made me want to cry a little. But as my eyes blurred with tears, I knew I wasn't just crying because of my physical injuries but also because everything with Andrew felt suddenly wrong, and I didn't know what to do about it. I was starting to worry I had married a man I didn't really know. Or maybe I had let Ethan get too far into my head.

Well, there wasn't anything I could do from bed, so I forced myself to get up, taking it slow because every movement was painful. I finally managed to get into a warm shower and stayed there for a long time. Over the next hour, I managed to get dressed and do my hair and makeup, looking far more presentable than I actually felt.

Andrew texted me he'd be back around eleven thirty. Realizing, I still had a half hour to myself, I started to unpack Andrew's bags. It felt like a wifely thing to do. I wasn't spying. I was being helpful.

My mental pep talk didn't really matter as there was nothing more than clothes in Andrew's suitcases. I don't know what I had been expecting. He certainly wasn't hiding a painting in his carry-on. But as I went to hang up Andrew's bomber jacket, something fell out of his pocket, and I stared in surprise at the phone on the ground.

It wasn't the phone he normally used. It looked plain and cheap. I picked it up, my hand suddenly shaky as I stared at the partial text still visible on the screen. It was from someone named Al and read: *If you cut me out, you'll be...*

I tried to click on the rest of the message, but it asked me for a password, and I didn't know Andrew's password. I tried a few number combinations, like his birthday and mine, but neither worked. Why would it? If he had a second phone, he would make sure it was locked up. He wouldn't want someone to read his private messages.

I sat down on the bed so hard, pain shot up my leg again, but I barely felt it this time. I was numb. Al was probably Allison, and she was angry because she thought Andrew was cutting her out of something. *What? What would they be doing together?* And it sure felt like the end of her message *you'll be...*was the start of the phrase that had been written on the wall of the bridal suite:

You'll be sorry. I'd thought the message was for me, but maybe it was for Andrew.

Looking down at the phone again, I wished there was a way I could get into it, that I could read the rest of that message, that I could see what else was on the phone. Maybe I could ask Ethan. Perhaps he could get into it, but then I'd have to give it to him. And what would happen when Andrew went looking for it?

I got up from the bed, returned the phone to the pocket of his jacket, and hung it in the closet. Then I zipped the empty suitcases and shoved them inside before closing the door. My breath was still coming fast, my head spinning with questions I couldn't answer. Maybe he just had a second phone for work. But that sounded like another excuse, and if I asked him about it, no doubt he'd come up with a similar explanation, something that would make me feel stupid for even asking about it.

The door to the suite suddenly opened and closed, and I hastily moved into the bathroom and shut the door, turning on the sink, as I pulled myself together.

A knock came at the door, and Andrew's voice rang through the air. "Lauren? I'm back."

"I'll be right out." I let the water run for another thirty seconds, staring at myself in the mirror, feeling like I was looking at a stranger. *Was Andrew the person who'd suddenly changed or was it me?*

"Lauren, I need to get in there," Andrew said. "We have to leave in fifteen minutes."

His voice pulled me back to reality. I shut off the water and rubbed my cheeks to bring some color back into my face. Then I put on a smile and opened the door. "Sorry. I'm moving a little slower today."

"It's okay." His gaze scanned my face. "You look better. Do you feel better?"

"No. I'm still in a lot of pain."

"I had a feeling..." He pulled a bottle from his pocket. "I

took this when I hurt my back a few months ago, and it gave me a great deal of relief. I think you should take one or two."

"I'm not good with strong painkillers. They make me feel sick."

"One won't hurt you, and it could really help." He held out the bottle to me. "Hang on to this in case you change your mind."

"Okay. I'll think about it," I said, moving back into the bedroom. I grabbed a sweater to throw over my white denim jeans and tank top and then put the medication into my bag. For now, I wanted to keep a clear head, and if that meant living through some pain, so be it.

We left the room a few minutes later. Andrew had taken a very fast shower and then thrown on khakis and a polo shirt. He had arranged for a golf cart to meet us in front of the lobby so I didn't have to walk down to the harbor.

He grabbed my hand as we sat down in the cart and gave it a squeeze, followed by his broad smile. "This will be fun," he said.

"I hope so. Who all is going?"

He let out a little sigh. "Should I start with the one person you're most interested in?"

"I assume that's Allison."

"Yes. Victor invited her, not me. They met this morning to discuss her designs."

"Great," I murmured.

"Colin and Harper are also coming, so you'll have a friend there besides me."

"What about Jay?"

"Victor told me I could bring him along, but Jay wanted to kayak. He'd rather be paddling a kayak than sitting out on the water sipping cocktails with a bunch of rich people," he said dryly.

"Maybe he's starting to feel like the odd man out with Harper and Colin spending so much time together."

"I don't think he cares about that."

"Do you think Colin likes Harper?"

"Looks that way to me. But who knows? They seem to be having fun."

"Harper got her heart broken last year. I hope it doesn't happen again."

"She's known him for two days. I don't think her heart is involved," he said.

He was probably right, but I could still remember the joy in her voice when she'd told me she thought she could fall for Colin. Well, she was a grown woman, and she could make her own choices.

As the cart hit a bump, I winced.

"I'm sorry you're still in pain," Andrew said. "I really think you should take the pills I gave you."

"I'll be okay," I said, happy when we arrived at the harbor. It was getting more difficult to talk to Andrew the way I used to talk to him. I wondered if we could ever get back to the way we'd been. Probably not until we got off this damn island. For now, I was going to have to fake it, and I was getting shockingly good at that.

CHAPTER THIRTEEN

The yacht was nothing short of breathtaking. Sleek and gleaming, its hull shimmered in the midday sun, and the faint scent of saltwater mixed with the tang of freshly polished teakwood. At nearly a hundred and fifty feet long, it was a floating palace, complete with multiple decks, a sprawling sun lounge, and gleaming chrome railings. Staff in crisp white uniforms moved with quiet precision, offering champagne flutes and chilled towels to guests who had already arrived.

Andrew and I were the last to board. As we stepped onto the main deck, we were greeted by a hum of chatter and clinking glasses. I scanned the faces quickly, taking in Victor, Paula, Bennett, Colin, and Harper, who were gathered near the bow, along with a handful of others. Allison stood close to Bennett, laughing lightly at something he said, her posture loose, her confidence tangible. I couldn't help noticing how seamlessly she fit in, as if she'd been part of this circle for years.

Andrew offered Allison a polite nod when she greeted him, but it was perfunctory at best. There was an uneasiness between them. It was subtle enough I doubted anyone else noticed, but I felt it like a thorn beneath my skin.

"Lauren," Victor said warmly as he approached, his smile

wide and welcoming. "Good to see you up and about. Andrew told us you weren't feeling well last night. How are you?"

"I'm doing better. Thanks for asking."

"I can't believe Sally threw you. She's one of our gentlest horses."

"She was spooked by something," I replied.

"That was unfortunate," Victor said. "I'm glad you weren't seriously hurt."

He seemed genuinely upset by the idea of me being injured, which touched me. I knew I was being included in these activities because of the marketing campaign, but his words did make me feel like he saw me as an individual, not just a business associate.

"I'll be fine," I said. "How far out will we be going today?"

"We'll cruise for about an hour and then turn around and come back. It's a little choppy today, but hopefully not too many bumps."

"I'm excited to be out on the water," I said as the yacht moved out of the harbor. "Thank you for inviting us."

"Of course. Why don't you come and meet my friends?" he suggested, leading us over to a spacious sitting area on the top deck, offering an uninterrupted view of the sparkling ocean.

The seating arrangement was elegant but casual, with curved sofas upholstered in soft cream fabric and low glass-topped tables. A silver-haired man in his sixties lounged comfortably with an air of affluence, a tanned arm draped over the back of the couch. Beside him sat a woman at least twenty years his junior, dark-eyed and striking in a turquoise sundress that showed off her toned arms.

"This is David Grimes," Victor said, clapping the man on the shoulder. "And his lovely girlfriend, Kirstie."

"It's nice to meet you both," I said, sitting down beside Andrew on a small loveseat adjacent to their couch.

Victor and Paula took the armchairs across from us, completing the cozy but carefully staged tableau. Kirstie leaned forward slightly, her lips curving into a flirtatious smile that seemed more practiced than genuine.

"Victor and I have known each other for over forty years," David said, his voice deep and smooth. "He's like a brother to me."

"Longer than I've been alive," Kirstie chimed in with a laugh, resting her hand lightly on David's knee.

"Don't remind me how old I am," David replied, though his smile was indulgent.

"You're the one who outdoes me in the gym every day," Kirstie said, giving him an adoring look.

They made a striking pair—David with his tailored linen shirt unbuttoned just enough to reveal a hint of a tanned chest, and Kirstie with her sleek ponytail and gleaming skin.

"You arrived this morning?" Andrew asked.

David nodded. "We were supposed to get in last night, but our flight out of New York was delayed, so we stayed in LA overnight and caught the morning ferry. We've barely had time to see the resort, but from what I've seen so far, it's spectacular."

Victor's face lit with pride at the compliment. "It's paradise, David. One of the best resorts I've ever developed, and I plan on spending a lot of time here." He paused, his gaze drifting toward his wife. Something unsaid passed between them—perhaps tension over Victor's decision to spend more time on the island. Paula's tight-lipped smile seemed to suggest she wasn't entirely on board with her husband's plans, but she remained silent.

"While I'm interested in exploring the resort," David said, cutting through the sudden tension in the air. "I also can't wait to see the new pieces in your collection, Victor. You've been unusually secretive about what you've recently acquired."

Victor laughed and gave his friend a sly smile. "I wanted to tempt you into coming out here. You've been hard to pin down for a get-together."

"Kirstie and I have been traveling a lot," David said.

"Well, I'm happy you were able to make the time now."

"Can you give me a hint about what new treasures you've picked up?" David asked.

I was curious what Victor would say, but our conversation was interrupted by the arrival of Megan and her media team. I hadn't realized they were even on the yacht.

Andrew immediately went into groom mode, putting his arm around me as we posed for the camera. After several shots with the group, Victor encouraged Megan to take us around the yacht and get more photos and videos done before lunch was served.

For the next forty minutes, we took romantic photos all over the yacht, wrapped in each other's arms, kissing each other, and posing in odd ways to catch the light at just the right angle. With each passing minute, the pain in my hip spread to my leg and back, and when we were done, I was pretty much in agony.

Andrew glanced at me and frowned. "What's wrong? You look like you're going to cry."

I wanted to cry from the pain, but I couldn't do that. "I wish I could get off this boat and go lie down."

He wrapped his arms around me and gave me a hug. "You need to take the medication I gave you. Then we'll get some lunch. You'll sit. You'll rest. You'll take a breath. You can do this."

I drew in a deep breath and let it out. "I know I have to do it," I said.

"This is what we signed up for," he reminded me.

He walked me over to the table where I'd set down my bag. While I retrieved the medication, he got me a bottle of water. I took two pills and then said, "Okay, let's go to lunch."

The pain started to ease about halfway through lunch, to the point where I actually felt like I could converse and eat something without throwing up. I was sitting between Andrew and Harper, who had pretty much let me just be quiet. Harper was talking to Colin on her other side, and Andrew was engaged in conversation with the outgoing Kirstie. I was relieved that

Allison was seated at a second table on the other side of the deck with Megan, Bennett, and the media guests.

"More champagne?" a steward asked, interrupting my thoughts.

"I'm okay."

"Have another glass," Harper said, speaking to me for the first time in a while. But that was probably because Colin had gotten up and left the table. "It might help you relax."

At her words, the steward filled my glass, and I took a small sip. Then I said, "How are things going with you and Colin?"

"So good," she said happily. "We get along really well. He's smart and funny. I feel like he's always one step ahead of me, which is challenging. It makes me realize how my ex was really never at my level intellectually. I always had to explain things to him. But Colin gets me, and I like that he's sarcastic, too."

"I'm glad you're getting along."

"We are." Harper glanced around me to see if Andrew was listening, but he'd left the table, probably to go to the restroom. Kirstie was talking to her husband now.

Still, Harper lowered her voice as she said, "Allison and Andrew fought last night at the bonfire."

My gut tightened. "How do you know that?"

"I overheard part of it before she dragged him down to the beach."

"What did you hear?"

"He told her to leave the island, but she said she wouldn't go, and he can't make her. I asked Colin about their relationship, and he said she and Andrew hooked up last year, and she's still stuck on Andrew. Colin thinks she's trying to use Andrew to get closer to Victor, which seems to be working. She is on the yacht with us."

My gaze moved to the other table, where Bennett and Allison had their heads together, conversing about something. She had definitely gotten into the Carrington inner circle, even though Bennett had seemed leery of her yesterday when he'd asked me about her. Apparently, her charm and beauty had wiped away all his doubts.

"Lauren?" Harper asked, bringing my gaze back to hers. "You're not worried about her and Andrew, are you?"

"Not worried, exactly. But I wish she didn't keep turning up everywhere we go. He said it was over between them before he even met me."

"It is weird that he invited her if they had hooked up. Who invites their ex to their wedding?"

"He said she pushed to come because she wanted an introduction to Victor in a more casual setting. He was helping her out." I paused as Andrew slipped back into the seat next to me.

He gave me a curious look. "What did I miss?"

"Girl talk," I said vaguely.

He smiled. "Okay, keep your secrets. The captain has invited anyone who is interested to come up to the bridge for a tour. Do you want to go?"

"No. I don't want to walk anywhere else."

"I want to go," Harper said eagerly. "Colin probably does, too, but I don't see him."

"He's already on his way up there. He told me to get you and meet him up top."

"Are you okay here by yourself?" Harper asked as she stood up.

"More than okay," I said, happy when they both left. The pain was finally starting to let go and my muscles were beginning to relax, so relaxed that I definitely did not feel like trying to walk anywhere. Despite the woozy feeling overtaking me, I was happy to get some relief from what had been unremitting pain.

I sipped on my champagne and spooned up the cooling, tasty sorbet that had been placed for me, and I was startled when Allison suddenly slid into the chair next to me.

"Lauren, we finally have a chance to talk," she said. "I heard about your accident yesterday. That sounds terrifying."

"It was scary, but I'm okay."

"You don't look that good. Are you in pain?"

"It's getting better." Clearing my throat, I decided that I might as well try to get to know her better since she refused to go away. "I'm glad we're getting a chance to talk. I was wondering how long you and Andrew have known each other."

"Several years," she replied, giving me a thoughtful look. "He hasn't told you anything about me, has he?"

"He said you've worked together on occasion."

She took a sip from the champagne glass in her hand, then gave me a smug smile. "Andrew and I have been more than work associates, more than friends. I think you probably suspected that. And I'm guessing he didn't tell you he invited me to the wedding, did he? I could sense you were surprised to see me, maybe even a little unhappy."

I wasn't going to admit to that. "Andrew told me you're trying to work for Victor, that your invitation was to get you an introduction to the Carringtons."

"That was part of it," she said. "And it looks like Victor is going to hire me. Well, actually, Bennett is. We had a great conversation this morning. Do you know Bennett well?"

"Not well at all."

"He's an interesting man. Smarter than I thought he would be. And very ambitious. I've always liked that in a man. It's what I like about Andrew, too. He has big goals, and he knows how to get what he wants. He is also patient...not reckless, but very deliberate. Every move he makes is calculated."

Goose bumps ran down my arms. I needed to shut her up because she was bringing my worries back, and my head was starting to feel too thick to think clearly. "Look, I don't know what was between you two, Allison, but Andrew and I are married. We love each other, so if you have a problem with either of us, maybe you should leave the island or at the very least, stay away from us. I won't let you come between me and my husband."

"Oh, honey, I am not the problem you should be worrying about," she said with a condescending and secretive smile.

Allison acted like she knew something I didn't, and I had a feeling she probably did, which made me feel even worse and a little sick to my stomach.

"I need to use the restroom. Do you know where it is?" I asked.

She hesitated, then said, "It's downstairs." She tipped her head to the nearby stairwell. "You should go now. You look very pale. I hope I haven't upset you. I actually feel a little bad for you. You have no idea what's going on."

Her words swirled around in my head. "Excuse me," I said, putting a hand to my mouth as another wave of nausea hit me. I hurried to the stairs, descending to the next level. A hallway greeted me, and an open door at the end of it. I stumbled down the corridor until I entered the empty stateroom and moved as quickly as I could to the bathroom. I immediately threw up, feeling even worse after that.

I washed my hands and splashed cold water on my face, but it did little to clear the fog clouding my brain. The icy sting of the water prickled my skin, but it felt distant, muted, like everything else around me. It wasn't just the ache in my hip and leg that bothered me—it was also the dizziness, the heavy, lethargic pull that gripped my body and wouldn't let go. My limbs felt like dead weight, and each breath was labored. I gripped the edge of the marble sink for balance, my fingers slick against its smooth, wet surface.

The thought of walking back up the stairs felt impossible. For a fleeting moment, I was tempted to collapse onto the perfectly made bed in the stateroom. But no. If I lie down now, I might not get back up. I couldn't pass out on Victor's yacht, surrounded by media people, cameras, and everyone who'd been watching my every move since the wedding.

I forced myself to move, stepping back into the narrow hallway. The sway of the boat made everything worse, my equilibrium spinning with every slight tilt of the floor beneath my feet. I dragged my palm along the wall, using it like a lifeline as I stumbled forward.

Then I heard voices.

Male voices, muffled, coming from behind a closed door a few steps away.

I froze, steadying myself against the wall. Maybe they could help me upstairs—or at least back to Andrew. But something in the hushed tones stopped me from knocking.

"Your greed is making you reckless," one man said.

"I know what I'm doing," another man replied, his tone firm, dismissive. "The reward is more than worth the risk."

I frowned, my pulse skipping. The voices were familiar, but in my muddled state, I couldn't place them.

"What about the investigator?" the first man asked.

"I'll take care of him."

My stomach dropped. *Take care of him?* Were they talking about Ethan?

I pressed closer to the wall, tilting my head toward the door.

"I hope you know what you're doing," the first voice said again. "This could all go very wrong."

"Or very right," the other man countered. "Thank you for your help."

"I owed you one."

"More than one."

"Well, you always know where to collect."

"I do. We should go."

I realized with a jolt they were about to come out. Panic surged through me. *If they caught me standing there, eavesdropping, what would they do?* My heart thundered as I stumbled away from the door, my hand catching the corner of the wall to steady myself.

I saw a side door to the lower deck and pushed it open, stepping into the sharp, salty wind. The ocean breeze whipped my hair across my face, stinging my skin like needles. The fresh air hit my lungs like a slap, momentarily shaking me out of my fog.

Who had been in that stateroom, and what had they been talking about? My mind wrestled sluggishly with the fragments of conversation. And who had been speaking? One had sounded like Victor or maybe Bennett. Although, it could have been someone else entirely.

I moved unsteadily down the corridor, the deck beneath my feet slick with sea spray. Before I realized it, I was standing on a swim platform at the stern of the boat, the waves crashing a few feet below me. The sound of the ocean was deafening here, a rhythmic roar that drowned out the faint laughter and music from the upper deck. I was completely alone.

The world tilted again, the platform swaying violently beneath me. I stumbled toward the railing, my palms slamming against the cold, wet metal. My breath came in short, gasping bursts as I fought to steady myself. My vision blurred. The horizon tilted. *What on earth was wrong with me?*

I leaned heavily against the rail, the cold steel biting into my palms. The water churned below, dark and ominous, the foam-tipped waves pulling and tugging as if they wanted to drag me under.

I needed to go back upstairs, to find Andrew. He would help me. He would take care of me.

I turned—or tried to. My feet felt heavy, uncooperative. I staggered, disoriented, and suddenly realized I was standing at the very edge of the platform. One wrong step and I'd be in the water. My heart thudded in warning, a sharp pulse of clarity cutting through the haze.

And then I felt a presence behind me. A hand on my back. Relief flooded through me. *Andrew.*

I swayed slightly, leaning back into the touch. *He'd catch me. He always did.* But there was no warmth behind me. No strong arms pulling me to safety. The hand pressed harder against my back, shoving me forward with sudden, brutal force. My arms flailed as I lost my balance. I tried to grab the railing, but it was too far away. A strangled scream tore from my throat as I tumbled forward.

For one heart-stopping moment, there was nothing. Just the cold, salty air rushing past me. And then I hit the water, and the ocean swallowed me whole.

CHAPTER FOURTEEN

The icy water stopped my heart, and for a terrifying moment, it felt like it might never beat again. The darkness of the ocean wrapped around me, a relentless, suffocating force pulling me deeper and deeper. It was so damn cold. And so very dark.

It felt like a bad dream, a terrifying nightmare, but one I'd never had before. Usually, my nightmares were about driving down steep hills and not being able to brake. That was a favorite. Or another one where I was lost in a maze and unable to find my way out. But this one was different. I didn't know which way was up, and I was fast running out of breath.

Some desperate need to survive cut through the fog in my brain. Simple, horrifying facts brought me back to reality. *I was drowning. I needed to swim. I needed to get air.*

I found energy I didn't know I had and started kicking and clawing at the water. There was a dim light above me. That had to be the surface. It felt like an eternity before my head broke free, and I sucked in a gasping breath—only for a wave to crash over me, pulling me under again.

When I came back up, the saltwater burned my eyes and throat, and I coughed and gagged, struggling to stay afloat. My arms and legs were already aching from my previous injuries as well as the cold and the effort of treading water. But I had to keep going.

As a wave bounced me higher on the sea, I finally had a chance to look around. To my horror, I saw the yacht at least a hundred yards away from me, if not more. Reality hit me hard. I was in the middle of the freaking ocean alone, and no one knew I was there.

Panic threatened to overwhelm me, so I started swimming but quickly realized there was no way I could catch the boat. Then I started screaming, trying to wave my hands. But I didn't think anyone could see me.

The truth hit me hard. *I was going to die!*

I could tread water but for how long? The waves were crushing. It was so cold, and I was already exhausted. I took a rest for a second, trying to float on my back so I had a minute to regroup, to get my strength back. As I looked up at the blue sky and felt the almost blinding sun on my face, I felt like I was hallucinating, because there was my mom's face right in front of me, her beautiful dark hair so much like mine. Some said we had the same smile, but I'd always thought hers was bigger, better. She was smiling at me now.

"I'm coming to see you," I said. "I didn't think it would be this soon."

"It can't be this soon," she told me. "You have more to do, Lauren, more life to live. You have to keep fighting."

"It won't matter. The boat is gone. They must not know I went overboard." I paused, thinking about that. *Did someone push me? Did I fall?* I remembered being dizzy and off-balance, but I couldn't remember now exactly what had happened. It was all a dark blur. I closed my eyes, thinking maybe this was fine. I could just go to sleep and be with my mom again.

"Lauren, open your eyes," my mother said. "Don't give up. I did not raise you to be a quitter. Remember what I always told you?"

I opened my eyes and saw her face again. "You said other

people give up, other people leave, but not us, we never stop. We never quit. That's why you fought to the end."

"I wanted so badly to stay with you," she said.

"I miss you so much."

"I'm with you now, Lauren. I'm going to get you through this."

"How? I can't swim to shore. I can't even see the shore."

"They'll come back for you."

"It might be too late by then. I'm so cold and tired. It's been an awful few days. I don't think I married the right person. In fact, I'm not sure I even know who he is."

"Then you'll find out when you get back on the boat. You can do this. You *have* to fight."

"We could be together now, Mom. That wouldn't be so bad, would it?"

"It would be the worst thing in the world, because I love you so much, and I want you to have a life. You have so much more to live for. I want you to have children and grandchildren. I want you to experience all life has to offer. As for Andrew, you'll figure that out. But you have to give yourself a chance to do that. Come on, Lauren, swim."

I was getting numb from the cold, and as another wave dunked me under for a second, I didn't think I had it in me to keep trying, but when I resurfaced, my mom's face was still there. She was yelling at me now, her voice getting louder and louder. She kept calling my name.

And then I realized it wasn't just her voice—it was lots of voices, echoing across the sea.

The yacht had turned around. It was coming back in my direction. I saw people on the top deck, more on the swim platform. They were yelling my name over and over again.

It wasn't over yet!

I came off my back, kicking hard with my legs as I tried to lift my arms in the air. I screamed as hard as I could, even though it felt like the wind was throwing my voice back at me.

But thankfully, the yacht kept coming closer and closer. The people were getting bigger, the voices louder. And then I heard a shout. I saw a deckhand on the swim platform. He grabbed some sort of ring and jumped into the water, followed by another guy.

I tried to swim toward them, but I couldn't get far. I was so tired, so weighted down.

Another man jumped off the platform and into the water. It wasn't a deckhand. I thought it might be Andrew.

It felt like forever, but it was probably only minutes before the first swimmer reached me. He put the ring over my head and pulled my arms up over the sides of it so I was held aloft, and it felt like a miracle to have something holding me up.

The second deckhand reached us next, helping the other pull me toward the boat. We'd gone only a few feet when Andrew appeared in front of me, treading water. He looked absolutely terrified, his face grim, his eyes wide.

"Oh, my God, Lauren," he said. "I can't believe this happened."

I started crying as soon as he said my name.

The two deckhands pulled me toward the boat while Andrew swam next to us. When we reached the yacht, there were more crew members to pull me aboard. A blur of people crowded around as I lay on the swim platform for a moment, exhausted and in pain but, thankfully, alive.

And then I was placed on some sort of stretcher and the crew was taking me down the hall and into one of the staterooms. Andrew and Harper followed the medical crew into the room and got me out of my wet clothes and into bed. Some kind of special blanket was placed over me, which immediately helped me feel warmer, but my teeth were still chattering, and I couldn't stop shaking.

There seemed to be concern about hypothermia, and my temperature was taken on my forehead and in my ear several times by someone who told me he was a medical officer. He also checked my heart rate and oxygen levels every few minutes.

Andrew and Harper tried to talk to me, but I could barely generate a weak smile in return. I was so cold. Gradually, I began to feel warmer, and my tremors eased along with my chattering teeth.

The medical officer gave me a smile and said, "You're doing good. Your temp is coming up. How do you feel?"

"I-I don't know," I said, happy I could at least get some words out. "Better, I think."

"That's what we want," he said.

"You're going to be okay, Lauren," Andrew said, drawing my gaze to his.

"You're wet," I said, seeing beads of water on his face, and his wet shirt was clinging to his chest. "You should change."

"I'm fine. I'll change when I know you're going to be all right."

"You can do that now," the medical officer told Andrew. He turned to a deckhand standing just inside the door. "Can you get him some clothes?"

"Already done," the deckhand said. "Sir, if you want to come with me..."

Andrew hesitated. "I'm not sure I should leave yet."

"I'm doing okay," I told him, my voice stronger this time. "I'm not shivering so badly. You should change."

Before he could move, Victor stepped into the room, his blue eyes dark with concern. "How is she doing?" he asked the medical officer.

"Much better. Her temperature is out of the danger zone, but she should get checked out at the medical center in Avalon."

"Does she need to be flown to an LA hospital? I've got a helicopter on standby."

My eyes widened at Victor's question. "I don't want to be flown anywhere," I said. "I'll be fine when I warm up."

Victor ignored me, focused on the medical officer's response, not mine.

"We'll be back at the harbor in fifteen minutes," the man

said. "If she maintains this level of heat and oxygen, she should recover quickly."

"All right." Victor let out a heavy breath. "What happened, Lauren? How did you end up in the water?"

I licked my salty lips, not sure how to answer that question, and I was suddenly very aware of everyone in the room: Andrew, Harper, Victor, the medical officer, the deckhand by the door, and now Bennett was squeezing into the room, too. I could hear chatter in the hall. There were probably more guests and staff hovering outside the door. They all seemed concerned and worried about me, but was all that worry about my welfare or about what I might say?

"Lauren?" Harper pressed. "How did you fall in?"

I didn't like her question. Everyone kept assuming I was the problem. I'd fallen off the horse. Now I'd fallen off the yacht. *Did they really think I was that clumsy?* Anger rose within me as I realized how close I'd come to dying, and it wasn't my fault. Someone had pushed me off the platform. They'd taken advantage of my unstable, woozy condition and given me a shove.

And that was after Allison had told me to go downstairs to use the restroom, after I heard two men talking about something in one of the staterooms, and maybe one of those men had seen me stumble away. *Had I heard something I wasn't supposed to?* At this moment, I wasn't sure of anything, because it was all a blur.

But they were waiting for an answer, and as the seconds ticked by, I knew I had to say something. *But what if whoever had pushed me into the ocean was standing in this room?*

God! I didn't want to believe that.

But how could I trust anyone?

"This is concerning," Victor said. "Her level of confusion. Maybe we need to get her to Los Angeles. Andrew, what do you think?"

"Wait," I said, finally finding my voice. "I took some pain medication earlier for my hip, and it made me a little woozy. I felt disoriented when I went looking for the restroom, and at some point, I ended up on the swim platform. I'm not sure exactly how I got into the water, but my head is clearing, and I'm sure it will come back to me. I need a little time."

I wasn't going to make an accusation in this group. That would only add more drama and maybe put my life at even greater risk. It was better to blame everything on the medication at this point.

"I never should have given you that medication," Andrew said. "You were in so much pain."

"I probably shouldn't have drunk champagne at the same time," I added.

The tension in the room eased at my words, as I'd given them a plausible explanation and taken all the blame onto myself.

"We'll let you rest then," Victor said. "I'm so sorry this happened to you, Lauren. I feel completely responsible for even allowing that area of the yacht to be open and untended. I had no idea it was possible for anyone to get that close to the water while we were cruising. I am going to ensure that whoever is responsible is punished and never works on my boat again."

His rage felt thoughtful but also irrelevant. I didn't plan on ever getting on this boat again, so I didn't really care about his plans for future security. I actually just wanted to close my eyes against the lights and the questioning gazes, take some deep breaths, and try to get my bearings.

"That's enough. Lauren needs some space," Harper said, taking charge. "She can answer all your questions later, but right now, everyone who doesn't need to be here should go. Andrew, why don't you get out of those wet clothes so you can come back and sit with Lauren? In the meantime, I will stay with her, and everyone else can go back to doing whatever they were doing."

At her sharp words, the room cleared, leaving only Harper, me, and the medical officer. I turned to him. "How am I really?"

He gave me a reassuring smile and said, "You're going to be fine."

I let out a breath. "Okay, good. I needed to hear that."

"I'll be back in a few minutes to check on you."

As he left the room, I looked at Harper. "Thanks for going bitchy Harper on everyone."

She smiled. "No problem." She sat down on the side of the bed. "I'm not going to ask you any questions, because clearly you are not up to answering, but I wanted to let you know that everyone was really concerned about you when I realized you were missing."

"You realized that first?"

"Yes, I came down from the bridge to look for you, and you weren't at the table. I went downstairs and didn't see you, but I saw Allison, and she said she'd actually been looking for you, too, because you'd seemed like you were feeling ill and had gone down there to look for the restroom. I started searching for you, and then I saw one of your shoes on the swim platform. I knew something terrible had happened. I started screaming, and they finally got the boat turned around. It felt like it took forever."

"It felt like that to me, too." I paused as Andrew came back into the room dressed in a gray sweatshirt and sweatpants.

Harper got up from the bed. "I'll leave you two alone."

As she left, Andrew stretched out on the bed next to me, putting his arm across my body as he gave me a slow, warming kiss. I wanted to savor his kiss, his embrace. I wanted to feel safe with him. But my brain was flashing on odd moments of memory, and I didn't know if they were real.

Had I heard Andrew talking to someone downstairs? Or had that been someone else?

I'd felt someone behind me on the swim platform. I'd thought it was him. But then I'd felt a push in the middle of my back.

I pulled back at that thought.

He gave me a surprised look. "Lauren?"

"Sorry. I was just remembering when I went into the water."

"I thought you didn't remember."

"It's hazy in my head. I'm not sure."

"You don't have to remember right now. Don't think about it."

Did he not want me to remember because he'd been there? That was crazy. That would mean he'd pushed me in the water, and he wouldn't have done that. If he'd wanted me to die, he wouldn't have jumped into the sea to rescue me.

Although he had jumped in after the two other guys. Maybe he'd thought it would look bad if he didn't try to save me. At that point, the deckhands had a better chance of bringing me back safely to the yacht. *It had probably made for a good photo, though*, I thought cynically. No doubt Megan and her team had been shooting my entire rescue. Not that Victor would want any of this to get out. It would be another secret to keep. There were getting to be so many of those, I didn't know how I could keep up with all of them.

Andrew propped his head up on one elbow as he gazed down at me. "You really gave me a scare, Lauren. I thought I was going to lose you."

"I thought I was going to die, too. The yacht was so far away, and I was alone in the middle of the ocean. But when I looked up at the sky, I saw my mom. She kept talking to me. She kept telling me to fight."

"I'm glad her spirit was with you."

"Me, too. I don't know if I could have held on without her there encouraging me."

"I never should have left you alone at the table. I had no idea you were feeling that bad. You should have said something before I went up to the bridge."

"I wasn't feeling that bad then. It got worse and worse. I felt like I was going to throw up, so I went downstairs to find a restroom."

"Why didn't you use the one off the main salon? Why go downstairs?"

"Allison told me the nearest restroom was downstairs."

His gaze darkened. "Allison told you to go downstairs? Why were you talking to her?"

"Because she came and sat next to me after you left the table."

He frowned. "What did she say to you?"

"I don't know. I still feel disoriented, Andrew." I did remember some of my conversation with Allison, but I didn't want to get into it until I had more time to think about what she'd said. And I was also so damned tired. "Can we talk about it later?"

"Of course."

"I need to close my eyes for a minute." As I shut out his handsome face, I wanted to believe that Andrew was the man I'd fallen in love with, the best man I'd ever met. I didn't want to think about all the doubts, the lies of omission, the extra phone, Ethan's warning words, or Allison's calculating smile.

But as I tried to rest, I kept hearing voices in my head, and there was a smell. *Perfume. Had Allison been downstairs, too?* Or had she been behind me on the swim platform? "Oh, my God," I murmured as my eyes flew open.

"What?" he asked. "Did you remember something, Lauren?"

I looked into his blue eyes, wanting to tell him everything, but then I remembered his secret phone, the message from someone named Al, the way Allison had implied there was so much about Andrew I didn't know.

I licked my lips. I had to answer his question. I had to tell him something. "There was someone behind me on the swim platform, and I think I smelled perfume, maybe the same kind of perfume that Allison wears. Then I felt a hard shove." I shuddered with the memory of flying off the platform and into the freezing water. "I didn't fall in the water, Andrew. Someone pushed me. And I think I know who it was."

He met my gaze and shook his head. "Allison wouldn't do that."

"Maybe you don't know her as well as you think you do."

"She wouldn't try to hurt you, Lauren. She wouldn't do that to you or to me." He paused. "Are you sure you didn't fall? You said you were woozy and out of it. How do you even know if you actually smelled anything?"

He wasn't completely wrong. I had felt disoriented and confused.

"Is it possible you stumbled and fell in?" he asked. "That seems a more likely scenario than someone pushing you into the sea during an elegant lunch cruise."

The way he said it made my doubts seem far less believable, and I could see he wanted to believe that the medication had made me fall into the water. I kind of wanted to believe that, too. Because the idea of someone deliberately trying to hurt me was terrifying.

But when I closed my eyes, I could feel the push from behind, and I knew with a terrible certainty that there was no way I had just fallen into the ocean.

CHAPTER FIFTEEN

When we arrived back on the island, the resort's private car was waiting to take Andrew and me directly to the island medical center, which was a modest, one-story building nestled near the edge of town. Andrew helped me inside because I was still a bit unstable on my feet.

Inside, the waiting room was bright but clinical, with chairs arranged neatly along pale- yellow walls adorned with posters about sun safety and hydration. The facility was clearly designed for minor emergencies and routine care.

There was no one waiting, so after checking in with the receptionist, a nurse took me into a nearby exam room. The doctor arrived a few moments later—a woman in her forties with kind eyes and a reassuring smile, who introduced herself as Dr. Gordon. She gave me a thorough checkup as well as IV fluids to combat any dehydration, warm blankets to raise my body temperature, and then told me I'd be monitored for the next two hours to ensure I didn't develop secondary symptoms like hypothermia-related shock or fluid in my lungs.

At my look of concern, she quickly assured me it was unlikely any more problems would occur, but she wanted to be careful.

After she left, Andrew sat down in a chair next to the bed

and took my hand in his. "Well, this is not the honeymoon I thought we'd have," he said lightly. "But we'll have quite a story to tell our kids and grandkids one day."

I wasn't sure how to react to his words. He was acting like I'd had an unfortunate accident, when I'd told him I thought someone had pushed me into the water.

"Victor spoke to me when you were getting in the car," he continued, his gaze turning more serious. "He's going to send Martin Demora over here to talk to you about what happened. Victor doesn't want to get the local deputies involved unless you're sure there's something that needs to be investigated. I told him your mind was very fuzzy about what happened, the result of the medication you'd taken, and it was unlikely you could give a detailed statement right now."

Was that because he didn't want me to give a detailed statement? Didn't want me to share my suspicions with anyone else, because I'd be pointing the finger at Allison, his good friend, or whatever the hell she was to him?

"Megan suggested we go with the medication explanation," Andrew added.

"Sounds like everyone is focused on spin control," I said, a little disappointed by everything I'd just heard. It made sense that Victor and Megan would immediately think about that, but Andrew's willingness to go along so easily with the story bothered me. But then, everything about him was starting to bother me. I didn't feel like I could trust a word he was saying.

"I know you think you were pushed, but it seems so unlikely, Lauren. Who would do that?"

"I told you who."

He shook his head. "I don't believe that."

"I know you don't," I said heavily.

A frown crossed his lips. "I'm not picking her over you."

"It feels that way."

"Your story just doesn't make sense. It was Harper and

Allison who first noticed you were gone. They raised the alarm. They were running all over the boat, looking for you."

"Well, that's what I would do if I'd pushed someone into the ocean and didn't want anyone to think it was me."

"You said yourself you were out of it. You could barely walk. You couldn't focus. You were disoriented."

"And someone took advantage of that."

"Or you're confused about what happened. Look, if you want to talk to the police, if you want to tell everyone what you told me, I'm not going to stop you. And I'll stand by you, but I'm trying to protect you, and right now, I'm not sure you have the mental capacity to protect yourself. I don't want you to regret something later when your mind clears. You love your job and this company, and accusing someone of trying to kill you on Victor's yacht without any proof whatsoever could be risky." He paused, letting his words sink in. "But if that's what you want to do, then I'll back you up. I'm on your side. You don't seem to believe that, but it's true."

It was hard not to believe Andrew when he was speaking with such force and a clarity that I had to admit I did not have at this moment.

I let out a sigh. "You're right. I'm not thinking clearly right now, so I don't want to make any official statements."

"I really think that's for the best."

He'd no sooner finished speaking when the door opened, and Martin Demora walked in, the resort's head of security.

"How are you doing, Mrs. Chadwick?" Martin asked, his sharp gaze running across my face and down my blanket-covered body.

"Much better," I replied.

"Mr. Carrington told me what happened and asked me to check in with you. He's very concerned about what happened on the yacht and wants to make sure everything is being handled appropriately. Is there anything you want to share with me about how you ended up in the water? I understand you took some pain medication prior to your fall?"

"Yes. I was thrown by a horse yesterday, and I was experiencing a lot of pain in my hip and leg."

"I've been made aware of that incident. Tell me more about today."

"There was a photo shoot on the yacht, and I had to do a lot of walking and posing. I was in a great deal of pain. I wasn't sure I could get through lunch. Andrew offered me a stronger painkiller, and I took it."

"What kind of painkiller?"

"It was hydrocodone," Andrew answered for me. "I had a prescription for a back injury I had several months ago, and there were a few pills left. Lauren was in a great deal of discomfort. I didn't know the medication would affect her so strongly."

"You do know it's illegal to share prescribed medication with someone else," Martin said.

"I didn't think it would lead to this," Andrew said sharply.

"Do you have the medication?" Martin asked me.

His question gave me pause. "It was in my bag, but I don't know where my bag is. It might be on the yacht. I don't believe I had it with me when I went downstairs or into the water. It was probably at the table where I was sitting for lunch."

"We'll track it down," Martin said. "Hydrocodone can cause dizziness, nausea, and disorientation, especially for someone who doesn't have a tolerance for it. If you mixed it with alcohol, that would amplify the effects."

"I did have some champagne," I admitted.

"Is there anything else you want to say?" Martin asked.

Having just been reminded of what was at stake for me and the company I worked for, I shook my head. "No. I want to rest and forget about what happened. Thank you for coming."

"If you change your mind or think of something else, please feel free to come to me. Mr. Carrington is very concerned about what happened to you, and I can assure you that anything you have to say will be welcomed and taken seriously."

"I appreciate that."

Martin nodded and left, closing the door behind him. Andrew turned back to me. "I'm sorry I gave you the medication, Lauren. That was a mistake. I could have lost you today. You could have died out there."

"Please don't remind me."

"I would have never been able to forgive myself, Lauren." He shook his head, regret in his serious and apologetic gaze. "It would have been my fault. I'm the one who's supposed to protect you. I'm your husband. I let you down. I wish I could go back in time and do it all over again."

His words were like a balm to my bruised spirit. He was looking at me with love and speaking with so much guilt that it was hard not to believe he was being honest, that he did love me. That he would never want anything to happen to me. That he wouldn't choose some ex-girlfriend over me. On the other hand, he had pushed me to take the medication. And he had asked me to keep quiet about my suspicions.

The turmoil of my thoughts made my head spin again.

"I need to rest," I told him. "I don't blame you. I just want to feel better. And then we can talk more, okay? I'm going to be here for two hours. Why don't you go back to the suite? Or better yet, go find my bag. My phone and wallet were inside. I'd like to get that back."

"Are you sure? I hate to leave you alone."

"I'm going to try to sleep. I'm very comfortable now. I'm feeling warm and tired, and I think a nap will do me good."

"Okay. I'll go find your bag and let everyone know you're doing better."

"I am doing better," I assured him, because I really wanted him to go so I could think without him trying to shape my thoughts. "I'll be fine."

Andrew gave me a tender kiss and then left. I blew out a

breath of relief with his departure, knowing there was something wrong with feeling that way about him. But, at the moment, his presence was more disturbing than anything else.

I was about to close my eyes when a knock came at the door, followed by a familiar voice, which for some reason I found more comforting than the one belonging to my husband.

"Come in," I said.

Ethan Stark walked into the room, and the concern in his sharp green gaze made my gut clench, because his worry for me actually felt real, which was another disturbing thought. *How could this man's emotions feel more honest than my husband's?*

"I can't believe you ended up in the ocean," he said, moving closer to the bed. "You must have been terrified."

"I thought I was going to die. And I might have if it had taken them longer to find me." A lump grew in my throat, and moisture filled my eyes.

He put his hand over mine, the warmth of his touch steadying my emotions. "What can I do to help, Lauren?"

"There's nothing you can do."

"Isn't there?"

As his challenging gaze met mine, I knew that he was thinking the same thing I was thinking. "You don't believe it was an accident, do you?" I asked.

"Do you?"

I slowly shook my head. "No, but I'm not sure. I took some pain medication for my hip, and it made me confused and disoriented. I was stumbling around on the lower level of the yacht, and I ended up on the swim platform. It didn't seem like anyone was around, but I felt someone come up behind me, and I think they pushed me into the water."

"Did you tell anyone else that?"

"Andrew. He didn't want to believe me. Especially because I said I smelled perfume—Allison's perfume. He told me there was no way Allison would do that."

Ethan gazed back at me, and I finally saw belief and acceptance of my story. Maybe that was because he didn't like Andrew or his friends. But at least he was listening.

"Is there anything else you remember?" he asked.

"No." I paused. "Wait. I did overhear a conversation in one of the staterooms, but I couldn't tell who was talking or exactly what was said. I think the voices were male. I'm pretty sure one of them said something about the risk being too great, and the other one dismissed that concern. It's a blur in my mind. I didn't want to get caught eavesdropping, so I moved down the hall to a side door that led to the lower deck. I thought the air might clear my head. A few minutes later, I was in the water, and I didn't know what had happened." I took a breath. "The cold ocean did shock my brain back into focus, though. It woke me up enough to swim to the surface, to try to survive."

"Why didn't you tell Martin this? I asked him what happened, and he said you insisted it was an accident, the result of a reaction to medication."

"Because no one wants this to be anything but an accident. The grand opening is in two days. Victor doesn't want negative press about this. He doesn't want people to think that a guest on his yacht might have been thrown overboard."

"Who cares about negative press?"

"The Carringtons do, and I do, too. I've worked hard on this campaign, and I don't want the resort's opening to be ruined, especially since I don't know what happened. Maybe I did imagine the shove at my back."

"You're backtracking pretty quickly, Lauren. Is it the resort you're trying to protect or your husband and his friends?"

I gave him a troubled look, reminded that sometimes he was more of an enemy than a friend. "I can't make an accusation without proof. It's not going to be good for anyone."

"Probably not," he said, surprising me with his agreement. "At this point, if someone did push you in, it's best they think you don't know that. Ignorance could be your protective shield. I'm just sorry you told Andrew."

I was a little sorry I had, too, but I wasn't going to admit that.

"I'm going to look into what happened, Lauren, but I will be careful in how I do that."

"Okay." I paused, suddenly remembering something. "One of the men in the stateroom...he said something about you."

A question flared in his eyes. "What?"

"I think he said, what are you going to do about the investigator? And the other person said not to worry, he had it under control. What could they have been talking about?"

"Probably something to do with the security of Victor's collection." He paused. "Are you sure the voices you heard didn't belong to Andrew and Colin?"

"They were muffled, and all this happened when I was feeling my worst. I was trying not to throw up again and to stay on my feet."

He frowned again. "I heard Andrew gave you his prescription medication."

"He thought I needed something stronger. I didn't want to take it, but the pain got so bad, I didn't think I could get through the day without some relief."

"Going forward, you need to be very aware of anything your husband is giving you."

"He didn't push me in the water."

Ethan gave me a hard look. "Are you absolutely one-hundred-percent certain of that?"

"He jumped into the sea to rescue me," I murmured.

"And I'm sure that daring gesture was captured on video, but you didn't answer my question."

"I don't want to answer it," I said.

"You just did."

"My husband is not trying to kill me." The words came out of my mouth with a rush of emotion, and before I could stop them, the tears quickly followed. Suddenly, my entire body was racked with sobs.

Ethan sat down beside me and put his arms around me, pulling me into a hug, as a waterfall of tears streamed down my face. Ethan held me until I was spent. Then he handed me the box of tissues on the nightstand, and I blew my nose a dozen times, probably looking even worse than I had before.

"I'm sorry," I said as I dried my eyes. "I didn't expect that."

"You were due. You've been through a lot the last couple of days."

"I have been. And the worst thing is, I don't know what's coming next."

"Maybe you should get off this island, Lauren."

"I can't." I gave him a helpless look. "I'm committed to the campaign, the grand opening. I'm not just the bride; I'm also an employee. I don't want to lose my job."

"After what happened today, I don't think Victor would make you stay. And surely they have enough photos of the two of you to sell the resort."

"Probably, but Victor has done so much for me. I don't want to let him down. I have to pull myself together and get through the next few days. I can do that, right?"

His lips tightened. "I don't know. I don't like what's going on, and I don't trust your husband or his friends."

"I don't trust him, either," I admitted. "I want to, but things keep happening to me. And then there's the phone—"

"The phone?" he interrupted.

I realized I'd never told him about that. "I found a second phone in his jacket pocket. There was a text on the screen from someone named Al. I couldn't read anything but the first several words: *If you cut me out, you'll be...* I couldn't get into the phone, so I couldn't read the rest of it. I think it was probably from Allison, and I'm beginning to think the first warning on the wall of the bridal suite was for him, not for me."

"Maybe so," he murmured thoughtfully. "Could be the crew isn't all on the same page." Clearing his throat, he added, "You need to get away from both of them, Lauren. Because you might be caught in the middle of their war."

"I can stay away from Allison, but not Andrew. We have dozens of photos to shoot every single day and people to meet and greet. We have to act like a happy couple. It's in my contract."

"Your life could be in danger. That's more important than a contract. But if you're determined to stay, you need to be very careful. Pay close attention to everyone around you and try not to be alone or in any other precarious type of situation."

"Trust me, I'm going to stay on solid ground and in a crowd whenever I'm not in the suite."

"But you'll be alone with Andrew then."

"I don't think he's the one who's been trying to hurt me. I think it's Allison. Maybe to get back at him, I don't know, but that's the way it looks to me."

"She does appear to be the best suspect," Ethan admitted. "I'll see what else I can find out about her."

"You should go now. Andrew will be back soon."

"Okay." He got up from the bed and gave me a long look. "Take care of yourself and call me if you feel even the least bit uncomfortable. It doesn't matter if Andrew is there or not. If you call, I'll come."

I felt immensely reassured by his words. "Thank you."

"You're more than welcome. Keep your head up, Lauren."

"I will."

By the time Andrew took me back to the suite, it was almost five o'clock. He'd brought my bag, and I'd seen a bunch of texts from Harper, Jamie, Megan, and several from other coworkers, which I would respond to later. I wanted to take a hot bath and get rid of the dried ocean salt on my skin.

Andrew ran the tub for me while I rested on the bed. He put

in a generous dash of bubble bath and then he helped me get into the bath, sitting on the side of the tub as I sank into the warm and sweet-smelling soapy water. I was afraid the water might remind me of being in the ocean, that feeling of drowning, but there was such a difference between this moment and those moments that I couldn't make the comparison, and I was grateful for that.

"You don't have to watch me," I told him, feeling oddly uncomfortable with a man I'd practically lived with for the past several months.

"I don't want you to pass out in the tub, so I think I'll stay right here."

"That won't happen. My brain feels clear again."

"I'm glad to hear it, and once again, I'm sorry I pushed you to take a pill. I didn't think it was a big deal."

"I don't blame you. It was my choice."

"Have you remembered anything else that you want to share with me?"

"No." I didn't want to get into another tense discussion when I had no new facts to relate.

"Are you sure? You can talk to me. I hope you know that."

"As long as I don't talk about Allison."

He frowned as anger flared in his gaze. "She's not the horrible person you think she is."

"She told me she knows you better than I do. How was I supposed to take that? It certainly wasn't a compliment. And I can't help thinking she's right, because I certainly didn't know about her or Paris."

He let out a sigh. "She doesn't know me better on a personal level, just on a business level. She and I have never had the connection that you and I have. Our attraction was instant. Don't you remember how quickly and how hard we fell for each other? We stayed up talking all night after our first date. It was the best first date I'd ever had."

"I thought so, too," I admitted. But now, looking back, I

could see that what I'd thought were deep conversations hadn't been deep at all. We'd talked about books and movies and places we wanted to travel to. We'd shared little about our actual lives. We'd just lived in a happy bubble where we were having fun, having sex, and falling in love. But who had I fallen in love with? The little discrepancies, the omissions, the second phone, the trip to Paris...it was all adding up in a way that made me nervous.

And Andrew was making me nervous. Even now, he was staring at me and getting bothered by the fact that I still didn't trust Allison, which meant I didn't completely trust him. It had been a long day, and I didn't want to get into an argument.

"I want to get back to you and me," Andrew continued. "I hope you want the same thing."

"I do want things to be the way they were before," I said with complete honesty. Because those days had been good, much better than the last few I'd lived through.

His tension eased at my response. He put his hand on my shoulder and leaned in for a kiss. Then he said, "I'm glad you feel that way, Lauren. When I saw you in the water, so far away from me, I felt a distance I'd never felt before. I didn't like it. I want us to be together always."

"Then maybe you should tell Allison to go home. Or maybe you could ask Victor to terminate his deal with her," I suggested.

"That would raise questions, and I don't think Victor would appreciate me telling him what to do with his business."

"So, she stays," I said, feeling deflated by his response.

"Look, I'll talk to Allison about leaving. And if she doesn't want to leave, I will tell her that she needs to stay away from you and me for the duration of our time here. We're only here until next Sunday, unless you want to leave earlier?"

"We can't leave before Thursday at the earliest. The grand opening on Wednesday has events running all day and into the evening."

"Exactly. But it's Monday night and Thursday will be here

before we know it. Then we can go home or anywhere else you want. We can have a real honeymoon."

"That would be nice. Let's talk about it later. I'm hungry. Do you think you could order room service?"

"Of course. What do you want?"

"Anything sounds good. Chicken or fish."

"I'll order a bunch of stuff. Victor is picking up the tab, and I'm sure he'd want you to have anything your heart desires."

"As long as I tell the right story," I said cynically.

"You've always told me your job is important to you. But whatever you want to do, I'll support you."

I wasn't sure that was true, but Andrew knew I was going to go along with the spin, because that's what I had to do. "I'll be a good team player," I said.

"I'm sure that will be appreciated. I'll go order us some food."

As he left, I couldn't help thinking that while I loved my job, I didn't want to die for it. And I really hoped I was making the right decision by staying silent.

CHAPTER SIXTEEN

After my bath, I changed into my comfy PJs and made my way into the living room. Andrew was sitting at the dining room table, his computer in front of him. When he saw me, he immediately gave me a smile. "There you are. I was wondering if you'd fallen asleep in there."

"I wasn't going to take that chance after almost drowning earlier. What are you doing?"

"Answering work emails. I do have an actual job besides all of this," he said, an edge to his voice.

"I know that."

He gave me an apologetic look and ran a hand through his hair. "Sorry. It's been a day. Not as bad for me as for you, so I shouldn't complain."

"We can complain together."

"It's about all we've been doing together."

"I know," I admitted, meeting his gaze. "Not the romantic, sexy honeymoon either of us was envisioning."

"I don't care about that; I care about you. I'm not protecting you the way I should be."

"You had no idea I'd be in danger on that yacht, and neither did I. It wasn't your fault."

"I hope you truly believe that. Lately, you look at me with a question in your eyes. Is there something you want to know that you're afraid to ask?"

That was a loaded question. There were dozens of things I wanted to know, like why he had a second phone, but when a knock came at the door, followed by, "Room Service," I knew this wasn't the right time.

"I'll get that," he said.

As Andrew got up to answer the door, I took a look at his computer screen, which was not opened to his emails but to something that looked like blueprints. It probably was work, I thought, until I realized I was looking at the floor plan of what appeared to be Victor's villa. His name wasn't on it, but I recognized the large patio and outdoor living space I'd seen off the living room during my earlier visit.

My heart jumped into my chest, and I quickly moved away to the other side of the table, not wanting to be caught spying. The waiter came into the suite, pushing a cart. As he set up dinner on our table, Andrew closed his computer and moved it out of the way.

I took a seat at the table, trying not to let my face reveal any of my thoughts. I wasn't sure exactly what I'd seen, and I shouldn't jump to conclusions. Andrew was a real-estate developer. Maybe those plans were for another oceanfront villa at a hotel resort.

Shaking my head at that ridiculous explanation, I settled into my seat, still feeling pain in my hip, but it was surprisingly better than it had been. Maybe some good had come from the pain medication and my icy-cold plunge into the Pacific Ocean. That might have brought some of the swelling down.

My stomach rumbled as the waiter revealed some very delicious-looking dishes from steak frites to a grilled branzino and a roasted chicken. There were also plenty of sides, from mashed potatoes to Brussels sprouts and spicy green beans. It all smelled heavenly, reminding me of how long it had been since we'd eaten.

And I'd thrown up most of my lunch. But I wasn't nauseous anymore. In fact, I was starving, and the waiter had barely left before I picked up a serving fork, split the tender fish in half, and put it on my plate.

"This looks great," I said as Andrew sat across from me.

"I'm glad you're feeling hungry."

"I am." I dug in with an enthusiasm I hadn't felt in a while. Maybe it was because I was realizing how lucky I was to be alive. This day could have ended in my death. It could have been Andrew sitting alone at this table. Or he might not have been alone at all. Allison might have been with him.

I frowned at the abrupt turn of my thoughts.

"Is the fish okay?" Andrew asked.

"What?"

"You look like you just tasted something bad."

"No, it's wonderful. My mind keeps going back to being in the ocean and feeling like I wasn't going to make it, and I was so close to not making it."

"But you did. You're alive. You're relatively well. Getting better every day, I hope. Try not to think about it."

"I'm trying," I said as we ate the rest of our meal in relative silence. We'd never been so quiet with each other as we'd been the last three days. For six months, we'd shared so many lively, energetic, talkative meals, filled with laughter and stories, and love and kisses. But there was a distance between us now. I didn't know how to shorten it. And there was a part of me that didn't know if I should try to bridge the gap between us.

But we couldn't live in this awkward silence, so as I finished my meal, I decided to see if I could find out more about his business, about what he might have been looking at on his computer. "What are you working on? I thought you were taking time off for our honeymoon."

"Well, since that has been a bust, I decided to catch up on some emails."

"About..."

"A property I'm looking at in Florida," he replied. "There's an old beachfront hotel in the Keys going up for sale at a good price. With an extensive remodel, it has the potential to be a beautiful resort."

Maybe the blueprints *had* been for some other oceanfront resort. I relaxed a little at that thought. "That sounds interesting. Have you put in an offer?"

"Not yet. I need a partner, so I've been working on some potential investors." He paused. "I actually brought it up to Bennett when we were on the yacht earlier. He's interested in bringing in some acquisitions of his own to prove to Victor he is worthy to be the heir apparent. This property could be a good addition to the Carrington portfolio."

Yet another secret project he hadn't told me about, and it involved my company, which made it worse. "This wedding weekend is working out good for your business," I couldn't help saying.

He set down his fork, giving me a hard look. "I saw an opportunity to discuss the idea with Bennett. Why does that bother you? It's not like I haven't fulfilled every other obligation that has come my way. And, frankly, I've done it with more joy and enthusiasm than you have."

He had a point, but I was a little startled by his attack. "I wasn't criticizing; I was making a comment."

"A pointed comment."

"You're right," I admitted. "I'm just feeling like I'm the last person you talk to about anything. I work for Carrington Resorts. Why wouldn't you mention this to me?"

"It recently came up, and you work in marketing, Lauren. You make ads and posts for social media. You have nothing to do with real estate acquisitions."

Now I was irritated. "I do more than make ads and posts. I work with Megan on far bigger strategies to market our brands around the world. Do you even know what I do?"

"Apparently, you haven't been that forthcoming, either," he

said, turning it around on me. "I didn't think you were interested in my business, Lauren. You rarely ask about it."

"Well, I'm interested when it has to do with the Carringtons."

"Noted. I'll keep that in mind."

I let out a sigh, knowing we kept tiptoeing around the edge of a big fight, and if I hadn't almost died today, we probably would have already had that fight. Andrew's phone buzzed, and he picked it up to read a text.

"Who's that from?" I asked.

"Jay. Bennett wants to meet us for a drink. He wants to talk about the Florida property. I'll tell him I can't go. He can do it on his own."

"You can go if you want to, Andrew."

"I don't think I should leave you alone."

Actually, I thought being alone would feel better than being on edge with him. "I'll be fine. I'm going to get into bed and watch a movie and probably fall asleep in less than an hour. I'm exhausted. Every muscle in my body is aching, and the day is catching up to me."

"Which is why I should stay with you."

"No. I understand that your business is important to you, and you have gone above and beyond with this campaign. I'm sorry if I haven't expressed my gratitude enough. You have carried me through a lot of shoots."

The tension eased between us. "I've been happy to do it, Lauren. We got a great wedding out of it, and, yes, I have made a connection with Victor and Bennett that may prove valuable in the end, but that was just an unexpected benefit."

"Go meet Bennett and Jay. I'll be fine."

He gave me a speculative look. "All right. If you change your mind, call me, and I'll come back."

"Is Colin going with you?"

"No. He's taking Harper out to dinner in Avalon." He smiled. "They are definitely having a good time together."

"I'm glad."

"By the way," he said. "Two things. One, Megan texted me about our spa day tomorrow and asked if you are still going to do it. I told her I would check in with you, but I couldn't guarantee anything. She wants to shoot us taking advantage of all the spa has to offer...couples massage, facials, manicures, and pedicures. It actually sounds relaxing. But you can think about it."

I really didn't want to do anything but lie in my bed. But if I had to do something for Megan, the spa was probably the easiest thing to do. "I saw I had a text from her, so I'll respond and let her know that we'll do it. What's the other thing?"

"Victor called to check on you. I said you were feeling much better, and he was happy to hear that. He's very upset about you falling off his yacht."

I frowned at his description, but I was tired of arguing over semantics. "Well, it was thoughtful of him to check in."

"He also invited us to his villa tomorrow night for a private dinner he's hosting for his friends and associates who are on the island for the grand opening. He said it would be a photo-free event and that he just wanted us to come and meet everyone and have a good time. But only if you're up for it, of course. He said to tell you there was no pressure on you to attend. But he and Paula would love to see us there."

"Another party, huh?"

Andrew shrugged. "Yes, another party."

"It would probably be an excellent opportunity for you to network," I said.

"And you," he returned. "I can't imagine it will hurt your chances of moving ahead in the company. Victor feels like he owes you."

"I don't want him to give me anything I haven't earned."

"I think you've earned a lot more than he's given you," Andrew said pointedly.

"Well, that's true. You're right. We should go to the party."

A smile spread across his face. "I think that's a good decision.

I also think that tomorrow will be a better day," he added as he got to his feet.

"It couldn't be worse than today," I said, hoping that was true.

Andrew left ten minutes later, taking his computer with him. After he was gone, I went into the bedroom and checked the pocket of his jacket for the second phone, but it was gone, too.

Frowning, I got into bed and turned on the television, but nothing interested me. I rolled onto my back and stared at the ceiling, trying to make sense of what I knew.

Andrew was getting close to Victor and to Bennett. That could be helpful to him personally and professionally. Through this whole event and marketing campaign, Andrew had gotten into a high-level circle that might have taken him years to infiltrate otherwise. But that wasn't a crime. I'd put him in a position to make those contacts. I couldn't criticize him for doing that.

But was it just about business contacts? Ethan thought Andrew was a thief, and the fact that he had been studying blueprints for a property that looked a lot like Victor's villa made me nervous. There was plenty of treasure inside Victor's gallery to steal. But there was also a high-level security system designed to protect those treasures, and Ethan was surely doing everything he could to make the system foolproof. Even if Andrew had blueprints for the villa, how could that really help him get inside? And why would he even need blueprints? He'd already been in the gallery. He'd had an opportunity to check out everything in that room, including the security system.

If Andrew was a thief, and he was planning to steal something from Victor, why wouldn't he have done it already? Why wait?

Maybe it was because not all the cases were full...

Was Andrew waiting for something in particular to arrive,

something spectacular and legendary like the Heart of Eternity diamond that had been talked about at brunch? But surely anything that special would be impossible to get to, especially when Ethan was so focused on protecting that gallery. If Andrew was a thief, he would know the odds were stacked high against him.

The paintings that had been in Victor's office at the Newport Beach Hotel had been hanging on a wall in a locked room. There hadn't been this level of security at that location, so that had been a much easier theft. Who would attempt to rob Victor now when he'd basically put everything into a secure fortress?

I remembered what Ethan had told me about thieves, about motivations. Some people just wanted to prove they could do it. I hated to say that sounded like Andrew. He'd told me once he liked long odds. He preferred the challenge of doing something no one thought he could do. That's why he was risking so much to build his own business. He didn't want to work for anyone else. He wanted to be his own boss and wield his own power.

Shaking my head, I couldn't believe I was thinking about my husband being a thief. It seemed unbelievable. But then, everything that had happened the last few days seemed unbelievable, too.

My phone buzzed and I saw a text from Ethan, asking how I was doing.

I was touched by his concern. Instead of texting back, I picked up the phone and called him. He answered almost immediately.

"Lauren, are you okay?"

"I'm fine. Am I interrupting you?"

"No. I'm just leaving Victor's villa to go back to my room. What's up?"

"I saw what looked like blueprints on Andrew's computer. I thought they might have been of Victor's villa, but I'm not entirely sure. Andrew also told me he has a piece of property in Florida that he wants to buy, and he's talking to Bennett about it being a potential acquisition for Carrington Resorts. They're meeting now for drinks to discuss it. It's possible those blueprints were for another ocean resort, but I thought I should tell you."

"I appreciate that. Andrew won't be able to bypass the security system we've set up, even if he has the blueprints of the villa."

"That's what I don't understand, Ethan. It seems like your security system is foolproof. Wouldn't that stop someone from trying to break in?"

"I hope it does, but it could also be a challenge someone can't resist."

I thought about that, then said something else that was on my mind. "Do you think there's any chance that Victor is...I don't know...playing two sides?"

"What do you mean?"

"I was wondering if he was one of the two people I heard talking on the yacht about handling you. Do you think Victor could be using you in some way?"

"Some of his actions have been questionable," Ethan admitted. "Like his refusal to see Andrew as a potential criminal. It made me wonder if Victor and Andrew could have been working together. If he'd hired Andrew to steal the paintings and cover up the theft with a fire."

"A fire that cost him a lot of money?" I questioned. "Why would he have done that?"

"I couldn't come up with a good answer to that question, so I let that theory go."

"What about Bennett? Maybe you're chasing the wrong person. Bennett seems at odds with his father about his position in the company. He told me he hates his dad's collection. I bet he would enjoy taking something away from Victor that meant a lot to him. Paula might feel that way, too. She doesn't seem happy with Victor's plans to live on the island."

"You've got a lot of ideas going on in your head tonight, Lauren."

"It's easier to think about paintings and thievery than to remember what happened to me today. Every time I let myself go back to that moment when I had to fight my way to the surface of the ocean only to realize that the yacht was moving away from me..." I shuddered as I blew out a breath. "It sends a wave of panic through my body. I know I'm not going to drown now. I'm not going to die in the ocean, but it still makes me sick."

"That's understandable, Lauren. I can't even imagine what you went through."

"I really thought it might be over for me. The water was cold, and I'm a strong swimmer, but I couldn't have floated on my back forever." I shivered at the memory.

"I wish I'd been on that trip, that I could have stopped you from having to experience that, Lauren."

"Well, what I need you to do now is help me figure out what's happening. I need to stop whoever is trying to hurt me. I'm pretty sure they've tried twice, and I don't want the third time to be the charm. I told Andrew to ask Allison to leave the island, but he doesn't think she'll go. And he refused to ask Victor to send her away. He said it wasn't his place to get into Victor's business, which I understand, but I really need her to be gone."

"I'll talk to her tomorrow, see if I can get a better sense of what she's up to."

I felt an immense relief at his words. "I would really like that. Thank you."

"It's the least I can do. What are you up to tomorrow?"

"We have to do a photo shoot at the spa. Nothing bad could happen there, right?"

"Maybe stay out of the sauna," he suggested. "I don't like the idea of you in a heated room with a door that could be locked."

"I hadn't thought about that."

"A massage, facial, getting your nails done, that's all good. Maybe leave the Jacuzzi and sauna for another time."

"I will. Good night, Ethan."

"Get some rest. I think you're going to need it."

After I ended the call, I put my phone on the nightstand, still too tired to go through all my text messages. I flipped through several channels, looking for a distraction, finally settling on an old sitcom with very loud canned laughter.

As I watched the show, I felt very much alone and very worried about my future. I'd fought so hard to survive my fall into the ocean. I thought I'd be safe when I got back on the boat, but I didn't feel safe. I felt like I was waiting for something else to happen, something bad, something I probably wouldn't expect, and I was terrified that my husband might be part of whatever was coming next. *How could I have gone so fast from love to fear? How could I be thinking that my own husband might be trying to hurt me?*

I blew out a tense breath, trying not to get too worked up. I had no proof Andrew was responsible for anything that had happened to me, and both times he had come to my rescue.

But my mind kept adding up all the odd things I'd learned about Andrew, all the small moments recently when I'd seen an anger, a hardness, I'd never seen before.

My phone buzzed, startling me with an incoming call from a number I didn't recognize.

"Hello?" I said tentatively.

"Stop trying to get rid of me," a woman said. "It won't end well for you, Lauren."

"Who is this?" I asked, even though I knew.

"You know who it is. You're like a cat, aren't you? You have nine lives."

"What do you want, Allison? Is it Andrew? Do you want him back? Is that what this is about?"

There was silence for a minute. "I want him to pay for what

he did, and he will. You might, too, Lauren, if you don't stay out of this."

"Stay out of what?" I asked, but there was no answer as the call abruptly ended.

My heart was racing as I set down the phone. Allison had sounded very angry. Andrew must have talked to her. He must have told her to go. But now she was even more pissed. More determined to stay and make Andrew pay for something. I'd never met someone so vengeful before, and it was terrifying because I was more convinced than ever that she was the one who had shoved me off the yacht.

CHAPTER SEVENTEEN

I woke up Tuesday morning with a headache and a sore hip. I hadn't slept well after Allison's disturbing phone call. I'd wanted to talk to Andrew about it, but it was almost midnight before he returned, and by then I thought it was better to just let it all be until the morning.

But that conversation would still have to wait because Andrew was gone, leaving a note on the table next to me saying he was going for a run with Colin, and he'd be back by ten thirty for our eleven o'clock spa appointment.

I was dreading another day of smiling and pretending everything was romantic and wonderful, when it was anything but. It would take all my acting skills to fake our newly wedded bliss. I was going to have to tap into how I used to feel about Andrew, before I started to doubt everything he said, everything he did.

After showering and throwing on a sleeveless dress that Megan had approved for this particular photo shoot, I went into the living room, wondering if Andrew might have left his computer open or some other clue lying about, but there was nothing.

A knock came at the door, and I was happy to see Ethan through the peephole. I needed to talk to him about Allison.

I opened the door. "Good morning."

"It's not good," he said grimly. "Is Andrew here?"

"No. He went for a run with Colin. What's wrong?"

Ethan stepped into the room and shut the door behind him. "When did Andrew leave?"

"I'm not sure. He was gone when I woke up around nine. He said he'd be back by ten thirty for our spa appointment at eleven."

"What happened last night after we talked?" Ethan asked. "What time did Andrew get back to your suite?"

"I think it was around midnight. But I didn't speak to him. Did you talk to Allison yet? Because she called me last night and basically threatened me."

"What time was that?"

"Around eight. She said I have nine lives, and if I don't stay out of her business, I'm going to get hurt. She's the one behind everything that is happening to me."

"Lauren—"

"All the signs point to her," I said, ignoring his interruption. "Everything from the message in the bridal suite, to my horse getting spooked, to her conversation with me on the boat. She's the only one with the motive to hurt me."

"Even if it was her, there's nothing we can do now," he said.

I didn't understand his grim tone. "Of course there's something we can do. We can talk to the police, get her arrested, questioned. We have to stop her from trying to hurt me again."

"She's not going to hurt you, Lauren."

"How can you promise that?"

"Because she's dead."

My jaw dropped in shock. "What?"

"Allison is dead. She was found on the ground in front of the model villas under construction on the hillside. It looked like she slipped through some temporary flooring on a balcony and was killed on impact."

I heard what he said, but it made little sense. "Are you sure?"

"I'm positive. I saw her body. There will be an investigation, of course. But there were no active cameras in the area, and apparently, no witnesses. A maintenance person found her a little after six this morning. It looked like she'd been dead for hours. She probably fell sometime last night."

I shook my head in disbelief. "If she's dead, she didn't fall. Someone killed her." I frowned. "But who would kill her? I was so sure she was the one trying to kill me. Now she's dead, and I'm alive? I'm...stunned."

"Well, based on what you said, the person most likely to have killed her would be Andrew. If he thought she was trying to hurt you, and she was refusing to leave, they could have gotten into an argument. Maybe he shoved her. Maybe she fell. Either way, she ended up dead. Now, she's no longer a threat to you or to him."

"She did tell me she would make Andrew pay, but she didn't say for what." I felt sick to my stomach. "I can't believe any of this is happening. I can't believe someone killed her."

"I didn't say someone; I said Andrew. It sounds like they had issues that went beyond you."

"Andrew has never shown even a hint of violence. He's not a guy who yells or gets into fights. He's calm and controlled, and he's always looking for the upside." I stopped, realizing I was defending him again, and maybe what I was saying wasn't even true. I had seen more anger in him the last few days than I'd ever seen before.

"People often have more than one side," Ethan said. "Andrew had opportunity. He was out last night until midnight. At any rate, the coroner will figure out time of death, and then we'll determine where everyone was at that time."

"What did the Carringtons say? Did you talk to Victor?"

"Yes. I spoke to all three of them. They're very shaken up, to say the least."

"This is horrible. I didn't like Allison, and I wanted her to leave, but I never thought she'd die."

"The local sheriff's office has asked for help from the Los

Angeles County Sheriff's Department. A detective will be arriving at some point to investigate. If he or she asks you questions about Allison, you should be careful what you say to him because the only other person who had a motive to kill her is probably you."

I stiffened at his words. "That's crazy."

"Think about it, Lauren. You're in marketing. You understand spin. Your husband's ex shows up at your wedding, is flirting with him, trashes your bridal suite, pushes you into the water, is ruining everything, and you just want her to leave. You want someone to get her off the island."

My stomach churned even more at his words. "So, I killed her, or I told Andrew to do it?"

"Like I said, you should be careful what you say."

"I understand. What is Victor going to do? Will he call off the grand opening? Will he cancel all the reservations? His VIPs are coming in today. Tomorrow is the ribbon cutting, the kickoff party, and numerous other events. But how can we open the resort when there's been a murder on the grounds?"

"First, it's not being called a murder, but an accident. It will be reported that a designer working on the villa had an unfortunate accident and fell in a construction area she wasn't supposed to be in. And that the rest of the resort is in great condition, blah, blah, blah."

His words made total sense. That's exactly how it would be spun. And I'd be a part of that spin. I'd be called on to distract everyone with my romantic wedding story. "They're going to need me and Andrew to put on an even bigger show now. Victor won't want you questioning Andrew. Pointing a finger at him will be too risky," I said.

"I'm sure you're right. The investigation will have to be done quietly, but it will be done." He paused as the door handle turned, and Andrew walked in.

He was wearing running pants and a T-shirt that showed sweaty patches on his chest and under his arms. His face was also red and sweaty. He'd definitely gone for a run, which was actually a little odd, because I was the runner, not him. He usually preferred to go to the gym and do the elliptical or lift weights, but today he'd gone for a long run with his friend, and even that seemed suspicious.

"What are you doing here, Mr. Stark?" he asked.

"I'm afraid I have some bad news," Ethan said. "Your friend, Allison McGuire, died last night."

Andrew sucked in a breath. I watched him closely, thinking if he were guilty, he'd certainly show it in some way, but all I saw was shock in his eyes and tension in the taut lines of his jaw. "I don't understand. Did you say Allison is dead?"

"Yes. She slipped off a balcony at one of the villas under construction. It appeared to happen sometime last night, but she wasn't found until this morning."

Andrew bit down on his bottom lip as he shook his head in confusion. "You're sure she's dead?"

"I'm afraid so. Do you know what she was doing there?"

"She was working on interior designs to show Victor," Andrew said. "She had permission to go into the model. Is that where she was?"

"She was found in front of that building, yes."

Andrew shook his head again, as if he couldn't believe what he was hearing. "How could she have slipped off the balcony?"

"The railings were not yet installed, and the flooring was temporary."

"Are you sure it was an accident?" Andrew asked.

"We don't know," Ethan replied without showing any emotion. "Do you have reason to believe it wasn't an accident?"

"She works on construction sites all the time. She knows how to be careful. It seems suspicious."

"Her death will definitely be investigated," Ethan said.

"What's going to happen now?" Andrew asked.

"The sheriff's office is trying to locate her family. Do you have any contact information you can share?"

"No. Alli didn't talk to her family. Her parents were divorced. As far as I know, she hadn't seen them in years."

It was weird hearing him call her *Alli*. He'd never shortened her name before, but maybe that's because he'd finally let down his guard.

"I—I need some air." Andrew walked through the living room and out the double doors leading to the deck.

"He's shocked and upset," I said to Ethan.

"He seems that way," Ethan agreed, but his tone was so pragmatic I didn't know if he thought Andrew's reaction was real or just really good acting.

"He wouldn't have told you he thought it was suspicious if he'd had something to do with her death." I paused as my phone buzzed with an incoming text. It was Megan reminding us we were meeting in thirty minutes.

"Andrew and I need to get ready for our spa date." I let out a sigh as I met Ethan's gaze. "It feels wrong to go on with these photo shoots like nothing happened."

"Until you're told otherwise, that's exactly what you should do." He lowered his voice. "Don't press Andrew, Lauren. Leave the questions to the police, to me, to everyone else but you."

I shivered at the look in his eyes, the warning in his voice. "You don't want me to try to get information?"

"No. I want you to stay safe. Did you tell Andrew about Allison's phone call to you last night?"

I shook my head. "I haven't had a chance."

"Keep that to yourself for now."

I looked at the man standing out on the deck, the man I'd married a few days ago. He had his hands on the railing, and he was looking out to the ocean. I couldn't see his face, but I could feel his tension, his distress. "I don't think he killed her, Ethan."

"Until we know who did, you can't trust anyone, not even your husband."

CHAPTER EIGHTEEN

After Ethan left, I joined Andrew on the deck. His face was tight, his eyes somewhat bleak. He didn't look like someone who'd killed his ex. He looked like a man who was grieving.

"Are you all right?" I asked quietly.

He drew in a deep breath before turning to look at me. "Not really. I know you didn't like Allison, that you were suspicious of her, but I can't believe she's dead. I don't understand how this could have happened."

"I know. It's terrible."

"Terrible?" he questioned. "I'm sure you don't feel that bad."

I was a little taken aback by his sharp tone. "I wanted her to leave the island; I didn't want her to die."

"Well, it looks like she won't be bothering either of us anymore," he said harshly. He turned back to look at the sea, his jaw set in stone.

"Do you want me to tell Megan to push things back at the spa or cancel?" I asked quietly.

He didn't answer right away. Then he said, "No. We can't do that. We made a commitment. We have to honor it."

"These are extreme circumstances. You lost a friend."

"We're doing it," he said. "I'll take a quick shower and then we'll go."

As he moved past me, I put my hand on his arm. "Andrew, I am sorry. I know she was your friend."

"She was," he said tightly. "But there's nothing I can do about what happened, and we're obligated to show up at the spa, so I'm going to change."

"What about Colin and Jay? Do you want to talk to them?"

"I'll do that in the other room."

After he left, I rested my arms on the rail and gazed out at the view. The sea looked so calm from here...gently rippling waves, diamond lights dancing down from the sun and skipping along the surface. But it had felt turbulent and dangerous when I was in that water, and it could have easily been my grave. If the yacht hadn't turned around, if Harper hadn't noticed I was gone, I'd be dead now, too.

I was so sure Allison had been the one who shoved me into the water. Now I had to question if I was wrong.

And if she hadn't accidentally fallen to her death, then someone had pushed her, too.

Maybe the same someone who had tried to get rid of me.

But Allison and I didn't go together. We barely knew each other, and what we knew, we didn't like. *What possible connection could there be?*

The question ran around in my head, landing on one rather unbelievable theory...

What if Allison had been killed because she'd tried to hurt me?

Had it been revenge?

Or had it been a punishment for her failure to get rid of me? Maybe someone else had paid her to get me out of the way, but I hadn't died, and she knew too much.

If any of that was true, then Andrew was the connector. Actually, even without those motivations, he was the link between Allison and me. She'd died, and I hadn't. But someone had gone after both of us.

It couldn't be Andrew, I told myself, desperate to believe that. There had been real fear in his eyes when he'd jumped into the ocean to save me and later when he was watching me fight to warm up under heated blankets with an IV in my arm. There was no way he'd pushed me into the ocean.

Andrew was upset about Allison's death, too. I could see the pain in his eyes and hear it in his voice. He might have been angry with her. They might have had an uncomfortable breakup. He might have even been annoyed with how she was treating me. But I couldn't believe he wanted her dead.

It had to be someone else, and I could think of a few people who also hadn't wanted Allison on the island. Colin and Allison had been arguing the night of my wedding. Paula Carrington hadn't liked Allison ingratiating her way into Victor's life. Even Bennett had mentioned his concern about that. But Allison had been on the yacht yesterday, and if the Carringtons didn't like her, they wouldn't have invited her to have lunch with them and go on a cruise.

Which left me with...no one.

I had to be missing something. Or maybe I just wanted to overlook the number one suspect because he was my husband.

We arrived at the spa a few minutes after eleven. When we stepped inside the building that was set at the back of the hotel with a sparkling waterfall fountain at its entrance, it felt like we were entering another world. The reception area had floor-to-ceiling windows that framed a view of the ocean and the cliffs. The air was cool and smelled of lavender and eucalyptus, which was instantly calming. Soft, natural light poured through skylights, illuminating the pale stone floors and walls textured with warm wood paneling. On the outside deck, plush lounge chairs draped with crisp white towels were arranged near an infinity pool that seemed to spill into the horizon.

I wished we were here just to relax, but we'd barely checked in when Megan and her team entered with lights and cameras that were completely destroying the soothing atmosphere.

Megan came up to me, her expression tense and worried. "Sorry I'm late. I just had a long conversation with Bennett and Victor about an incident that occurred last night." Megan's gaze drifted to Andrew. "Are you aware of what's happened?"

"We are," he said shortly. "And I don't think this is the place to discuss it."

"No," Megan agreed. "But I know you were close to the individual in question, and I wasn't sure you were up for this today. You or Lauren," she added, giving me a concerned look. "You went through a lot yesterday."

"I'm feeling better now, and Andrew and I are willing to continue with the plan for today."

Relief ran through Megan's gaze. She was trying to be polite and compassionate, but she also had a job to do. "If you're sure," she said. "That would be great. I was hoping we wouldn't have to reschedule."

"Let's do it," Andrew said.

"I'm going to send Tony with you, Andrew. He'll take some shots with you getting ready for your massage and the men's lounge area. Why don't you get started? And then you'll meet back up with Lauren for the couple's massage, which will be done on the garden patio."

"Fine." Andrew headed toward the men's locker room so fast that Tony had to jog to catch up to him.

"Is Andrew okay?" Megan asked me, pulling me to one side of the reception area, away from the women behind the counter and also from Elisa, who would shoot photos of me in the women's lounge.

"He's upset," I murmured. "But he doesn't want to let anyone down. Neither do I."

"I know I've been a little rough on you at times and probably too demanding—" Megan said.

"Probably?" I interrupted with a smile.

She tipped her head. "Okay, definitely. There's a lot riding on this campaign, with Victor and Bennett being so heavily involved. I never saw Bennett as competition before because he barely worked. I thought he just wanted to enjoy his father's money, but suddenly he has his nose in everything, and he's continually second-guessing me. I've been doing marketing for years. He's been doing it for like three months, and he thinks he knows more than I do. But I have to deal with him because he's the boss."

"I know he can be challenging, but he is building relationships with very popular influencers and going after a non-traditional customer market for Carrington Resorts. Maybe he brings a fresh perspective that his father could use."

"I don't think they're getting along at all. I met with them earlier, and they were definitely jabbing at each other. They were also very upset about the discovery of Andrew's friend and how that might affect the grand opening."

"That's understandable. What is the plan?"

"Well, Bennett wanted to ignore it completely, but Victor felt sure someone on the staff or in the sheriff's office would leak it, so it was better to get ahead of the news by stressing it was an accident. Victor wants to control the narrative."

"I agree with Victor."

"So do I, and I said that, which didn't go over well with Bennett. Anyway, besides that incident, there's trouble brewing between Victor and his son, and I hope it doesn't erupt before we get through the grand opening."

"They both know how important this launch is. I'm sure they'll keep the peace."

"I hope so." Megan paused. "I feel badly about what happened to you yesterday, Lauren. I can't imagine how you felt watching the yacht sail away from you. You must have been terrified."

"I'm not sure that word is strong enough. I've never felt so scared in my life. I didn't think anyone knew I was gone."

"Harper made them stop the boat when she realized you were missing."

Andrew had told me the same thing, but I was still surprised Harper had noticed my absence. She'd been so into Colin; I hadn't expected her to be the one to realize I was gone. A tiny voice inside me wondered if that was because she'd seen me go in the water, like maybe she'd pushed me in and then had second thoughts about letting me die.

I shook that thought out of my head, knowing my insecurity was making me distrustful of everyone.

"I'm very grateful to her," I said to Megan, trying not to show any ambivalence on my face. "And thank you for the nice text you sent last night."

"It was the least I could do. One last thing, Lauren. We did film your rescue. I don't believe it will ever be seen by anyone, because it's not something Victor wants to publicize, but I wanted you to be aware we have that footage."

"I don't want to see it," I said quickly. "I'm trying to forget the whole thing, and I'm hoping this spa day might do the trick."

"Then let's get started."

The spa shoot took forever. It was after four when Megan finally called it a wrap. We'd had massages, manicures, pedicures, and facials. We looked good, but I didn't feel good, and I didn't think Andrew did, either.

As we left the building, I let out a sigh, happy to be outside and on our own again. It would also be nice to have a break before the party tonight. Not that I wanted to go to another party, but I was quite certain that Andrew did. This was an excellent opportunity for him to build a professional network, and it wouldn't be bad for me, either. I didn't think as much as Andrew did about the importance of a network, but I also wasn't trying to build my own business. And he'd done everything he'd been asked to do for the marketing campaign; I needed to do the party for him.

I looked over at Andrew, who was reading something on his phone. "Should we go back to the suite?" I asked, feeling a little uncertain about what I wanted to do next. While I was tired of having my photo taken and pretending to be rapturously in love with my husband, I also wasn't looking forward to being alone with him and probably ending up in another awkward conversation, because his mood today was all over the place, and I didn't know which mood was real and which was an act.

"What?" he asked, giving me a distracted look.

"Do you want to go back to the suite? We have a couple of hours before the party at Victor's villa."

"No. I need to talk to Colin and Jay about some work issues."

I wondered if they would discuss work, or if Allison's death would be the subject of their conversation, but I wouldn't ask him that. If he needed to mourn her death with people who knew her, then I wouldn't stand in his way.

"I'll be back at the suite around five thirty."

"Okay. I'll see you then."

He left without giving me a kiss. Apparently, he was tired of pretending, too.

Where did that leave us?

I had the feeling our marriage wouldn't last longer than our honeymoon. Not unless something changed, but so far, the only changes had been bad.

Instead of heading back to the hotel, I walked down the path to the harbor. I needed to clear my head, to get away from my own thoughts. I was surprised by the new cluster of small and large boats that had appeared since yesterday. Apparently, Victor's high-rolling friends had arrived.

The path along the oceanfront was flat and easy, and there were plenty of tourists about, especially as I neared the town of

Avalon. Maybe I'd stop at a café and get a drink and a snack. It would be nice to sit outside and actually feel like I was on vacation for a few moments. When I arrived at the nearest waterfront café, I was surprised to see Harper sitting alone, staring at her coffee with a pensive expression.

I pulled out the chair across from her and sat down.

"Lauren," she said, clearly startled by my appearance. "What are you doing here? I thought you were shooting your honeymoon visit to the spa."

"All done. Do you not see my glowing facial-treated face and my perfect nails?" I asked, waving my manicure in front of her.

"Nice," she said. "You look a lot better than the last time I saw you."

"That might have been the worst I ever looked," I admitted.

"When they first pulled you onto the boat, your skin was so white, you looked like a ghost," Harper said. "It's good to see the pink back in your cheeks. How's the pain from your hip?"

"It's still there but a thousand times better than it was yesterday, and my plunge into the ocean has had no lasting physical effects, just psychological ones."

"I'll bet." Harper gave me a questioning look. "Did you really just fall in, Lauren?"

"What else do you think could have happened?" I asked, curious to hear what she would say.

"I don't know, but when I went downstairs, Allison was very close to the swim platform. She said she was looking for you because you weren't feeling well. I believed her. I didn't have any reason not to—until today."

"Today?"

"Colin told me Allison is dead, that she fell off some balcony at the villa she was looking to decorate. He said it was a terrible accident. And I couldn't help thinking how many *accidents* seem to be happening."

"Most of them to me."

"You could have died, just like Allison." Harper drew in a

shaky breath. "I don't like the feeling I'm getting, Lauren, like something bad is going on at our resort. Every accident has a plausible explanation, but there have been a lot of accidents in the last two days. And we have a ton of people arriving today and tomorrow. I have to say, I'm not sure the resort is all that safe."

"I don't think our guests are in any danger," I said. "But I agree that there's something going on, and I'm a little scared for myself. I have to tell you that yesterday I thought Allison might have pushed me into the water. She'd been angry since she'd arrived, and I thought she was jealous of me and Andrew and maybe wanted to get me out of the way. But now she's dead, and I have a hard time believing it was an accident. So where does that leave me?"

Harper met my gaze, looking more serious than I had ever seen her. She hesitated, swallowing hard.

"What?" I asked.

"I was thinking the same thing, that Allison might have pushed you in the water. Colin told me that Andrew didn't like her the way she liked him, and he didn't think she'd ever gotten over him, even though she pretended she had." Harper took a sip of her coffee, then set the mug down. "But as you said, now she's dead. Did Andrew kill her because she tried to hurt you?"

"I can't believe Andrew is capable of that."

"It seems impossible," she agreed. "Maybe her death was an accident."

"Has Colin said anything to you about any of it? Did you tell him you thought Allison might have pushed me in?"

"I mentioned my theory to him last night, and he shut me down fast. It was the first time he was sharp with me. The anger in his eyes disturbed me. It felt too intense. We were supposed to go out on a kayak today, and he blew that off, saying he had work to do with Andrew. I thought Andrew was supposed to be honeymooning, not working, but I guess there's some deal that's time sensitive."

"I don't know. To be honest, Andrew and I aren't getting

along that well. I've been feeling like shit, and I keep hearing little things about him that he's neglected to mention to me, and I wonder what else he isn't telling me."

"I tried to warn you that Andrew might have secrets."

"You did," I admitted. "I probably should have listened. But I'm hoping once we get through this week, we'll be able to sit down and talk about everything."

"I thought you were free tonight, but Colin said you and Andrew are going to a party tonight. What's that about? It's not on the official schedule."

"It's a private dinner at Victor's villa. I think he feels guilty about me falling off his yacht and almost dying, so he invited us to the party. It's not a photo shoot, which is a relief."

"That sounds very cool and important. Is Megan going?"

"I'm not sure who from the staff will be there."

"Except for you." Harper's gaze darkened. "You really are moving up the ladder fast, Lauren."

"It's not a promotion or a salary bump; it's a party. You really shouldn't be jealous of me, Harper. I've almost died twice in the last three days. If anything, I should be jealous of you."

"You're right. I need to stop comparing my life to others," Harper said, giving me an apologetic look. "Something I have to work on. And I need to stop jumping into what looks like perfect, because perfect never seems to be true. I don't have as good a feeling about Colin as I did before. He's gotten cagey, and I don't like it."

"At least you're not married to him. I'm starting to feel the same way about Andrew. But at the moment, we are tied together. I have to hope whatever he's being secretive about isn't that bad."

"What if it is?" Harper challenged. "What are you going to do?"

I met her gaze. "I'm going to try not to have another accident."

CHAPTER NINETEEN

After leaving Harper, I returned to my suite. Andrew still wasn't back, and as the minutes ticked past five, I couldn't help thinking we'd both given up all pretense of being on our honeymoon. We'd kissed a few times, but only when the cameras were on us. Other than that, we'd never touched each other, barely spoken, and Andrew had chosen to spend our free time with friends on a work project, or whatever it was they were doing together.

I really hoped it was work, because I still didn't want to believe Andrew was a thief, and I definitely didn't want to believe he was a murderer.

While I was waiting for Andrew, I read the company email that Victor's office had sent out. It was noticeable that no one had taken to any of our group chats to discuss what had happened. Wherever people were talking, it was definitely not online.

I wondered what was happening with the investigation into Allison's death. She'd been so beautiful, so vibrant and alive. She'd bothered me, for sure. And I still thought she might have pushed me into the ocean, but I felt bad that she was dead.

The door to the suite opened, and Andrew came into the room and gave me a quick nod. "I'm going to change."

"Okay. How's everything going with your work?"

"Fine. We can talk about it later."

"Sure." I'd put that on the list with everything else we were going to talk about later.

Twenty minutes later, we were out the door. I'd put on a short black cocktail dress with high heels, which didn't make my hip feel any better, but this party was dressy, and I needed to play my part. Andrew wore a dark gray suit, looking as handsome as ever, but he was subdued, making no effort to take my hand or talk to me. He probably had Allison on his mind and figured I didn't want to hear about her. But the silence between us grew longer and wider with every passing day.

As we walked down the path, Victor's villa glowed against the darkening sky, strings of lights draped across the terraces creating a magical effect. When we got to the house, we were greeted by a server holding a tray of champagne. I felt uneasy about drinking more champagne after what had happened yesterday, but I took a glass just to have something in my hand.

We moved through the entry and living room and out onto the massive deck that had been transformed into an elegant outdoor living room with white sofas and oversized chairs arranged in intimate groupings. Flowers were everywhere, their scent mixing with the salty ocean breeze. Waiters moved smoothly through the crowd with elaborate canapés.

There were probably twenty or so people in the space, most of them Victor's wealthy friends who had arrived on the various yachts I'd seen in the harbor earlier. The jewelry on the women and the watches on the men probably cost more than I made in a year. I felt more than a little out of place. This was not my world. But Andrew didn't seem to feel the same. In fact, he'd perked up since we'd entered the party, exhibiting far more energy and interest than I'd seen all day.

"Hello, Lauren," Bennett said, appearing in front of us,

looking slightly drunk, a whiskey glass in his hand. "Ready to mingle with the rich and famous before your coach turns into a pumpkin?"

"I do feel a little like Cinderella," I admitted.

"But you already found your prince." Bennett gave Andrew a nod. "Sorry about your friend."

"I don't think we're supposed to be discussing that," Andrew said quietly.

"Oh, right." Bennett put his finger in front of his lips. "It's a secret. Shush."

"You might want to slow down on the alcohol," Andrew told him.

"Afraid I'll embarrass my father? Believe me, it wouldn't be the first time." Bennett took another deliberate and purposeful swig of his drink.

"Why don't we step inside?" Andrew suggested. "I'd like to chat with you for a minute."

Bennett shrugged. "Sure. Why not?"

Andrew and Bennett moved into the living room, with neither of them saying a word to me. As they disappeared, I felt even more awkward and clutched my champagne glass like it was a life vest. This party was for Victor's friends. I was only here because some people apparently wanted to meet the wedding couple, but I had no idea how to act or what to say. I was relieved when Paula moved toward me. At least I knew her a little.

"Lauren, you look beautiful tonight," she said.

"Thank you. So do you." I wasn't lying. Paula looked stunning in a dress that probably cost thousands of dollars and showed off her thin but busty figure in the best possible way. While her weary eyes and somewhat wrinkled hands showed her age, everything else appeared to have been nipped and tucked to make her look younger.

Paula took a sip of her champagne, then said, "Where is your handsome husband?"

"He's talking to Bennett."

"That's good. Maybe it will slow down Bennett's drinking. I don't know what's gotten into him tonight. He seems very agitated about something." Paula sighed. "It's probably Victor's unwillingness to listen to any of Bennett's ideas. Apparently, he brought him some project that your Andrew is developing, and Victor thought he was overstepping." She shook her head in frustration. "The two of them have always clashed. They're a huge disappointment to each other, and I'm caught in the middle. I sometimes wish that Bennett would do something else, start his own business, and I think he wants to, but then he has this intense desire to impress his father, too."

I didn't know what to say. It almost felt like she was talking to herself.

She suddenly started, as if realizing she had said too much. "My apologies. I'm sure you're not interested in our family dynamics."

"Families can be complicated," I said, even though I hadn't really experienced that myself. With my mom and me, there really hadn't been that many complications. We'd led a very simple life. Of course, having less money also made things simpler.

"Yes," Paula agreed. "Complicated is a good word. How are you and Andrew feeling now that you're officially married?"

"It's been a difficult few days."

"He was very worried about you when you fell off the yacht. We all were. Thank goodness you survived."

"I was lucky."

"Not as lucky as Andrew's friend," she muttered, taking another sip of her champagne. "That was an unfortunate incident. I liked her designs more than I thought I would. I underestimated her talent. I regret that. It's a shame she won't have the opportunity to bring them to life."

"It's tragic," I agreed, trying to think of how I could steer this awkward conversation in a better direction. "This is a beautiful party. Andrew and I feel very grateful to be included."

She tilted her head to the right, giving me a considering look. "What do you think of this life you're getting to experience? Is this party your dream?"

"I've never aspired to anything this grand. It's way out of my league."

"And yet you're here, drinking expensive champagne, meeting rich and well-connected people who can help you and Andrew with your careers."

"Only because of your generosity. You and Victor have been so kind to include us in everything."

"Well, that's not kindness, dear...that's business. Victor has been selling your story and now his friends want to meet the couple living out the romantic fantasy." She paused. "You should find your groom before someone suspects you're not as happy as you're pretending to be." She gave me a knowing smile. "I know what a fake smile looks like, Lauren. You need to get better at it, especially if you want to move in these circles."

"I think I will go find Andrew," I said. "Thank you again for inviting me."

"Well, every girl should have at least one trip to the ball."

As Paula left, I couldn't help thinking that was the second reference to Cinderella I'd heard tonight, and both from members of the Carrington family. I didn't get the feeling they were nearly as excited by the whole romantic wedding fantasy campaign as Victor was. It didn't matter. It was almost over.

As I entered the house, I ran into Ethan.

"Hi," I said, feeling a little breathless as our gazes met. I'd always felt nervous around him, but lately, the nerves seemed to come from a different place. We'd gotten closer than I'd expected, and he'd become one of the few people on the island I felt I could trust.

"You look beautiful, Lauren," he murmured, a gleam in his eyes I hadn't seen before.

Or maybe I hadn't wanted to see. *Because I was married*, I reminded myself. Clearing my throat, I said, "Thanks. Why are you here tonight?"

"Victor will open his gallery to his guests shortly."

"Has he filled in the empty cases?"

"Yes. Every last one. And the last one is...well, you'll see it soon enough." He paused. "Where's your other half?"

"Talking to Bennett. They're working on some deal together. But Bennett seemed like he was already a little drunk, so I don't know how that's going to go."

"Has Andrew talked to you about Allison?"

"No. He's been very distant, focused on getting through what we need to get through, and nothing else. I think he stopped pretending, even though I never thought he was pretending. But now I do. I just don't know why he would have ever wanted to fake something with me. Why marry me? Why go through all this? I'm not rich. I don't have anything of value."

"You have connections," Ethan said. "Marrying you got him into the marketing campaign and gave him access to not only this resort and this villa, but also one of Victor's private and very exclusive parties."

"And now that he has those connections, maybe he's ready to walk."

"I doubt he'll walk too fast. He'll want this to play a while longer, make sure he's on solid ground with the Carringtons before he pulls the plug on his relationship with you."

I stared at him. "You make it sound like a foregone conclusion."

"I'm sorry. I thought we were done pretending."

His pointed words made me draw in a sharp breath, but then I gave a nod. "You're right. My defensive reflex has been to say you're wrong, to act like everything will be okay and that I haven't made the worst mistake of my life, that I still know the man I married. But I don't. I have no idea who he is anymore, and that's shocking to me. Now and then, the old Andrew pops up with his dazzling, caring smile and his attentive manner, but that's happening less frequently, and since Allison's death, it hasn't happened at all. He can barely stand to look at me. I don't know how we're going to get through the next twenty-four hours, much less the next few days or weeks. I can't imagine once we leave this island that we'll want to spend even one more second together. Maybe I should stop pretending right now. What am I waiting for?"

He put a hand on my shoulder when I finally ran out of steam, giving me a concerned look. "As much as I would like you to stop everything and get the hell out of here, I know it's not that simple, and so do you."

"Maybe I'm making it too complicated," I argued. "It's getting to be really hard to be with him, especially alone. Although, it seems like he's trying to avoid those moments, too. But you're right again. I can't bail now. I have to get through tomorrow's events so I don't lose my job, because I'm going to need it when this is all over."

He gave my shoulder a squeeze. "It's not too much longer, Lauren. You can do it."

"I have to do it. What is happening with the investigation? Is Allison's family coming here to the island?"

"No. The sheriff's office located her father. He's in Europe and said he would pay for everything, but he wouldn't be coming."

"That sounds cold."

"He said he hadn't seen her in fifteen years. Her mother hasn't returned any calls. She had no siblings."

"But she had friends. She had three guys on this island who cared about her. And when I looked at her social media, she seemed very popular. I'm sure a lot of people will mourn her death."

Ethan shrugged. "Social media doesn't always reflect the true picture of someone's life or their relationships. I spoke to Colin and Jay earlier. They expressed all the right emotions. But there was also a wariness in their answers, as if they didn't want to be looked at too closely. It was the same feeling I got from Andrew. I honestly don't know how any of them really felt about her, but there was definitely a relationship between all of them."

"I think Andrew cared about her. That's why he's upset now. Even though they weren't currently involved, they had a past."

"Does that bother you?"

"There are so many things that bother me, Ethan, I couldn't even tell you where that falls on the list."

He gave me an understanding smile. "Well, you don't need to worry about anything tonight. You should try to enjoy this incredible party."

"This is not my scene, Ethan. I didn't grow up with money. The only luxury I ever saw was in the hotels where my mom worked. But I was the kid who knew the back rooms, the kitchens, and the laundry—not the five-star guest rooms, the ballrooms, or the fancy parties."

"Well, this is your world now, at least for tonight."

I sighed. "I know. At midnight, my coach will turn into a pumpkin, and I'll be dressed in rags."

"And where will your prince be?" he asked.

"I honestly have no idea."

I gasped as the house and patio were suddenly plunged into darkness.

Someone else cried out in alarm. A glass shattered. I put my hand out, and it landed on Ethan's solid chest.

He put his hand over mine, steadied me, then said, "I need to find out what's going on. Stay here. Don't go anywhere else, Lauren."

Before I could promise I wouldn't move, he was gone.

CHAPTER TWENTY

I felt someone bump into me in the dark. They didn't say a word—not a sorry, not an excuse me—and then they were gone. Through the floor-to-ceiling windows, I could see people on the patio pulling out their phones, tiny constellations of light appearing in the dark. The gentle hum of the air conditioning died, leaving behind a weighted silence broken only by nervous laughter and whispered conversations. I reached for my own phone, but before I could activate the flashlight, emergency generators kicked in, casting the great room in a dim glow.

Then Victor appeared in the center of the room. "We've had a minor electrical problem, nothing to worry about," he said, scanning the crowd with sharp eyes. "I'd appreciate it if you would all stay where you are. I don't want anyone to get hurt while we're getting the electricity back on. It should just be a moment."

After his reassuring announcement, Victor crossed the room to speak to David Grimes. They huddled together, speaking in low voices, before heading toward the stairs.

My nerves tightened. *Did this sudden blackout have something to do with Victor's private collection in the upstairs gallery? Was the darkness a cover for a robbery?*

I wondered again where Andrew was. I wanted to know that he was in this room, that he wasn't upstairs, that he wasn't the thief Ethan thought he was. But I couldn't see him anywhere, and I felt more uneasy with each passing moment.

No one else seemed as tense as I was. But I had a bad feeling in my gut, and I couldn't seem to shake it, so I did what I'd told myself I wouldn't do—I drank my champagne, hoping the bubbles would ease my stress. Unfortunately, the sparkling liquid made my stomach churn even more.

While the other guests carried on with their practiced party smiles, I noticed security personnel moving with military precision down the hallway and up the stairs. Their hands hovered near concealed weapons, and their expressions carried none of Victor's artificial calm.

"Where's Andrew?" Paula's voice at my elbow made me jump. I hadn't seen her come in from the patio.

"I'm not sure." I hated how my voice wavered. Clearing my throat, I added, "He was with Bennett earlier."

Paula's lips thinned into a harsh line. She turned and cut through the crowd toward the stairs, but one of the security guards intercepted her. Their conversation was brief and one-sided—Paula's face darkened with each word until she spun away, radiating fury.

As I turned my attention back to the living room, Andrew emerged from the shadows, and when our gazes met, he gave me a casual nod and threaded his way through the crowd toward me.

"Where were you?" I asked, the question coming out sharper than I'd intended.

"In the restroom. I got lost in the dark. Any idea what's going on?"

"Victor said something about an electrical glitch that should be fixed shortly." As if on cue, the lights came back on.

"Perfect timing," Andrew said with a smile.

"What do you think that was all about?"

"Who knows? Maybe a power surge?" He adjusted his tie. "I could use another drink and some food. I'm starving."

He wasn't acting like a man who had anything to hide. He wasn't trying to leave or avoid anyone. But I still had the feeling the blackout and his disappearance were tied together.

"I see apps being served on the patio," he added. "Let's go see what food we can snag before dinner starts."

I followed him outside, watching as he grabbed a crab puff from a server.

"Want one?" he asked.

"I'll wait for dinner. What did you and Bennett talk about?"

"The work project."

"Anything new?"

"Not really. He wants to do the deal on his own, but I told him it has to be the Carrington Group or nothing. He didn't like it, but he understood. I'll sit down with him and Victor on Thursday, after we get through the grand opening."

His words reminded me of my recent conversation with Ethan. How much had Andrew gained through my Carrington connections? Looking back at our early days together, I searched for signs I might have missed. We'd been going out for weeks before we'd talked about the marketing campaign. Before that, I'd been a mid-level employee working for a large corporation. I'd had no contact with Victor, Paula, or Bennett. *Had Andrew been conning me from the beginning? Or had our love affair been genuine at first, and it was only later when he saw opportunities that his ambition had taken over? That he'd pushed ahead on marriage because he saw where I could take him?*

"What's going on in your head?" Andrew suddenly asked, his gaze sharpening. "You're quiet."

I shrugged, knowing I couldn't have a personal and deep conversation now. "Just tired and a little stressed. The lights going out was unnerving."

"I'm sure it was nothing. No one seems concerned but you, Lauren. You should try to relax. Have another glass of champagne. We might as well try to salvage something out of our honeymoon," he said, a dry note in his voice.

"Are we still having a honeymoon? You've been so distant today, Andrew. I'm sure Allison's death hurt you, and I want to be there for you, but I don't know how to talk to you about it."

"We're not discussing Allison," he said, his voice turning to ice. "It was an accident. And we can't change anything, so we move forward."

"I want to move forward."

"Then do it," he snapped, losing patience with me. "I get that this has been a rough couple of days—"

"Rough?" I interrupted. "I could have died yesterday, Andrew."

"I know that. I was there. And I was terrified that even if we found you, it would be too late. But it wasn't. You're alive. You're okay. And you should be happy and grateful we get to be at this beautiful party tonight. But everything we have to do is a hardship to you, and I'm getting tired of having to pump you up through luxury experiences like an incredible massage or an exclusive party for the rich and famous. Do you know how many people would like to change places with you right now?"

I stared at him in amazement, shocked by his harsh words. "It's my fault that I feel bad after getting shoved off a yacht in the middle of the ocean and left to die?"

"We both know that's not what happened," he said tersely. "It's what your drug-addled brain made you think happened."

"Either way, I was in the water struggling to survive, not you. It's pretty easy to judge me for an experience you didn't have."

He exhaled sharply, then raised his hand in what looked more like surrender than apology. "Okay, you're right. I guess I'm trying to move past the bad stuff so we can enjoy the good times. But you are fighting me every inch of the way, and it's exhausting."

"I'm not trying to fight, Andrew. I want things back the way they were. I want us to feel connected."

"We'll get there, but we both have to try. And that starts now. Can you look a little happier?"

"I can," I said, realizing he was partly right. I was tense, constantly searching for threats in the shadows, desperate not to be caught off guard again. It wasn't only because of Andrew's suddenly inconsistent behavior; it was everything that had happened to me.

"Good," he told me, his stiff shoulders relaxing with my words. "We love each other, right, Lauren?" His questioning gaze bored into mine, demanding the right answer.

"Right," I said automatically, even though love was the last emotion I felt right now. But arguing with him was only making things more uncomfortable.

"Then let's start over now. Let's move forward together. Tonight is a good night. Tomorrow will be even better. We have nowhere to go but up."

I wanted to believe in his certainty, but my mind kept circling back to the blackout. *What had really happened in those five minutes of darkness? And more importantly, what was coming next?*

Twenty minutes later, Victor gathered everyone in the living room once more.

"Before our meal, I have something special I want to share with you all, the newest piece in my collection." Victor's eyes gleamed with barely contained excitement. "Please follow me upstairs and into my gallery."

A ripple of anticipation moved through the crowd. As we ascended the stairs, I couldn't help but notice how the security presence had doubled since our last visit. Two guards flanked the gallery entrance, their weapons prominently displayed in tactical holsters—a clear message to anyone considering mischief. They collected our phones in a woven basket, citing a strict no-photo policy that felt more ominous than before.

The gallery's climate-controlled air washed over us as we entered the room and formed a semicircle around the previously empty display case that was now covered with a white linen cloth. Victor took his position behind the case, with Ethan hovering at his shoulder like a particularly vigilant shadow. Paula stood off to the side, her perfectly manicured fingers fidgeting with her diamond bracelet. Bennett stood with the rest of us, looking both bored and angry, as his father commanded the spotlight.

I glanced at Andrew beside me. The transformation in him was startling. Gone was the relaxed and somewhat distant man from the patio. His eyes now burned with intensity; his body coiled with anticipation.

"Tonight is a very special night," Victor began, drawing my attention back to him. "In the early eighteenth century, King Louis XV of France was known for his extravagance, and his queen and mistresses famously adorned themselves with lavish jewels. But there was one notable and spectacular blue diamond that was beyond anything anyone had ever seen. It was cut into the shape of a heart and worn in a large pendant by Louis's queen as a symbol of his love. It was called the Heart of Eternity, and also known as the Unbreakable Heart, because it could never shatter."

The irony of the name wasn't lost on me, standing there beside my increasingly mysterious husband. Some things broke in ways that had nothing to do with physical destruction.

"While it couldn't break, it could be stolen," Victor continued. "The diamond disappeared during the French Revolution. There were alleged sightings over the years, other smaller blue diamonds that were suggested to have been cut from that original stone, but nothing was ever proven. And then six months ago, in an old farmhouse in the South of France, a very old man died, and one of his heirs discovered a velvet pouch tucked away in an old army boot."

Victor paused, a master storyteller who knew exactly how to

hold his audience. I could feel the electricity, the anticipation in the room. It was palpable.

"Inside that box," Victor said, "was the bluest diamond this man had ever seen. He knew he had stumbled upon something very, very special, and he reached out to a jeweler to find out what it was worth. The jeweler was a friend of mine. He'd known of my interest in finding that diamond for years, and he was able to broker a private deal between the three of us."

"When I first envisioned this resort," Victor continued. "I saw it as a place for love to be discovered and rediscovered. For couples to fall in love, get married, and celebrate their anniversaries. This diamond is a symbol of eternal love, and it's why I wanted it to be the centerpiece of my collection here on the island. It won't be here forever, but while it's here, I wanted to share it with you—my closest friends. Down the road, my company will be working with a jeweler to create a blue diamond wedding pendant that will be available to purchase by the brides who get married here in the future. In fact, it will launch an entire wedding jewelry collection, which will be my next venture."

Bennett's sharp intake of breath caught my attention. His face had drained of color, this news clearly hitting him like a physical blow. Another decision made without his input, another reminder of his peripheral role in his father's empire.

"But today..." Victor's voice swelled with pride. "I am thrilled to say that you will be the first people in hundreds of years who will see the legendary diamond in all its glory." He cleared his throat dramatically. "Here is the Heart of Eternity."

He dramatically pulled the cloth away, revealing a diamond that seemed to capture and amplify every bit of light in the room. It sat alone on white silk, a pure expression of blue fire that made several guests audibly gasp.

The crowd surged forward instinctively, then froze as bells chimed when someone's hand brushed the glass.

"I'm sorry," Victor said, though he didn't sound sorry at all.

"You won't be able to touch the glass without setting off an alarm. Those of you in the front, please take a moment, and then move away so others can see the diamond."

Andrew and I were among the last to approach the case. The diamond was even more spectacular up close, seeming to pulse with an inner light that made it appear almost alive. Victor beamed at us with proprietary pride, while Paula's smile had calcified into something brittle and sharp. She probably sensed that her husband loved this diamond far more than he loved her.

"What do you think?" Victor asked.

"It's stunning," I managed, struck by how something so beautiful could feel so dangerous. "I've never seen anything like it."

"One of a kind," Andrew murmured, his gaze sliding from the diamond to Victor with admiration. "And quite the acquisition. I'm surprised you were able to keep it quiet this long."

"It was not easy," Victor admitted. "But I wanted to have this moment with a special group of people."

I was still surprised that Andrew and I had been included in that special group of people, but maybe it was because we went with the love story.

We gazed at the diamond for another minute before moving away to let the last few guests take a look. Andrew then wandered around the gallery, as did many other guests, pausing now and then to gaze at one of Victor's pieces. I stood off to the side, not particularly interested in seeing it all again. As I did so, I glanced at Ethan. His eyes were on Andrew, but after a moment, he turned and looked at me.

There was a determined grimness to his gaze. His job had just gotten more difficult, as he would now have to keep a legendary diamond safe from thieves. And Andrew, one of his favorite suspects, was walking around the room, taking a look at everything.

But the gallery had to be as secure as any room could be. I couldn't imagine how anyone could get inside to steal anything, and the case itself seemed impenetrable.

Another ten minutes passed before Victor said that the gallery would be closing, and they would see everyone downstairs for dinner.

As we left the room and collected our cell phones, I turned to Andrew. "That was a surprise."

"Yes. Victor outdid himself. It's amazing what kind of wealth he must have to acquire something like that."

There was an undertone to his words I couldn't decipher. *Was it envy that Victor was so far ahead of him? Or anger that one man could have so much?*

I had never realized the extent of Andrew's ambition until this weekend. I'd known he was trying to build a business, but now I saw how much he wanted the success and wealth that Victor had. Maybe everyone wanted that. Maybe I was the one who didn't dream big enough.

CHAPTER TWENTY-ONE

The party ended around ten, and we walked back to the main building in silence, my tension increasing with each step. It was easier to be with Andrew in a group than to be alone with him. I was too confused about him to want to be physical, but I was fast running out of reasons not to have sex. My hip wasn't as bad as it had been, and I'd recovered completely from my unexpected swim in the ocean. Andrew had told me he wanted to get back to our honeymoon, and I needed to want that, too, but the truth was—I didn't. But I couldn't say that tonight, not with all the events happening tomorrow. After that, we would definitely have to talk.

Maybe Andrew wasn't as set on getting back to our honeymoon, either, because he had his hands dug into his pockets, when before we'd always walked hand in hand everywhere we went.

Andrew must have read my thoughts because he suddenly took my hand and looked at me, giving me a smile that was nowhere near as dazzling as those he'd showered around the party tonight. But it was clear he was trying.

"Tired?" he asked.

"Yes," I said, not sure how he'd take that answer, but maybe I could use that excuse for at least one more night. "We did a lot of talking."

"Everyone loved our story."

"You've gotten better at telling it. You know all the right points to hit to get the perfect laugh, the perfect ah."

"Well, I've had a lot of practice the past few days," he said. "But it's almost over. After tomorrow, we can put that story away."

His fingers were warm around mine, but I didn't feel the heat that used to burn between us...only a cold dark chill. I knew now that our love story had no substance. It was just a story that I'd told myself.

And we were back to silence again. It lasted until we got into our suite.

As soon as we entered the room, Andrew dropped my hand and headed toward the refrigerator to pull out a bottle of water. I kicked off my high heels and sat down on the couch. He moved over to the dining room table and opened his computer.

So much for getting back to our honeymoon. But as he looked at his computer, I felt relief more than anything else. "I think I'll take a shower and get ready for bed," I said as his fingers moved across his keyboard.

"Sounds good," he murmured, without lifting his head to look at me.

I got to my feet and paused by the table. "Are you working?"

"I have some emails I need to answer. You should get a good night's sleep tonight, Lauren. Tomorrow will be a busy day, the culmination of all of this."

"I know. I'm glad it's finally here." I thought about leaning down and giving him a kiss, if for no other reason than to keep pretending we were a happy couple. But he was focused on his computer, and there didn't seem to be any point in faking a feeling that wasn't there anymore.

I jerked awake, heart hammering. The digital clock said two forty. For a moment, I lay perfectly still, trying to identify what had pulled me from sleep—a sound, a movement, something. The space beside me was empty, the sheets cool to the touch. Then I realized Andrew stood at the window, a dark silhouette against flickering lights that shouldn't have been there.

"What's going on?" My voice came out rusty with sleep as I pushed myself up. "Is something wrong?"

"Looks like a fire," Andrew replied, his tone oddly detached.

"What?" I was out of bed in an instant, crossing to where he stood at the now-open patio doors. The night air carried the acrid smell of smoke, and through the trees, emergency lights pulsed like a crimson heartbeat. Even through the thick foliage, I could tell they were coming from the direction of Victor's villa.

My stomach dropped. "Oh my God," I breathed. "It looks like it's close to Victor's place."

"There's a lot of smoke, but I don't see any flames."

I strained to see through the darkness, but he was right, there were no flames, just clouds of smoke curling through the strobing lights of the fire engines. Still, a wave of fear ran through me. *What if something had happened to one of the Carringtons? Would the morning bring another notice that someone was dead?* "Should we go down there?" I asked.

"No. I'm sure whatever needs to be done is being done. We'd be in the way." Andrew paused. "It actually looks like the smoke is dissipating. I think they've got it under control."

"I hope no one was hurt."

"I'm sure they weren't. I bet whatever happened is electrical, something related to the power outage earlier tonight. There was probably a short somewhere." He yawned. "I'm going back to bed. Are you coming?"

"In a minute," I murmured, unable to look away from the distant scene. The emergency lights suddenly cut out, plunging everything into darkness. Whatever had happened was over—or someone wanted us to think it was.

A chill that had nothing to do with the night air crept over my skin. I hurried back inside, securing the patio door with trembling fingers. The soft click of the lock felt like false security in a world where nothing was what it seemed anymore.

As I got into bed, Andrew's breathing had already settled into the rhythm of sleep, or a convincing imitation of it. I lay awake in the darkness, listening to that steady sound and wondering if I'd ever trust it—or him—again. I also had the feeling this might be the last night we spent in bed together.

After tomorrow, we wouldn't have to stay together if we didn't want to. Not that we could publicly separate. But we would be done as the perfect Carrington wedding couple, and we could quietly go our own ways.

Where those ways would lead, I had no idea.

Andrew was gone again when I woke around eight o'clock Wednesday morning. His disappearing act had become routine, but today it carried a different weight. No note, no explanation —just tangled sheets that mirrored the mess of our marriage.

Megan arrived as I finished dressing, her usually composed features tight with stress. "We have an additional problem to deal with," she said, barely waiting for the door to close behind her.

"Is this about the fire engines I saw on the property last night?"

"Yes. There was a problem at Victor's villa."

My heart jumped. "Is he okay? Was anyone hurt?"

"I heard the private insurance investigator is at the medical center with a concussion, but everyone else is fine."

The room tilted slightly as I took that in. "What?" My voice caught. "You're talking about Ethan Stark?"

"Yes, and that part is not for public consumption, Lauren. Victor wants everyone to believe there was an electrical problem at his villa, which produced copious amounts of smoke but no fire. Everything is fine now."

"But you don't think it's fine?"

"I suspect there's more to the story, but that's above my pay grade and yours. What I need is a distraction, and that's going to be you and Andrew all day long, selling your story, generating interest and conversation. We don't want any of our events to be marred by what happened at the villa."

"I understand. We'll do whatever you need us to do."

"Good. I texted you both the schedule for today."

"I saw that."

"We'll have the ribbon cutting at eleven thirty, lunch on the patio at noon, resort tours in the afternoon, and a myriad of other social activities for the press and our arriving guests. We're also hosting small, intimate cocktail parties starting at six thirty each night this week in the old lighthouse. Andrew and you will host tonight's party for VIP guests."

"Okay." My mind spun from all the events. "Is that it? Will the lighthouse party be the end of our official duties?"

"At the moment, that's the last thing I have you doing. Where is Andrew?"

"Uh, he went out to grab some pastries," I lied. "He'll be back soon."

"Let him know I need you two to be very engaging. I want them talking about your love story, not what happened at Victor's villa. And try to look like you're infatuated with each other. Yesterday, I could feel the tension between you two, and while it might not be evident in photographs and videos, it will definitely show in person, and we cannot have that."

"We'll do our best. This has been a lot, Megan."

"Well, from what I hear, you're getting a promotion at the end of it," she said, an irritated note in her voice.

"Really? Who told you that?" I asked in surprise.

"Victor said we should reward you for being such a great

representative for the brand. So don't let him down. Do your job."

"I will," I promised, excited about a promotion but wondering if whatever came my way from Victor wouldn't turn Megan and Bennett into my enemies. That didn't bode well for a long, successful future with the company. My job security was as fragile as my marriage security.

After Megan left, I grabbed my phone and called Ethan. Each ring stretched my nerves tighter until his rough voice came through.

"It's Lauren." The words tumbled out. "How are you? I heard you're at the medical center."

"I'm waiting for the doctor to release me," he replied tersely.

"What happened, Ethan? How did you get hurt?"

"What have you heard?" His question was careful, measured.

"That there was an electrical problem at Victor's villa that resulted in a lot of smoke but no fire and that no one was hurt but you." I paused. "Is that true?"

"It's the story the Carringtons will tell today."

"Can you tell me what really happened?"

"I don't know, Lauren. Can I trust you?"

My fingers tightened on the phone. "You can trust me, Ethan." My voice softened. "I care about what happened to you. I'm so sorry you got hurt, and I really need to know if Andrew was involved."

"I don't know if he was involved, but I suspect he was."

"Tell me what happened."

"The thieves disabled the villa's main alarm system," Ethan said, frustration evident in his voice. "But they missed something critical—the diamond's display case was on a completely separate circuit with its own power source and cellular connection. At one thirty-seven, that sensor triggered, sending an alert directly to my phone. No one else got it because the regular security network was down."

He paused, then continued, "When I arrived at the villa

around one forty-five, I found the perimeter guard unconscious near the back door. His keycard was missing. I called resort security and told Demora to contact the sheriff's office, but I couldn't wait for them all to arrive." His voice hardened. "I should have, though. I'd barely made it inside when the smoke hit me—thick and disorienting. The last thing I remember was a sharp pain at the base of my skull. When I came to, the deputies and resort security were there, and the gallery had been cleaned out."

"Oh, my God! Did they steal the diamond?"

"They stole almost everything. The thieves got quite a haul."

"I don't understand. What about the inside guards? Where were they?"

"Smoke bombs had been planted in the air vents throughout the house and triggered remotely. When they went off, a toxin filled the air that rendered everyone unconscious, allowing the thieves to enter the villa."

"That's crazy." I shook my head in disbelief. "Do you think the blackout earlier in the night was part of it?"

"Yes. That's probably when they set the bombs in the vents. It was a very sophisticated and clever plan," he admitted, bitterness in his voice. "I thought we had plenty of redundancies in our security system and our personnel. But we were outsmarted. And I am so pissed off I can hardly stand it."

"I can understand that. How are the Carringtons and the guests that were staying with them?"

"They're fine. Everyone was asleep when the toxin was released, keeping them asleep. As soon as the firefighters arrived and the house was vented, everyone started waking up. They were disoriented and confused, but, according to Victor, they're all fine. However, as you can imagine, he's very upset about the theft. My employer will be as well. What they took was worth many millions of dollars."

"I'm sorry about that, but I'm really glad you're okay, Ethan.

And that no one else was hurt. The robbery is awful, but I'm sure Victor will be compensated for his losses."

"At my employer's expense. I'll be out of a job after this."

"It wasn't your fault."

"It was completely my fault. I approved the insurance on the diamond even when Victor brought it out at the last possible second. I felt confident in the security system, but that confidence was misplaced." He blew out a breath. "You said Andrew was with you all night?"

I licked my lips, realizing I had no idea where he'd been between the time I'd gone to bed and when I'd been woken up by the fire engines.

"Lauren?" he pressed. "You have to tell me what you know."

"Of course. I was just thinking. Andrew and I went back to our suite around ten last night. He was working on his computer in the living room when I went to bed. I woke up at two forty. Andrew was standing at the patio doors. He told me there was a fire, and we went out onto the balcony to take a closer look."

"He could have been gone between ten and two forty then?"

"I suppose."

"What was he wearing when you saw him standing by the patio doors?"

"Uh..." I tried to remember if I had even noticed what he was wearing. "I think he was in black track pants and a black long-sleeve T-shirt."

"Is that what he wears to bed?"

"Not usually," I said slowly. "I think he was in bed before he got up. I feel like the covers were mussed, but I don't know for sure. I didn't really look." I blew out a worried breath. "What time were you hit over the head?"

"Probably a little before two. And you saw Andrew at two-forty dressed in clothes that could have been worn outside."

The implication hung heavy between us.

"He didn't act like someone who had robbed a vault of treasures," I said. "And if he had, why would he come back to the suite? Why wouldn't he have left? Why would the thieves stay on the island?"

"Maybe they didn't, and he did, to avoid raising suspicion." Ethan's voice grew harder.

"But he's taking a risk by staying."

"Are you sure he's actually still on the island? You said he was gone when you woke up. Maybe he just needed you to see him in the middle of the night to provide an alibi."

My breath caught. "I'll find out soon if he doesn't show up for the ribbon cutting at eleven thirty." I hesitated, my voice dropping. "What should I do if he comes back, Ethan? Do I keep pretending? Do I ask him anything? How can I help you?"

"You can help by staying calm and acting like you know absolutely nothing." The steel in his voice softened. "That's what I need you to do. I don't want you to be in any more danger, Lauren. And once today is over, you need to get away from him. I'll help you with whatever you need."

Something in his tone made my heart skip. "I appreciate that." I swallowed hard. "And Ethan, I'm really grateful you weren't badly hurt or worse. Your life is far more important than anything that was stolen."

A weighted pause followed. "Your life is important to me, too." The words came out rough, almost unwilling. "That's why I need you to be careful, Lauren."

"I will." I tried to sound confident. "If Andrew is the thief, I can't see why he'd hurt me now. He has what he wants, and it looks like he might have gotten away with it."

"For now," Ethan said, his voice dropping to a dangerous growl that sent an unexpected shiver down my spine. "But I will hunt the thieves down if it's the last thing I do."

I heard someone outside the door. "I think Andrew is back. I better go."

"Stay safe. I'll talk to you later."

As I ended the call, Andrew walked in, wearing jeans and a sweatshirt. He had a white paper bag in his hand and a cup holder with two coffees. "Good morning, beautiful," he said with his usual smile, no trace of tension in his blue eyes.

"Hi," I said, faking a smile in return. Ethan's warning rang through my head, reminding me that I had to pretend like nothing was wrong. "Looks like you got us some treats."

"Coffee and pastries," he said, setting everything down on the table.

He'd made my lie to Megan the actual truth. But truth and lies were a risky thing to discuss right now, so I kept that thought to myself.

"Who were you talking to?" Andrew asked.

"Megan," I lied as I moved over to the table to get my coffee. "She wanted to go over the schedule. She also told me there wasn't a fire last night at Victor's place, just smoke from an electrical problem. All the Carringtons are fine."

"That's good news. Did she say anything else?"

I shook my head. "No. In fact, she said that I should tell everyone exactly that if asked about the fire engines on the property last night."

"Always looking to avoid trouble." Andrew took out a chocolate chip scone and bit into it.

He seemed different this morning—happier, more relaxed—and I was hesitant to guess why. *Was he getting over the shock of Allison's death? Was he putting on a front because we needed to get through the day looking happy together? Or was his upbeat attitude the result of stealing millions of dollars of treasure right out from under Victor's nose?*

I really hoped it wasn't the latter.

"These are good," Andrew said, waving his scone at me. "You should try one."

"I will. Thanks for picking them up, along with the coffee. That was thoughtful."

"I'm still the same guy you married," he said lightly, as if I'd forgotten.

While he might be the same guy I'd married; I wasn't sure he was the same man I'd fallen in love with.

"I'm going to get changed for the ribbon cutting," he added. "Megan sent me the schedule, too. We have a long day ahead of us, but it's almost over, Lauren. What do you think about that?"

Several answers came to mind, but the first word to come out was, "Relieved. I'm tired of the cameras, the speeches, and always being on."

"You have to admit it's been exciting. Isn't that what life is supposed to be about? Taking risks, pushing the envelope, and living past your own expectations?"

"I guess." I wasn't sure what he was getting at, because he had to know I wasn't a risk-taking, push-the-envelope, live-past-my-own-expectations kind of woman. But he was gone before I could say anything. And it didn't matter. As he'd said, it was almost over. I just wasn't exactly sure what *it* was...the marketing campaign, the marriage, the con...

Or maybe it would be all three.

CHAPTER TWENTY-TWO

The scent of jasmine hung thick in the air as we rounded the corner to find Megan and her media team sequestered in a bush-enclosed patio left of the resort's grand entrance. Jeanette Bilson and the Carringtons were already there, their presence adding tension to the moment. Through a space in the bushes, I could see a crimson ribbon fluttering across the hotel's entrance, where an eager crowd had begun to gather, their excited murmurs carrying across the manicured grounds.

Paula and Bennett stood apart from the others, heads bent close in whispered conversation that seemed to stop whenever anyone drew near. Victor prowled the edges of the patio, phone pressed to his ear, his usually commanding presence fractured by barely contained fury. The loss of his treasures had clearly gutted him. But he wouldn't tell us about that, and we wouldn't ask. My stomach churned with the weight of secrets, but Ethan's words about the robbery echoed in my mind, each syllable a warning bell. One wrong word, one telling glance, and I could bring everything crashing down—or worse, put myself in the crosshairs of whoever had orchestrated this theft.

"Good, you're here and you're both smiling," Megan said as

she joined us, her gaze sweeping over us. "Holding hands would be even better."

"We'll do that as soon as we go public," Andrew replied, his voice clipped.

"Fine." Megan's lips thinned. "A few kisses here and there wouldn't be bad, either. Try to look like an actual honeymoon couple. Because right now, I'm thinking I could have paid some models to get a better result."

I felt Andrew stiffen beside me, his previous warmth turning to ice. The unfairness of her criticism burned in my chest. We'd been playing our parts perfectly, dancing on the knife's edge between public performance and private turmoil. I understood Megan's frustration—her carefully orchestrated media campaign was hanging by a thread. But with everything else going on, Megan's wounded pride would have to wait for another day.

Before either of us could respond to her criticism, Victor stepped forward, his presence commanding immediate attention.

"Lauren, Andrew—it's good to see you both," he said. "How are you today?"

"We're good," Andrew said, answering for me. "We saw the fire engines at your house last night."

"Yes. There was an unfortunate incident," Victor replied. "But everything will be fine."

"Hardly fine," Bennett drawled as he and Paula joined us.

"We're not going to discuss it today," Victor said, sending his son a stern look.

Clearly, Bennett and Paula knew about the robbery, but I couldn't quite tell how either of them felt about it. Neither one had seemed to appreciate the collection Victor had built. I think in somewhat different ways, they'd both been jealous of the time he'd spent pursuing treasures, which had probably taken time away from them.

Victor turned back to me and Andrew. "I want to thank you

both for everything you've done this past week and will be doing today. You've gone above and beyond the call of duty, especially you, Lauren. Even after everything you had to deal with, you put a smile on your face and did what needed to be done. That's the Carrington way, and I'm immensely proud of how you've handled yourself."

I was touched by his words. "Thank you, Victor."

"Here, here...to Lauren," Bennett said, giving me a few hard claps.

His eyes looked glittery and a little off, his hands unsteady. *Had he already started drinking?* That didn't bode well for a long day of events.

Apparently, Victor agreed with me because he gave his son a sharp look and said, "You need coffee."

"I need a lot more than coffee," Bennett returned. "But that's probably all you want to give me, isn't it?"

"Paula?" Victor said, giving his wife an impatient glance.

She shrugged. "What do you want me to say, Victor? It's been a long, stressful night."

Victor didn't look happy with her, either, but he put a smile back on his face when he turned back to me. "At any rate, I've spoken to Bennett and Megan about moving you up in the company, Lauren. You deserve a promotion, and as soon as we all get back to work next week, we'll make that happen."

"I appreciate that," I said.

"And Andrew, I've also been pleased with your efforts," Victor continued. "I want you to know I'm going to take a more thoughtful look at your latest proposal. We can go over that next week. I'm sure you're both eager to get on with your honeymoon after today."

I was sure Andrew was more excited about going over his business proposal with Victor than honeymooning with me. And it worried me that this growing connection between Victor and Andrew might make Andrew feel like he needed to stay with me, and I didn't want that to be the reason. Actually, I didn't want there to be any reason for us to stay together, because I was done. I was rather shocked at the finality of that thought, but it was the truth. I didn't trust Andrew anymore, and I couldn't love someone I didn't trust.

"I can't wait for us to work together," Andrew said, offering his hand to Victor, a smug smile on his lips.

I couldn't help wondering if Victor was shaking the hand of the man who'd robbed him of the things he held most dear.

The next few hours were a blur of photos, interviews, and conversations with an endless number of people I'd probably never see again in my life. Andrew played his part well, and so did I. But as much as we looked like a loving couple, I felt absolutely no connection between us. He never left my side, but his presence didn't feel like protection or love anymore. It felt like a trap, a prison, and I desperately wanted to escape.

After our last event of the day, an afternoon high tea in an oceanfront gazebo with four older women who had apparently paid a great deal for the privilege of meeting the honeymoon couple, Andrew and I finally had a chance to take a break for a few hours before our last event at six thirty.

We'd barely left the gazebo when Andrew told me he was going to meet up with Colin and Jay. I was fine with that. I needed time away from him and everyone. Then my phone buzzed with a text from Megan, and I realized I was not going to rest yet.

Megan wanted to meet me at the lighthouse so she could show me the setup and talk to me about my hosting responsibilities for the cocktail party. She said it wouldn't take long, but she needed me to come now. I texted back that I was on my way, but I wasn't with Andrew. She said she only needed me.

Lucky me, I thought with a sigh. Turning around, I headed down the path toward the old lighthouse that stood on the edge of the resort property, high upon a hill. I hadn't been inside yet, so it was probably good to get an idea of the layout. Because of the interior size, only ten guests would be joining us, which was great. I was enjoying the smaller groups much more than the bigger events.

As I walked up the path, I sent Ethan a text, asking him how he was feeling, and if there was any news.

He didn't text back, which was disappointing, probably more disappointing than it should be.

But Ethan felt like my only real friend these days. I hadn't heard from Harper since we'd spoken yesterday. Jamie had pretty much disappeared, although I'd seen her in passing at the ribbon cutting. She and Brad had gone to the other side of the island for a few days to rest and relax. They'd been on the vacation I should have been on.

But this was almost over. A few more hours and then I could get back to me, if I could remember who that was.

As I passed the villas that were still under construction, I saw yellow tape across the entrance to the model villa where Allison had apparently fallen. That sent a shiver down my spine, another reminder that she was dead, that she had lost her life on this pretty island. It chilled me to think about it, and I was happy to move past those buildings.

The path grew more picturesque as it wove its way through a grove of wind-twisted cypress trees, their shadows lengthening in the late afternoon sun. Sea birds circled overhead as a salty breeze lifted my hair off the back of my neck, and I wished I could simply enjoy the day. Soon, I told myself. This really shouldn't take long.

As I came through the trees, I saw a road coming from another direction that ended in a small parking area in front of the old lighthouse. The building rose before me like the beacon it was, its white and gray weathered exterior showing its age. It had been built almost a hundred years ago, and it was no longer the island's primary lighthouse. The more modern building was on the north side where the cargo ships passed. This one was more decorative than functional, although its slim tower still rose proudly into the sky.

I remembered writing marketing copy for this lighthouse. I'd called it historic, romantic, a perfect spot for sunset viewings, but I'd written those lines based on photos, not the real thing, and I had to admit it was much prettier in person.

As I approached the building, a gust of wind rattled the old storm shutters. And when I got closer, I could see fading paint and brass fixtures turned green with age. The door looked heavier than I expected, its old wood worn smooth by decades of oceanside weather.

I hesitated at the bottom of the short stairs leading up to the entrance. The late sun caught the lighthouse's windows, turning them into blazing squares of light that revealed nothing of what waited inside, and I felt fear creep down my spine, but that was silly. This was just another party venue, and Megan was probably waiting impatiently for me to arrive.

The door creaked as I pushed it open. "Megan?" My voice echoed in the circular room, where old navigational equipment lined the walls, and brass fixtures gleamed in the late afternoon light that streamed through salt-crusted windows. A spiral staircase wound upward, its iron steps disappearing into the shadows above. "Are you here?"

"Lauren?"

It was a man's voice that wafted down the stairs. "Bennett?" I asked in surprise.

"Come up to the office," he said.

I moved up the stairs, getting a little dizzy as I made my way up the narrow circular steps. Finally, I got to a landing and saw an open door leading into the lighthouse keeper's office. Bennett was standing behind an old wooden desk, a half-empty bottle of whiskey next to a file folder in front of him, a glass in his hand.

"Hi," I said warily. "I'm looking for Megan."

"Yeah, she's not coming," he replied. "Come in. Close the door."

I stepped further into the room, but I didn't close the door. "What's going on, Bennett?" I didn't like the angry, somewhat wild look in his eyes.

"It's time you and I had a talk, Lauren. Past time, actually."

"About what?"

"Well, it's not about a promotion," he said, lifting the glass to his lips and taking a long swallow. "That won't be happening, in case you're wondering. There are a lot of things that won't be happening."

I felt uneasy at the dark edge in his voice. "I should go."

"You're not leaving yet." He leaned down to pull something out of a desk drawer.

I froze in shock when I saw the gun in his hand. "What—what's going on?" I asked, fear running through me. "Why do you have a gun? Why did Megan ask me to come here?"

"I told her I wanted to talk to you about your future at the company. And I have a gun because you're not going anywhere."

"We can talk back at the resort, where it's more comfortable. In fact, we should have this conversation with Megan. She's my actual boss. And, clearly, you're upset about your father's suggestion that I be promoted. We can discuss that. There's no reason to be upset."

"Nice speech, Lauren. You're not as stupid as I thought, or maybe you are, because you're here, even after all the near misses you had this week."

I swallowed back a growing lump of terror in my throat as he took another swig of whiskey and then slammed the glass down, making me jump.

"What's going on, Bennett? Why are you so angry?"

"Didn't you ever wonder why my father wanted to throw you such an elaborate wedding? Why you were suddenly the centerpiece of a marketing campaign that would cost the company ten times more than any campaign we'd ever run? Why you were invited to the private events? You, a marketing rep, a nobody... but there you were rubbing elbows with the richest people in the world."

His jealous rage thickened the air, and I knew I had to tread carefully, or he was going to blow up. Obviously, his anger had been building for a while, and I suspected the alcohol he'd consumed had taken it to an explosive level.

"The campaign took on a life of its own," I said slowly. "But if you're unhappy about what was spent, talk to your father. I had no say in it."

"You think he'd listen to me? I don't. He's selling half the hotels in our group. I found that out earlier today from one of the people he's selling a property to. He lied about those sales being a rumor. He's selling off my inheritance because he doesn't think I can run the company. I can do a hell of a lot better than him. He's so obsessed with his precious art that he's been siphoning money we need for the company into his collection. I'm not going to tolerate it anymore. I'm not going to be treated like I'm no one, like I'm less than you."

"I'm sure your father doesn't think you're less than me."

"Oh, but he does," Bennett said, so angry his voice shook. "And I'm not going to let my inheritance be cut again." He shook his head as if convincing himself of what he needed to do. "Today, I take charge. My father thinks I'm a weak alcoholic addict who is stupid and out of control. He doesn't believe I'm a worthy successor, but I am more than worthy, and I am not going to wait for him to give me anything. I am going to take it. I will not lose what I am owed."

I didn't understand why his anger with Victor was pointed at me. "Why are we having this discussion? This is a family matter. And if you're taking control of the company..." I still didn't think that would happen, but I wanted him to believe I was buying his story. "Then you don't have to promote me. In fact, you can fire me now and never see me again."

He gave me a smirking smile. "I wish it was that easy, but it's not. You were right when you said this is a family matter. I discovered this weekend my family is bigger than I thought." He opened the file folder on the desk and pulled out a black and white photo, pushing it toward me. "Look at that."

I didn't want to get closer to the desk or to the gun in his hand, but I didn't have a choice. I took a few steps forward and stared down at the picture that appeared to have been taken in a photo booth. There was a man and a woman hugging each other and mugging for the camera, their smiles bright, loving. My gaze narrowed, my breath coming faster as I realized the man was a much younger Victor Carrington, and the woman...

My heart stopped. *No, it couldn't be...*

"You recognize her, don't you?" Bennett asked.

"I—I'm not sure."

"Yes, you are. Tell me who that is, Lauren."

"It looks a little like my mother," I said in confusion.

"It is your mother, Sarah Gray."

"I don't understand," I said, turning my gaze to him. "My mother didn't know Victor."

"Oh, she definitely knew him. In fact, she knew him intimately." He pushed the rest of the file across the desk, and I looked down at what appeared to be a legal document, an addendum to Victor's will.

"What is this? Why are you showing me your father's will?"

"Because he's not just *my* father." Bennett gave me a hard look.

"What are you talking about?"

"Look at it. Look at your name on the document, Lauren. My father had a secret daughter, and he recently made an addendum to his will so that you will get a share equal to mine upon his death."

Shock ran through me at his words, and I put my hands down on the desk to steady myself. I wanted to say he was wrong, but I was staring at my mother's face, looking at legal papers with my name on them.

How could my mother be in a loving photo with Victor Carrington?

How could I be his daughter?

The questions ran around and around in my head, creating panic and anxiety. I could barely breathe, barely think, but I had to think.

My mom had never mentioned she knew Victor, much less that she'd dated him or slept with him. And my father had died in a car accident before he knew she was pregnant. He hadn't abandoned me. He'd never known about me.

Why would she lie about that?

As soon as the question ran through my head, her entire story fell apart.

She'd lied because she'd had an affair with a married man, gotten pregnant, and was probably ashamed. But she had to have told Victor about me. Otherwise, I wouldn't be in the will. *Why hadn't he said anything all this time, all these years?*

Again, I came up with an answer I didn't like.

Because he hadn't cared enough about me to be my father. He hadn't wanted to know me, and he sure as hell hadn't wanted anyone else to know about me, at least not until after he was dead.

"Are you finally getting it?" Bennett asked, taking another swig of whiskey, drops of it sliding down his chin. "In case you're having trouble doing the math. I'm thirty-one. You're twenty-seven. I was four years old when you were born."

I shook my head, still not wanting to believe what I was looking at. "You have to be wrong. My dad was killed in an auto accident. He was a construction worker. My mom said his name was Gary."

"Did you ever see a picture of Gary? Did you meet his family, his parents?"

"He didn't have a family." I felt like a fool repeating her lies, because that's clearly what they were. I felt sick to my stomach. "I can't believe she made up a story about my father."

"Bravo," Bennett mocked. "You finally caught up. And to think you're the smart, committed employee my father is so proud of. It's a joke."

"But your father never told me I was his daughter. Why would he keep it a secret? Why would my mother do that? Why would she pretend she'd never even met him?"

"I'm sure he paid her off."

"I doubt that. I didn't grow up with money. I had no privilege. I wasn't entitled, like you."

"Well, you're entitled now. Because Daddy is changing his will, so you get half of everything." He paused. "I have to say, I didn't believe it at first, either. I thought she was trying to play me, but then she gave me the file, and all the proof was right there in front of me."

"Who are you talking about now?" I asked.

"Allison. She told me everything."

"Allison?" I echoed. "How the hell would Allison know? Where would she get the photo, the file? Maybe it's all fake, Bennett. Maybe she was conning you." I latched on to that theory with desperation.

"I thought the same thing at first, but the papers aren't fake, and there's a note in that file you haven't read yet from my father, expressing remorse for not taking care of you. Since your mother died, he wanted to make sure you ended up with something. That's why he was changing his will now."

"With something? With money?" I demanded, rage running through me. "But not with him acknowledging I am his daughter? *My God!* Everything I've gone through this week. I could have died twice, and he never once acted like he was anything more than a concerned employer, but I'm his daughter, and he almost lost me at sea, and that wasn't enough to make him say something?"

Bennett seemed to enjoy my confusion and even more so, my disgust at his father—our father. "Well, he's never been father of the year. But I've had to deal with him putting me down for thirty-one years. I've paid my dues. I don't give a shit that he hasn't told you anything, that you're his secret shame. I care about his money and the inheritance that is supposed to be mine. That is the only reason I still talk to him, and I will not let you have a dime."

I didn't need to ask him how he was going to prevent that, because the gun in his hand was a very strong clue.

"I know exactly how to stop that from happening now," he continued. "You are going to have yet another unfortunate accident, Lauren. You came here early to check out the venue at Megan's request. When you got here, you ventured too close to an old wooden rail. As you grabbed the rail, it broke. You slipped and fell to the ground, just like poor Allison did. The caterers will probably find you when they arrive around six."

My breath caught in my chest as I saw the crazy and proud light in his eyes and realized one horrific fact. "You killed Allison?"

"She killed herself. She got too close to the edge of a balcony. It was her own fault. She shouldn't have gone out on that deck. There was a warning sign. But she was determined to get a job from my father, so she pushed things too far, and let's say she slipped."

"Because you forced her to slip." I saw the truth in his eyes. "Why, Bennett? Why would you want her dead?"

"She wanted too much for this information. She had to go. And so do you."

I swallowed hard. "You can't do this, Bennett. Think about it...I'm your sister. Are you really going to kill your own sister?"

"You're my competition," he said coldly. "I'll never get what I want now that our father is fascinated and impressed by you. I wondered what the hell he was thinking, spending so much money on you, and then it all fell into place when Allison showed me the file. He wanted to give you the perfect wedding because you are his daughter. That's why everything had to be five-star, first-class. He didn't do it for the campaign. He did it for you. He did it out of guilt."

Shaking my head, I said, "That can't be true. He never cared about me before. If he had, he wouldn't have kept me a secret... he would have been there for me."

"He couldn't admit you were his daughter. My mother would have left him, and a divorce between them would have cost him too much. That was always her leverage. He needed her money."

"I thought it was his money. The company was started by his father."

"Who basically bankrupted it. He convinced my mother to invest her trust fund in the company, and she agreed, as long as he never left her, never divorced her, never embarrassed her. That's why he couldn't publicly acknowledge you until he was dead, until he didn't care anymore about his business or his collection. Actually, let me change that order to collection and then business. Do you know how much of our company's money he has spent on old manuscripts and swords? It's ridiculous. And I have no idea what he spent on that diamond..." Bennett shook his head in disgust. "And then he didn't even have the brain power to protect it from being stolen."

"Were you part of the robbery? Was that your way of getting back at him? Steal what he loves most? Keep it for yourself? It makes sense."

Maybe Ethan and I had both been off base. Maybe Andrew had never been involved in any of it, and it had always been Bennett, who hated that his father loved his collection more than he loved his son.

"Let's go," Bennett said, waving his hand toward the door.

"Where?"

"Up the stairs to the viewing deck. We'll spin your accident like we spun Allison's tragic fall, which we're now referring to as a mishap. That was a good word Megan came up with. She's a hell of a lot more valuable to our company than you are. You're just going to be another mishap. Walk."

"And if I don't?"

"I'll shoot you right here."

Our gazes clashed, and I saw the murderous intent in his eyes. "If you shoot me, no one will believe it was an accident."

"No, it will look like murder, but I've planted some information that will tie Andrew to Allison's death, so it won't be difficult to pin this on him, too. He has motive to get rid of both of you. Allison was his ex. You two were fighting. You caught him cheating, and whatever... There are plenty of narratives we can tell."

"What kind of information did you plant?"

"Stop stalling. Move or I shoot!"

Neither choice was good, but one gave me slightly more time to think of a way to escape. I walked toward the door, my mind racing as I searched for an option. But there was no way I could sprint down that narrow circular staircase and get away from him or a bullet, so I had to go up to the viewing platform.

Bennett was right on my heels every step of the way, the gun pressing hard into my back, the smell of alcohol on his breath making me want to gag. He was definitely drunk. Maybe he wasn't as rock steady as he should be. Maybe I could find a way to shove him over the railing and save myself.

When we reached the circular viewing platform, I saw the broken rail, the empty space, the long fall awaiting me, and I stopped abruptly, panicked at what was coming. Bennett pushed me forward. I stumbled from the force of his hand, and it brought back memories of another shove, the one on the swim platform.

"Did you push me before?" I asked, turning back to look at him. "When we were on the yacht? Was that you?"

"No. That was Allison. I told her if she got rid of you, I'd pay her double. But she failed. You survived. You're quite good at that."

"And Sally, my horse? Did you throw a rock at her?"

"That wasn't me. That was Allison. She wanted to scare you

and show Andrew what a weak person you were. And that's enough questions."

He forced me to take another step forward, then another, until I was almost at the edge, and terror ran through me. I didn't see any way out. This might really be it. Bennett had already killed once. He would do it again. I looked over my shoulder, giving him an imploring look. "You don't have to do this. I won't accept the money. I won't acknowledge Victor as my father. You don't have to worry about me. I don't care about the inheritance."

"He cares. And I don't trust you. You'll say anything to save yourself."

I saw a shadow slip onto the deck. Then someone came running out of the shadows, moving so fast that Bennett didn't hear him. A gun came down on the back of his head. Bennett's eyes flew open in shock as he fell at my feet.

My jaw dropped when I saw who had taken out my attacker.

"Andrew," I breathed, looking into my husband's beautiful blue eyes. A tremendous relief swept through me. "Oh, my God! You're here!"

"Looks like I got here just in time."

"How did you know where I was?"

"When you weren't in the suite, I called Megan. She told me Bennett was meeting you here."

"You saved my life—again," I said in amazement. Maybe I'd been wrong about him. Maybe I should have never lost faith in him. "Thank you." I moved into his embrace, closing my eyes as he gave me a long hug.

As we broke apart, he picked up Bennett's gun and tucked it into his waistband, while he still kept his weapon in his hand. That made me wonder when and where he'd gotten a gun. I hadn't seen it in his suitcase when I'd unpacked for him. And why had he brought a weapon here? *Had he known I was in trouble?*

Suddenly my relief turned to wariness.

"Let's go inside," Andrew said.

I was more than happy to get away from the broken railing, so I followed him down the stairs. He stopped at the landing and waved me toward the office.

"I'd rather get out of here," I told him.

"In a minute. I need to show you something."

I didn't think I could handle any more surprises, but he was blocking the stairs, so I went into the office. Once inside, Andrew grabbed my hand and pulled me toward the desk.

"What are you doing?" I asked, seeing the hard look in his eyes, feeling the tension in his grip.

"It's over, Lauren."

There was a finality to his words that renewed my anxiety. "The marketing campaign?"

"Our love affair."

There was no smile on his face now, no warmth in his gaze, just icy coldness. He might have saved my life, but something was off. The man I'd fallen in love with was gone. Maybe he'd never really been there at all. "Okay," I said. "Can we talk about it at the resort?"

"I'm not going back to the resort. You might not be, either, but that depends on a few factors."

"You're scaring me, Andrew. Could you put the gun down?"

"I'm afraid I can't. Sit in the chair behind the desk, Lauren."

"Why?"

"Just do it," he bit out, pulling me toward the chair, then letting go of my hand long enough to shove me down on the seat. A second later, he pulled something metal out of his pocket, cuffing my right wrist to the arm of the chair with a motion so quick I barely registered what he was doing. I stared down at the metal cuff in shock, then back up at him. "Now what?" I asked.

"Now we wait."

"For..."

"Your father to come."

My heart leapt against my chest. "You know who my father is, too?"

His answering smile had once dazzled me, but now I saw past the sparkle to the evil. He might have saved my life, but that was only because he needed me to be alive for some reason...a reason I was about to find out.

CHAPTER TWENTY-THREE

After making sure I was secured to the chair, Andrew left the room, closing the door behind him. I didn't know if he was going to finish off Bennett, or if he was going to wait downstairs for Victor to arrive.

As the minutes ticked by, my anxiety increased...as well as my anger. I couldn't believe I'd been so blinded by love I hadn't seen who Andrew really was. People had tried to warn me, but I'd been stubbornly defensive of our love story, which had turned out to be a bad fairy tale.

I yanked at the wooden arm of the chair where he'd cuffed me. The lighthouse's dampness had rotted the wood over the decades, and I could feel it giving slightly each time I pulled. I twisted my wrist, ignoring the bite of the metal cuff, using it to help splinter the wood. There was no one coming to rescue me. I had to find a way to save myself.

When the door opened, I halted my movement.

Andrew gave me a sharp glance, then said, "Your father will be here soon."

My gut clenched. "Victor is really my dad?"

"I see Bennett filled you in." His gaze moved to the open file on the desk, and a new gleam of anger appeared in his eyes.

"Allison stole that from me and stabbed me in the back. I couldn't believe she would betray me like that."

"You had the file first?" I asked, wondering how many more surprises were coming my way.

"I found it in Victor's office. It looked interesting, so I swiped it along with the paintings on his walls before I started the fire."

I stared at him in bemusement, still unable to correlate this man with the one I'd fallen in love with. "You started the fire? I defended you so many times to Ethan. I told him he was wrong. You weren't a thief. You weren't an arsonist. You were a hero. You saved me."

"And I didn't have to."

"Did you rescue me because you realized I was Victor's daughter?"

"I didn't know who you were when I heard you scream for help. I hadn't read the file that closely, so your name meant nothing to me." He shrugged. "I saved your life because you were pretty, desperate, and because I could. The next day, when I realized you were the woman named in the will, I knew you could be very useful to me."

"That's why you came to my hospital room, why you started this whole charade." I was amazed by how carefully orchestrated everything had been. "What if I hadn't been caught in the fire? Would you have sought me out?"

"Yes. I would have found a way to use you, because you were Victor's dirty little secret. That gave me power over a powerful man."

"For six months, you spent every day with me convincing me we were in love," I said. "You texted me, called me, took me out on dates, had sex with me, told me you loved me." I gave him a long questioning look. "That took time and effort. Why go through all that?"

"Because you were my way in." His voice was patient, like a teacher explaining something obvious to a slow student. "I could use you to get to Victor, and there were so many ways I could exploit the information I had acquired. I could blackmail him for money, connections, art. I could force him to use his power to get me whatever I wanted. But I wanted to go slow and find the right angle. I needed to see how close I could get to him without revealing what I knew."

"And that angle was the marketing campaign."

"Exactly. Having our wedding thrown by the Carrington group gave me the perfect opportunity to get on this island, to network with Victor, and to gain access to his gallery."

"How did you know Victor would go for it?"

"Once he saw your name, how could he refuse? You are his daughter. He could justify throwing you a wedding under the guise of business. It was the perfect plan."

I hated how *good* of a plan it was. "I still can't believe how well you faked loving me."

Andrew shrugged. "I'm a patient man. The reward was worth the effort."

It was clear now that I was nothing to him. Just a job. A con. The means to an end." I clenched my fists. "You're a terrible person, Andrew. I can't believe I was so blind."

"You wanted to believe in the love story, and I was damn good to you, Lauren. You really don't have that much to complain about."

My eyebrows shot up in amazement. "I'm cuffed to a chair. You're waving a gun in my face after lying to me for six months, and you don't think I have much to complain about?"

"You'll be fine if your father pays up. You can go back to living your sad, lonely, depressing life, and I will be a very rich man."

"Aren't you already rich? Didn't you rob Victor last night? I know there was a robbery, and I'm pretty sure you and your friends were the thieves. So, why are you still here? Why continue with the pretense today? What more is there to get?"

"The Heart of Eternity," he said flatly.

"I thought you took it last night."

"The stone in that case turned out to be a fake." Andrew's lips tightened. Victor thought he outsmarted me, but now I'll play my ultimate card—you. I'm going to trade you for the diamond. Then I'll disappear."

"What if Victor won't give you the diamond? What then?"

"He'll turn it over in exchange for your life. He has a soft spot for you."

I almost laughed at the absurdity of that statement. "Are you kidding? He doesn't care about me at all. He has never done anything for me."

"Except throw you the most luxurious wedding a woman could want."

"That was for the business, not for me."

"It was for you, too. Victor wanted to ease his guilt for not being there for you. Why do you think we were invited to all his private parties? And that last party gave me much-needed access to his house. I wasn't sure how I would plant the smoke bombs until I realized we were going to be there. All I had to do was turn off the lights."

Andrew was so sly, so conniving, and so evil...

How had I ever thought I'd loved this man? How had I ever believed he'd loved me?

His mask was completely gone now. This wasn't the man I fell for. But this was who Andrew really was—a greedy, ruthless thief who would do anything to get what he wanted.

"Did you know Allison took the file and went to Bennett? That she was trying to make her own deal?" I asked.

"I knew she was pissed I was marrying you and suspicious I had another plan that didn't include her."

"Which you did."

"I couldn't have her involved. She was too volatile, too reckless."

"She trashed our suite, didn't she?"

"Yes," he admitted. "I told her to back off after that. I agreed to introduce her to Victor if she stopped trying to mess things up between you and me."

"But that wasn't enough for her."

"No, it wasn't. I didn't realize how far she would go until you ended up in the water. She refused to admit culpability, but I knew it was her doing. I told her that if she tried to hurt you again, she would regret it. She promised to leave you alone. When she turned up dead, and I realized the file was also missing, I knew she'd betrayed me, and that person had killed her."

"She sold the information to Bennett."

"I figured it was him."

"When I survived, Bennett killed her because she'd failed, and she knew too much."

"If he hadn't taken her out, I would have," he said coldly. "She almost ruined everything. I needed you alive. You were no use to me if you were dead."

"That's cold."

He gave an uncaring shrug. "It's the truth."

"I'm surprised you know what the truth is. You won't get away with any of this, Andrew."

"Oh, I think I will," he said with a laugh.

"Ethan Stark knows you're the thief and that Colin and Jay helped you. He'll spend the rest of his life hunting you down."

"Stark won't find me. I'm very good at reinventing myself."

I thought about that. "Is anything about you real? Was anything about *us* real?"

"No."

A pain ripped through me at that single, devastating word and the callous look in his eyes. "I thought you were so charming, kind, and attentive. You were always reassuring and caring. You tried to give me whatever I wanted."

"I was playing a part, and, frankly, it was exhausting. I've never had to reassure a woman so much in my life. You need to grow a spine, Lauren, get some guts."

My pain was replaced with anger. "I have a spine."

He rolled his eyes. "No, you don't. You get nervous standing up in front of a crowd. I practically had to hold you up at our rehearsal dinner. When we met, I quickly saw that you were a lonely, weak, insecure, and needy woman. That made you the perfect mark."

My hands clenched into fists. If I hadn't been cuffed to the chair, I would have punched him in the face. Although, I'd never hit anyone. *Did I have it in me?* Of course, I did. I wasn't as weak as he thought I was. I'd taken care of my mother when she was dying. I'd faced a lot of hard things in my life, and I'd survived. "Maybe you don't know me as well as you think you do."

"Maybe you don't know yourself. You like to hide behind other people, behind work. You hate the spotlight. You're like a little mouse that scurries away when the lights go on."

"You're a terrible person, Andrew."

"I'll be terribly rich very shortly," he replied, my harsh words not making a bit of difference to him.

"Victor won't trade the diamond for me."

"You better hope he does, Lauren. Because I've played my card, and if I don't get what I want, then I'm going to burn everything down. And you will not be saved from that fire."

A shiver ran down my spine because I believed every word he'd said. He was a man with nothing to lose, and I was a woman with everything to lose.

He straightened as his phone buzzed. He gave me a pleased smile. "Your father has arrived."

Heavy footsteps approached, followed by Victor's voice demanding to know where I was.

Then Colin shoved Victor into the room, positioning himself against the door, gun raised. The facade of friendly college buddies had vanished. Andrew and Colin now looked every inch the criminals they were. I wondered if Harper had known anything about this, or if Colin had just been using her to monitor what I might know.

"Lauren," Victor said, his eyes pleading for understanding. "I don't know what he's told you—"

"He told me you're my father. Is that true?"

"Yes. But I didn't know about you for a long time. I thought your mother got an abortion. I didn't find out you existed until you were twelve."

"Twelve was a long time ago," I said sharply.

"It was a complicated situation."

"You two can catch up later," Andrew interrupted. "Where's the diamond, Victor?"

"You stole it last night, didn't you?" Victor replied.

Andrew gave Victor a hard look. "You know I stole the fake. Where is the real diamond? And don't tell me you didn't bring it, because if you didn't, Lauren will take a bullet for you. That one won't kill her, but it will hurt like hell. She'll feel like she's dying. And you'll get to watch her suffer before I put her out of her misery."

I shuddered at his words. I didn't want to believe that this man who had once been so tender and loving to me could talk so ruthlessly about hurting me.

Victor seemed to be weighing Andrew's intent. Finally, he reached into his pocket and pulled out a velvet pouch.

"Toss it to me," Andrew ordered.

Victor hesitated, then tossed the pouch. Andrew caught it with one hand. He tucked his gun into his waistband while Colin kept his weapon trained on Victor.

I caught my breath as Andrew opened the pouch and pulled out a gleaming blue stone. Even in the dim light, it still took my breath away. Andrew pulled out a jeweler's loupe from his pocket. Before he could examine the stone, there was a thud from above us. We all looked toward the ceiling.

Bennett must have woken up, I thought, wondering if by any chance that could be good for me, but it seemed doubtful since he'd wanted to kill me only minutes earlier.

I wondered why Andrew hadn't killed Bennett when he'd had

the chance. He'd gone back up there after he'd cuffed me to the chair. But while Andrew was ruthless, he also seemed deliberate. When he came up with a plan, he stuck to it. If he hadn't had a reason to kill Bennett or thought he might be useful later, he might have left him alive.

"He should be secure, but check it out," Andrew told Colin, confirming my thoughts that Bennett was still alive.

As Colin left, Andrew retrieved his weapon, holding it in his left hand while raising the loupe to his eye. While Victor's gaze darted between us, I focused on working the metal cuff against the splintering wood of the chair arm, each movement as silent as I could manage.

Andrew was so absorbed in the diamond he didn't notice. A splinter jabbed into my wrist, but desperation drove me on.

Suddenly, Andrew swore and hurled the stone against the wall. I jumped as it shattered into a thousand glittering pieces.

"You thought you could fool me again?" Andrew's voice was deadly quiet. Then he lunged forward, driving his fist into Victor's face, slamming him backward into the wall.

Andrew struck again, splitting Victor's lip, sending blood dripping down his face.

I redoubled my efforts on the chair arm, ignoring the splinters piercing my skin. A deep crack appeared in the wood.

Victor was trying to defend himself, but Andrew was beyond reason, each blow fueled by his rage at being deceived. He'd promised to burn everything down, and I knew with terrible certainty that he'd kill Victor—and then me—if I didn't stop him.

With one final wrench, I felt the wood give way. I was free.

Andrew spun around at the sound. I leaped to my feet, swinging the broken chair arm like a club. It connected with his wrist, sending the gun in his hand flying.

The weapon skidded across the floor, disappearing under a heavy cabinet.

Andrew swore and instinctively reached for the second gun—the one he'd taken from Bennett.

I jumped on him. We collided, slamming into the desk, both of us grappling for control of the weapon. His fingers closed around the grip, but so did mine. I twisted, using every ounce of strength I had. His grip was stronger, but I had one advantage—desperation.

I found the trigger and squeezed.

The blast knocked me backward, and the gun flew from my grip as I hit the floor.

Andrew sprawled nearby on the ground, blood spreading across his chest as he gasped, pressing his hand against the wound.

Victor stirred against the wall. I could hear his pained breath, but his eyes were still closed.

I needed to move, to get Victor and myself out of here before Colin returned.

Before I could get to my feet, heavy footsteps pounded down the stairs. I scrambled to pick up the gun I'd just used to shoot Andrew. I pointed it to the door as it flew open.

Thankfully, I didn't pull the trigger, because it was Ethan.

Relief flooded through me as I lowered my weapon and let out a breath, feeling safe for the first time since I'd arrived at the lighthouse. "I shot Andrew."

"I can see that."

"Do you think he's going to die?"

"It looks like you hit him in the shoulder." Ethan put his weapon away.

"You might need that, Ethan. Colin is around here somewhere."

"I already took care of him. He's tied up on the deck with Bennett. Bennett begged me to release him, but I wasn't sure what was going on, so I left him where he was."

"Good. Because Bennett tried to kill me."

"I want to hear everything, but first..." He squatted down

beside me, giving me a concerned look. "Are you all right, Lauren?"

I nodded, fighting back tears that seemed ready to fall now that the fight was over. "I am now."

"The sheriff's deputies are on the way. Demora will also be here shortly."

"What about Jay?"

"He was arrested on a boat in the harbor with Victor's treasures. No one else is coming to hurt you, Lauren."

I blew out a breath. "Thank God."

Ethan stood up, then held out his hand to me. I appreciated the warmth of his fingers as they wrapped around mine, and he pulled me to my feet.

Once I was standing, Ethan grabbed Andrew's gun and checked on Victor, who was slowly returning to consciousness. Then he returned to me, his gaze moving to my arm, to the one cuff still on my wrist, the other dangling. There were long scratches on my arm that had puffed up and some were bleeding, but my injuries were minor, and I was grateful for that.

"Now tell me what happened," he said.

"Bennett lured me here so he could kill me."

Ethan's eyes widened. "Why would Bennett want to hurt you?"

"He found out I'm Victor's secret daughter. The evidence is there on the desk." I tipped my head toward the file. "Andrew stole those papers from Victor's office the night of the hotel fire. He didn't know I was the woman mentioned in the addendum to Victor's will until later. He just happened to rescue me because I was there, and I was trapped. That part of our relationship wasn't planned. Everything else was."

Ethan shook his head in amazement. "That is not what I expected you to say."

"I know, right? It's unbelievable. Anyway, at some point, Allison found the file. She thought Andrew was cutting her out, so she tried to make her own deal with Bennett. Once Bennett knew about me, he wanted me dead and told Allison to get rid of me. She got her opportunity on the yacht, but she failed."

"And then Bennett killed Allison," Ethan murmured.

"Yes. And like Allison, I was going to have a tragic fall that would look like an accident." I paused, thinking about everything I had learned. "Bennett didn't want to share his inheritance with me. There's a document in that file that shows Victor wants to give me half his estate upon his death."

"That's wild. And you said Andrew saved you from Bennett?"

"Yes. When he came to my aid, I thought I was wrong about Andrew, that he was saving my life again. But then, Andrew brought me in here and cuffed me to the chair. He told me he'd discovered the diamond he'd stolen from Victor last night was a fake, but he had one last card to play."

"You," Ethan said, meeting my gaze.

I nodded. "Andrew told Victor he would trade me for the diamond. Otherwise, I would die. But..." My voice trailed away as I realized the truth. "But Victor didn't bring the real Heart of Eternity; he brought another fake. Andrew threw it against the wall when he realized it wasn't the real thing." I tipped my head to the blue glass on the floor. "The fake diamond shattered, and Andrew flipped out. He went after Victor. I thought he was going to kill him. I knew had to stop it, but I was cuffed to the chair. Fortunately, I could see the old wood was giving way, so I did everything I could to break free, and I was just in time. I used the arm of the chair to hit the gun out of Andrew's hands, but I still had to fight him for Bennett's weapon, which he also had. I don't know how I got the best of him, but I was filled with a strength I didn't know I had. I found the trigger, and I pulled it."

Ethan's gaze filled with admiration. "I always knew you were strong. You wouldn't have survived this week if you weren't."

Andrew yelled louder as the pain gripped him. "Need help," he begged, giving me an imploring look. "Don't let me die, Lauren."

I walked over and looked down at him, at the man I'd vowed to stand by and love forever. "Why shouldn't I let you die? You were going to kill me."

"Because you're not a murderer, Lauren. You're a soft, sweet, kind person."

"Oh, please." I stared down at his handsome face and realized how ugly he really was. "You told me to grow a spine. Well, guess what? I already have one. I also have a heart, and I want you to know something, Andrew. You did not break it. You did not break my heart or me. I am not like the fake diamond you threw against the wall. I'm the real thing, and you never deserved me."

As I finished speaking, I heard the sirens, and a moment later, help arrived from the sheriff's office, the fire department, and hotel security. As one of the deputies unlocked the cuff on my wrist, Ethan related what I'd told him about the situation. Then we made our way downstairs and out of the lighthouse to give the others room to work.

It was after five when we got outside, and the sun was sinking lower in the sky. It was a beautiful view and one I appreciated even more because a short time ago I wasn't sure I would see another sunset.

"It really is over now," I said as I let out another relieved breath.

Ethan met my gaze and nodded. "It is. I'm sorry for everything you went through, Lauren. I wish I'd found evidence against Andrew six months ago so I could have saved you from all this pain."

"I don't blame you for anything. I blame myself for being so easily taken in. Andrew caught me at a low moment in my life. I was an easy mark. I was lonely after my mom died. I'd spent so much time taking care of her, I'd lost friends, I'd been away from the workplace. I had to start over, and burying myself in work kept me busy, but I wasn't really living. When Andrew saved my life, he changed me. And even though I know it was all fake now, he did bring me out of my shell. I guess that's something."

"Don't let him off the hook. I liked what you told him up there. Because the woman I see standing in front of me now doesn't look broken at all."

"I don't feel broken anymore, but the truth is I did feel that way after my mom died. Andrew saw my weakness, and he exploited it."

"You're not weak anymore."

"I know. I proved that to myself when I survived being stranded in the ocean, and I proved it again tonight." Taking a breath, I added, "I really don't want to have to prove it again."

"You won't have to. Andrew and his crew are going to prison. Bennett will be charged with murder and attempted murder. And Victor...well, I guess he didn't break any laws. But his future with you is probably up in the air."

"He won't care about that. It's not like he's losing anything. He never had me in his life." I shrugged. "And since you've recovered his collection from Jay, and he still has a diamond worth millions of dollars, I think he'll be fine."

"What about the secret you two share?"

"I'm not sure what to do about that. He said he didn't know of my existence until I was twelve, but even then, he didn't acknowledge me. Bennett told me Victor could never leave Paula because he'd lose too much financially. I guess she'd invested her own money in the company." I paused. "Bennett said Victor spent a ton of money on my wedding because it was for me, for his daughter."

"Maybe he did spend more because you were the bride. He wanted to throw you the perfect wedding."

"That doesn't make up for not being my father. And he didn't even bring the real diamond to trade for me. What does that say?"

"I have no idea," he said, giving me a sympathetic shrug. "I guess your mother never told you about your father."

"She made up a fake story, too. I wish I knew why." I paused as the paramedics brought Andrew out of the lighthouse and put him in the back of an ambulance. He seemed to be unconscious now, and I was fine with that. I didn't want to look at him again. I'd seen enough.

Two sheriff's deputies then escorted Bennett and Colin to a waiting vehicle. Bennett's shoulders were slumped in defeat. Colin appeared more defiant, but it didn't matter how either of them felt. They'd lost, and I'd won. That felt good.

Victor was the last to leave the lighthouse. He was able to walk on his own, albeit with the help of Martin Demora.

Victor's steps slowed as he reached us, and his gaze met mine.

"Lauren," he said, sending me an imploring look. "I know you may never want to talk to me again, but I want to thank you for saving my life. You are a remarkable woman." He gave me a regretful smile. "Very much like your mother, in fact."

I didn't know what to say to that.

Then he reached into his pants pocket and pulled out a velvet-covered box. "This is for you."

"What is it?"

"Just take it. Please."

I hesitated, then took the box from his hand and opened the lid. I was expecting to see the necklace from his mother that he'd had me wear at the wedding, but it wasn't that at all. It was the large and spectacular blue diamond heart—the Heart of Eternity. I gasped as it glittered in the light.

"That's the real one," Victor said. "I didn't want to give it to Andrew unless I absolutely had to."

"You could have gotten us both killed by holding back."

"It was a calculated risk. I'm usually good at those, but I must admit Andrew was a formidable competitor. Ethan had his doubts all along about Andrew, but you seemed to love him, and I didn't want to believe you'd fallen for a criminal. But I started to worry after you fell off the yacht."

"I was pushed off the yacht by Allison." I paused. "She was working with Bennett. He told her to get rid of me because he found out I was your daughter. Your son didn't want to give up half his inheritance. When Allison failed, he killed her. And tonight, he tried to kill me."

Victor shook his head in bewilderment as he stared at me through troubled eyes. "It's hard to believe such terrible things about my son."

"You can believe me or not; it's the truth."

"I had no idea Bennett knew about you," Victor murmured. "But now it makes sense why he's been in such a rage the last few days."

"If Bennett had gotten rid of me, you would have been next, Victor. He wasn't going to wait for you to die a natural death, he would have taken you out before you could do anything else to lessen the value of the company. He just had to make sure I died first so that addendum wouldn't come into play." I paused. "The ironic thing is that Andrew stopped Bennett from killing me because he needed me to be alive when you showed up. I don't know how I survived both of them, but somehow I did."

"We should get you to the medical center, Mr. Carrington," Martin said, interrupting our conversation. "You can talk about all this later."

I tried to hand Victor back the diamond, but he waved it away.

"The diamond is yours, Lauren. Use it to do something important, something meaningful to you. You deserve it."

"I don't want anything from you."

"I know," he said, meeting my gaze. "And that's exactly why I want you to have it."

I stood there speechless as Martin helped Victor into the waiting vehicle. Then I turned to Ethan. "Will you take this, please? I don't know what to do with it."

"You'll figure it out, but I can put it in the hotel safe for now.

No one will know it's there, so it should be safe, especially since we've rounded up all the thieves."

I handed him the velvet box and felt a heavy weight fall from my shoulders, leaving me with a feeling of freedom and lightness I hadn't experienced in a very long time.

The role-playing was over and so was my marriage, maybe even my job. I had no idea where I was going from here, but for the first time in forever, the uncertainty didn't scare me. Shockingly enough, Andrew had given me back something I'd lost, and that was faith in myself.

"What do you want to do now?" Ethan asked. "Can I walk you back to your suite? Do you want me to call one of your friends so you can talk all this out?"

"No. I'm already talking to one of my friends, maybe my most honest friend." I gave him a bemused smile. "Who would have thought you would turn into that? When you showed up at the rehearsal dinner, I believed you were my worst enemy. You didn't trust me at all."

"I didn't. But the more I got to know you, the more I realized you didn't have it in you to lie, at least not well. I could see that you were blinded by love, and while I didn't know what the game was, I knew you were an unwitting player."

"I was blinded," I admitted. "And I feel like a fool, Ethan. How could I have blown by every single red flag? I got so angry with Harper for continuing to tell me I was moving too fast. And I was pissed at you for the same reason. But you were both right. I was the one who was wrong."

"Don't be so hard on yourself. You opened yourself up to an emotion you wanted to feel again. Love is powerful. It can cloud your judgment."

"I'm done with love."

"You say that now but give yourself some time. Don't let Andrew steal your capacity to love and to laugh, to feel joy and connection. You deserve all that and more."

"Thanks. I might deserve it, but I'm not in a rush to go down that road again."

"You can take your time. You're not on anyone's schedule anymore."

"Thank God!" I paused. "You don't think Harper knew what Colin was up to, do you?"

"I don't. I believe he was using her as a reason to stay on the island and also to keep a separate connection to you, in case you said something to her you wouldn't say to Andrew."

"That makes sense."

"We'll find out for sure. So, what next?"

I thought for a moment. Then said, "I don't want to go back to my suite and look at Andrew's things in my bedroom closet. And I don't want to walk around the resort where there will probably be a lot of curious stares, because I'm sure the news of what happened here is already spreading. Megan will have her work cut out for her if she wants to spin all this. And no matter how hard she tries, it will all come out eventually. The Carrington dream wedding couple wasn't real at all. The groom was a con man, and the bride was an idiot. Kind of hard to sell that." I let out a breath. "I'd like to walk into town and be a nobody. I want to order a cheeseburger and fries and walk barefoot on the beach and listen to music and feel normal again."

"That sounds like a plan."

"Would you care to join me, Ethan?"

He smiled. "I would, but only if you're paying, because you now own a diamond worth about twenty million dollars, which is way above my pay grade."

"What?" I asked in astonishment. "Seriously? It's worth that much?"

"It could be even more." Ethan paused. "You could do a lot of good with that money, Lauren. I wouldn't give the diamond back to Victor. Does he really need something else to impress his friends when you could change a lot of lives? Wouldn't that be more fun?"

"That would be fun. Okay. I'll think about it. We'll put the diamond in the vault, and then I will buy you dinner. You can even order a beer if you want," I added with a smile.

"Oh, I am definitely ordering a beer. Maybe two."

"Or three," I said, meeting his warm gaze. "Because this beer-drinking girl has had more than enough champagne."

EPILOGUE

Four weeks later...

I stood at my mother's grave in a cemetery in west Los Angeles, holding a bouquet of blue forget-me-nots in my hand. As I gazed down at her tombstone and read the inscription *Sarah Gray, Loving Mother*, my eyes filled with moisture. Kneeling down, I put the flowers in the built-in vase by the tombstone. I hadn't been to her grave since a few weeks before my wedding, and that felt like a lifetime ago.

I should have come before now, but I'd felt too emotional, too close to everything that had happened. And there had been a lot to deal with in the past few weeks as I learned more about Andrew and his friends.

Andrew, Colin, and Jay had been transferred to the county jail in Los Angeles and charged with multiple crimes. Jay had decided to talk in exchange for a lighter sentence, and it turned out the three of them had met in their early twenties and had been stealing for over a decade, their skills and ambition increasing with each passing year. Andrew's real estate company had made a few development deals in the past several years, but it was primarily a front for laundering money made through fencing stolen works of art.

Allison had worked with them on multiple occasions, but they had never really trusted her. As Andrew had told me on the island, she was too impulsive and too reckless. She and Andrew had had a sexual relationship that had lasted far longer and gone far deeper than he'd shared with me, which explained why she'd gotten so angry with him. She'd felt betrayed by his marriage to me, and his secret plan to use me against Victor for his own personal gain.

Harper had known nothing about Colin's life as a thief and had been devastated to realize she'd fallen for another bad guy. It would take her a while to trust someone again, but I hoped she would get there. I hoped we would both get there. I'd told her we couldn't let these men steal our future happiness. They'd already taken too much from us.

As for Bennett, he had been charged with murder and attempted murder and was being held without bail. Paula had apparently checked herself into some sort of luxury mental health sanctuary as she tried to deal with the fact that her son had killed someone and her husband had a bastard daughter.

According to Megan, who had also been in touch, the marketing campaign had been completely scrapped. The photos and video we had shot would never be seen, but news of my relationship to Victor had come out, creating more interest in the Carrington family. Ironically, the extensive coverage had resulted in more people booking rooms at the resort, wanting to see the lighthouse where Bennett Carrington had tried to kill his half-sister.

Over time, people would forget. But I would never forget any of it.

However, I would move on. I had a life to live, a life I had almost lost, and I wouldn't waste it. My mom wouldn't have wanted that for me.

Tracing her name with my fingers, I said, "I wish you'd told me about Victor, Mom. I'm trying to understand why you didn't want me to know who my father was. And I'm angry that you can't tell me now, that we can't discuss it. I want to hear your version of the story, not just his. How will I know if he's telling me the truth?" I sighed, feeling a futile yearning for a voice that could never come again.

"It might not be the same story your mother would tell you, but it will be true," a man said from behind me.

Shocked, I got to my feet and faced Victor Carrington. I still had trouble thinking of him as my father. We hadn't spoken since I'd seen him at the lighthouse, and I wasn't sure I was ready to do that now.

The polished veneer he usually wore had cracked. His blue eyes, normally sharp and confident, were shadowed with exhaustion and uncertainty. Silver had begun threading through the dark hair at his temples, and the perfectly tailored suit that had always seemed like armor now hung on his frame as if he'd forgotten to eat for days.

"Will you let me tell you the story, Lauren?" Victor asked, bringing me back to the present.

"How did you know I was here?" I asked.

"I went to your apartment. A woman watering the plants out front told me you'd gone to the cemetery to see your mom."

"I'm surprised you would know which cemetery that was, or did my landlord share that information, too?"

"I knew where your mother was buried. I visited a few weeks after the funeral."

I started at that piece of information, remembering the odd bouquet I'd found on her grave on one of my visits. "Did you bring her flowers?"

"Lilies. They were her favorite after forget-me-nots. I couldn't bring her forget-me-nots, because she did all she could to forget me. And I couldn't blame her."

"How could you blame her? You deserted her when she was at her most vulnerable."

"It wasn't exactly like that. Sarah left me before she knew she was pregnant. We had a very short affair. I couldn't give her what she wanted."

"Because you didn't love her, or because you loved your wife's money more? Bennett told me Paula invested in the company and that you could never leave her without losing a lot of money."

"I did love your mother, but I also cared about my wife and my son," he said. "I had no idea Bennett would grow up to be a monster. He was a toddler then."

"Did my mom ask you to leave your wife?"

"No. Sarah felt guilty for getting together with me in the first place. We got swept away by a passion neither of us expected to feel. We knew it was wrong, and we were only going to hurt each other the longer we stayed together."

I frowned, not sure if I should believe what he was telling me. "When my mom told you she was pregnant, what happened? Did you suggest an abortion?"

"It wasn't like that. We talked about options. I said I would pay for whatever she needed to end the pregnancy or to continue it, but that I couldn't publicly confirm your existence. That was a dealbreaker."

"Because that would have ended your marriage and maybe your business."

"Yes. And Sarah knew that."

I was a little surprised he wasn't trying to sugarcoat his actions. "Well, at least you're not lying."

"I'm telling you the truth. I assumed Sarah had decided to terminate the pregnancy and had paid for it herself, because I never heard from her again."

"She would have had too much pride to beg for scraps from a man who didn't want to acknowledge her or her child." I was beginning to understand my mother's choices a little better.

"That's what she told me when I ran into her twelve years later at the Christmas Tree Lighting at Rockefeller Center."

"Rockefeller Center?" I echoed. "That was our big trip to New York. She wanted to show me a white Christmas. You were there, too?"

"I was with Paula and Bennett. I went to get them hot chocolates and coffee, and there she was. You were standing next to her in line. I looked at you and I just knew you were my daughter, that she'd had my child. Before I could say anything, you went to look at the tree, and then Sarah turned and saw me."

"Did you speak to each other?"

"We did. She confirmed what I'd already guessed. She also told me that while you carried my blood, you weren't my daughter, and you never would be. It wasn't only because she wanted it that way; it was because I wanted it that way. And she dared me to say she was wrong."

My body tightened as I asked, "What did you say?"

"I told her that if I had known about you, I would have supported you. And I was willing to do that going forward."

"You were talking about financially and nothing else." It wasn't a question because I already knew the answer.

"I was," he admitted. "Sarah told me she didn't need my support, and she didn't want someone in her daughter's life who couldn't love her the way she should be loved. She didn't want you to feel less than Bennett. She didn't want you to be a secret. As far as you knew, your father was dead, and she wanted it to stay that way. The two of you had a great life, and I needed to keep out of it. Then she walked away, and I never saw her again."

"What about me? At some point, I grew up. I turned twenty-one. I was my own person. You could have tried to see me."

"I would have been taking a risk."

"That I would tell Paula or Bennett who I was?"

"Yes. But I also wanted to respect your mother's wishes."

I shook my head, not buying that reason at all. "That's not why you did it. You wanted to keep me a secret to protect your business, your marriage, and your reputation. It was all about you."

"Well, I already admitted that, didn't I?" He gave me a small smile. "You are your mother's daughter, Lauren. Sarah was strong and independent, determined to live life on her terms. And you're as brave as she was. I saw that on the island more than once. To be completely honest, you were probably better off being raised by your mother than me. I didn't do a good job with my son, that's for sure."

"I don't know that you can blame yourself entirely for Bennett's actions. He's a man, not a child. Although, I think he inherited your greed."

"I'm sure he did. I always knew Bennett didn't have the will to do what was hard. He was always looking for a shortcut. That's why I didn't give him more responsibility in the company, and why I was thinking of selling properties to put our financials in better shape. I didn't work as hard as I did for the last thirty years to have my son ruin all of that. I also knew I couldn't trust him. He's been in and out of alcohol and drug rehabs since he was fifteen. He's good for a while and then something snaps, and he goes off the deep end. I worried for years that I'd get a call one night that he'd overdosed. However, I never thought I'd find out he'd killed someone. That part is still difficult to digest."

"Have you spoken to Bennett about it?"

"Briefly. He doesn't want to talk to me, although, he has spoken to Paula a few times."

"How's she doing?"

"Not well. She wants to hide from all the bad publicity, so she's gone to stay at a sanctuary in France for a few months. She's embarrassed and ashamed of her husband and her son."

"I'm sure she's hurting. Will you stay together?"

"We've been married a long time, so probably..."

"I've wondered if she suspected something was off about your interest in me. She acted rather oddly when she let me wear your mother's necklace for my wedding."

"She wasn't thrilled with the idea. And she thought I was spending too much money on the wedding." He shrugged. "She might have been suspicious of my interest in you, but we didn't discuss it."

I had a feeling they rarely discussed anything, but I didn't care that much about his relationship with Paula. However, I was curious about one thing. "Is there a chance Bennett is going to wiggle out from these charges or get them lessened? Will you use your influence and wealth to save your son from life in prison?"

"No." His answer was blunt and unequivocal. "I want to be clear about that, Lauren. I'm not going to try to get Bennett a deal, because I won't let him ever be in a position again to hurt you."

"You should take me out of your will. Then he won't have any reason to hurt me."

"You're my daughter. I haven't been there for you, and I want to do better. I want you to have the life you deserve. And you will be in my will."

My gaze moved from Victor to my mother's tombstone, then back again. "I want to make one thing clear; I've had a good life, Victor. I might not have grown up rich, but I was taught the value of work and how to take care of myself. I was babysitting when I was twelve and serving up scoops of ice cream when I was fifteen. I had jobs after school and every summer. My mom helped me pay for college by working two jobs."

My eyes filled with tears, and I took a moment to regain my composure. "She gave me everything I needed, and she was the best mom in the world. She was my hero. I loved her more than I could ever express." I drew in a ragged breath, then added, "I came here wanting to yell at her for keeping you away from me, but I can't do that because she did what she thought was right. And if she was wrong, there's nothing I can do about it now. It certainly doesn't change how I feel about her."

"She was trying to protect you."

"And maybe herself, too," I said honestly. "My mom was a stubborn, proud woman. When you were willing to walk away from her, she was done with you. You weren't getting back in, no matter what. She was a fiercely loyal person, but if someone crossed her or did me wrong, she could be ruthless."

"I'm glad she was a good protector and that you had a great life with her."

I cocked my head to the right, a question on my lips that I'd wanted to ask since I'd learned he was my father. "Did you have something to do with me getting hired at your company?"

He shook his head. "I had no idea you worked for me until Megan brought me the marketing campaign, and I saw your name and your face. I couldn't believe you were one of my employees. Since you hadn't used your connection to me, I assumed you still didn't know I was your father."

"I didn't. I had been working in marketing, but I had never tried to go into the hotel industry because my mother hadn't wanted me to follow in her footsteps. However, when I saw the position at Carrington Resorts, it reminded me of her. I'd grown up in hotels, and working in one felt comfortable, like a second home." I cleared my throat. "That decision led to all of this..."

"Your job is still available, Lauren. If you want it."

"Too much has happened for me to go back to my old job."

"I actually have another idea, if you'll hear me out."

"What's that?" I asked warily.

"The Carrington Foundation. I'd like you to manage our philanthropic efforts. I believe you would be the perfect person to oversee where our money can best be used outside of our profit margin."

"I know about the foundation, but I've never been that impressed with it."

"Because it hasn't been impressive or a priority. I want to make it both of those things."

"Why? Because you think your company will need positive spin?"

He smiled at my blunt statement. "Partly, yes, but also

because I want you to be involved. You're my daughter. And this is the family business. I want you in it."

I had a lot of mixed emotions about his offer. "You already gave me a very valuable diamond. I don't need to work at all."

"I was wondering what you were going to do with that, but I didn't want to ask. It's yours to do whatever you want with it."

"Well, I'm not going to put it in a glass case for people to look at or try to steal. I'm going to sell it, and I want to use the money for good."

He nodded, his expression neutral. "Okay."

"That doesn't bother you?" I challenged. "You don't want it back after searching for it for so many years?"

"Like I said, it's yours. You don't have to work for me at the foundation, but I'd like you to consider it. I want us to have a relationship, however that might look."

I hesitated for a long minute, but in truth, I'd already made my decision. "I'd like to get to know you better. That's as far as I can go right now."

Relief ran through his eyes. "Good."

"There is another question I have for you."

"You can ask me anything."

"How did you have so many good fakes of that diamond?"

He smiled. "David's girlfriend Kirstie is an artist and a gemologist; she's very good at making fakes."

"Kirstie?" I asked with surprise. "Seriously? I would not have guessed that about her."

"People rarely look past her beauty. I was worried that someone might try to steal the diamond, so I asked David to have her make me several fakes. He gave them to me when we were on the yacht."

"It was you and David in the stateroom," I said as the last piece of the puzzle fell into place. "I heard parts of your conversation. You said something about taking care of Ethan. What did you mean by that?"

"I wasn't aware anyone had overheard our conversation," he

said. "I did tell David that I didn't want Ethan to know about the fakes. I couldn't trust anyone, not even Ethan. It was too risky."

"It was risky to bring the second fake to Andrew. He almost killed you and then he would have come after me."

"I didn't think he would react so quickly and so violently. Have you spoken to Andrew?"

"No, and I won't. I've already filed for an annulment. I can't wait to be completely free of him. I was a fool to fall for his con. I won't be that trusting ever again."

"Andrew fooled me, too. I did look into Andrew's background because of Ethan's concerns, but I didn't find anything that set off alarm bells. And I knew you weren't a thief, so I dismissed the idea that you and Andrew might be working together." He paused. "I should have done a more thorough investigation, and I should have trusted Ethan's instincts. I'm sorry Andrew hurt you the way he did."

"He hurt me, but he didn't break me." I repeated the words I'd said to Andrew that last day. "I'm going to be fine."

"I'm glad. I'll go now so you can have time alone with your mom. But I hope I'll hear from you soon." He paused, giving me a smile. "You know, there are very few people who don't say yes to me immediately."

"Maybe that's not such a good thing."

"Maybe not. But I think I'll enjoy getting to know someone who isn't afraid to speak her mind and tell me when I'm wrong."

"Be careful what you wish for."

He laughed, then headed down the small hillside to his waiting car.

After he left, I turned back to my mother's grave. I wished he could give me time with my mom, but she was gone. And he was here. It wasn't fair. She should have been here, too.

But her spirit would always be with me, and I would have the life she wanted for me. I just couldn't follow completely in her footsteps with regard to Victor.

"I'm going to get to know my father, Mom," I said aloud. "I'll enjoy spreading his wealth to those less fortunate, and I'll see what kind of relationship we can have. I'll be more careful about who I trust in the future. But I know I won't be fooled again, because now I know who I really am. It's ironic that it took a con man to make me see that." I leaned down once more and traced her name with my fingers, then I put my fingers to my lips and blew her a kiss. "I'll be back soon. I love you."

When I got into my car, my phone rang. I answered it, feeling happier than I'd ever thought I would be to get a call from Ethan Stark, who had once been my nemesis.

"Hi, Ethan."

"How's it going, Lauren? It's been a few weeks. I wanted to check in on you."

"It's good. I brought some flowers to my mother's grave today, and Victor showed up with all kinds of tempting offers. He wants me to head the Carrington Foundation and be a part of his life."

"That sounds interesting."

"I don't need his foundation to spend his money. I have his diamond locked away in a vault at my bank."

"That's true. You have options."

"And I'll think about all of them. We had a good talk. He seemed sincere in wanting to have a relationship with me, and I feel like I want to at least get to know him better. But I don't want money or a job to be a part of that."

"That makes sense. You don't need to rush into anything. You can investigate, research, and make sure you choose what's right for you."

"That's good advice. What are you doing these days?"

"Victor made me an offer, too. He wants me to be in charge of security for all his properties, both business and personal."

"What do you think about the job?"

"I'm tempted. It would be broader in scope than what I've been doing, and I'd get to travel around the world."

"That could be fun. You should investigate, research, and make sure to choose what's right for you," I said, repeating his earlier statement.

He laughed. "In other words, take my own advice."

"Exactly. You're a smart man."

"And you are a smart woman."

"I am. So, where are you now?"

"I'm headed to New York to talk to the current head of security for Carrington Resorts, who is retiring at the end of the month. The research begins. What are you doing tonight?"

"I'm having drinks with Harper and Jamie. I'm not sure where that friendship will go in the future, but they didn't have anything to do with what happened to me, and at times they did try to warn me about Andrew, so we'll see." I paused. "Maybe you and I could get together if you ever come back to California."

"I'll be back," he promised, sending a little tingle down my spine. "As long as you're there."

"I'm here."

"But I want to make it clear that next time we go out, Lauren, I'll be buying. I don't want money to come between us, either."

"Is there going to be an *us*?"

"I guess we'll find out."

"When we're done investigating and researching," I said with a laugh.

"Exactly. So, I'll see you when I see you."

"Yes, you will. Have a good trip, Ethan."

"Have a good night, Lauren."

As I ended the call, I smiled to myself. I didn't know when I'd be ready to take another chance on love, because I needed to be on my own for a while. But if I did want to take that chance, it might be on a cynical, pragmatic, and sexy man who had once been my enemy but had turned out to be my best friend.

ABOUT THE AUTHOR

Barbara Freethy is a #1 New York Times Bestselling Author of 87 novels ranging from contemporary romance to romantic suspense and women's fiction. With over 13 million copies sold, thirty-three of Barbara's books have appeared on the New York Times and USA Today Bestseller Lists, including SUMMER SECRETS which hit #1 on the New York Times!

Known for her emotional and compelling stories of love, family, mystery and romance, Barbara enjoys writing about ordinary people caught up in extraordinary adventures. Library Journal says, "Freethy has a gift for creating unforgettable characters."

For additional information, please visit Barbara's website at www.barbarafreethy.com.

Printed in Great Britain
by Amazon

58502268R00169